Burying Ben

Burying Ben

Ellen Kirschman

ISBN: 978-1-60809-176-8

Published in the United States of America by Oceanview Publishing
Longboat Key, Florida

www.oceanviewpub.com
10 9 8 7 6 5 4 3 2 1

PRINTED IN THE UNITED STATES OF AMERICA

Dedication

This book is dedicated to my colleagues at the International Association of Chiefs of Police – psychological services section, the American Psychological Association – public safety section, the Society for Police and Criminal Psychology, and the West Coast Post Trauma Retreat. Through hard work and compassion, you make a big difference in the lives of those who are sworn to protect and serve the rest of us.

Acknowledgements

Storytelling is how cops learn to be cops. Their experiences, funny and tragic alike, inspired me to write this book. I hope they will forgive me for stealing their stories and lifting their personalities.

I am grateful to the people who helped me learn the ropes. My law enforcement consultants Lt. Zach Peron, Lt. Bob Bonilla, Sgt. Natasha Powers, Retired Chief Lynne Johnson, Judge Mike Ballachey, Phil Shnayerson, Esq., Wayne Schmidt, Esq. and Marty Mayer, Esq.; my fellow psychologists Gary Olson, Dave Corey, and Phil Trompetter; my fellow writers Mike Orenduff, Harriet Chessman, Maud Carole Markson, Jan Harwood, the Wombistas, and my sister-in-law, Doris Ober, who has stuck with me from the awful first draft.

My backup team is composed of talented professionals: Laurie Harper of Author Biz, my agent Cynthia Zigmund of Second City Publishing Services, who is wise, supportive and always answers her phone, and the fine folks at Oceanview Publishing who have given *Ben* a second chance. They are a pleasure to work with.

Finally, and forever, to Steve, who is always there when I need him.

Prologue

Suicide. It's the one thing therapists dread the most.

We try to prepare. We make our clients promise to call us before they kill themselves, even though they know, and we know, there's not a chance in hell we'll be by the phone waiting for their call. Patients may be depressed, but they're not stupid. We get them to sign contracts, useless documents designed to cover our asses. And they do, just to shut us up. I'm not questioning the solace that comes from covering one's ass. Or the wisdom. The therapist who can show her dead client's family, lawyers and the newspapers that she made her client promise not to kill himself without contacting her first and has a piece of paper to prove it is a lot better off than I am this morning.

Ben Gomez is dead. Last night he checked into a motel in the Sierra foothills, got into bed fully dressed with his badge pinned to his shirt, pulled a blanket over his head to contain the mess and shot himself in the head with his duty weapon.

I imagine him squirming under the covers, tugging at his clothes as they catch under him. How long did he lie there? What was he thinking about? Who was he thinking about? Was he debating against putting the cold metal gun under his chin? Or did he do it instantly?

And then what? Noise? Color? Flashes of light?

I liked Ben Gomez. He and I had something in common. It brought us together when we first met and held us in a fragile balance, as if tethered by a fraying rope. It was the recognition that we both had an uncommon sensibility the others around us didn't have. We were outsiders, displaced persons trying hard to fit in without losing too much of our souls. It wasn't much of a bond. And it didn't hold.

"Dot? Are you still there?" Chief Baxter's voice echoes through my bedroom. The telephone in my hands seems miles away, as though I am looking at it through the wrong end of a pair of binoculars. I put the phone up to my ear. I have no idea how long the chief has been waiting for me to respond.

"Sorry to have to tell you this over the phone." The words leave his mouth reluctantly, I can almost hear little ripping sounds. It is not his style to apologize. "I need you to come in to the station before the troops get the news. I'm going to wait until the 6:00 a.m. shift change to make the announcement." He doesn't wait for me to reply. I'm the department shrink. It's my job to be there in a crisis, whenever and wherever

Even if the crisis is my fault.

Chapter One

It is a day of firsts. My first day on the job and my first dead body. Chief Baxter wants me to see it. His whole face is concentrated with the effort to make his point, as though he were explaining blood spatter analysis or the biomechanics of tasers. He is wearing gold cufflinks shaped like barbells. Short and barrel chested, he looks like a well-dressed fireplug. I can imagine him as a street cop, pugnacious and badge heavy.

"Don't sit around your office and wait for cops to come to you. That's why I'm giving you a car and a scanner. Get out in the field."

He speaks in short staccato bursts as though he is transmitting over the radio, dropping any unessential words. A slight spray of saliva leaves shiny droplets on his desktop. He walks around the desk and stands close to me. I smell his pine-scented aftershave and mouthwash.

"This is why I have credibility. I make it my business to suit up and get out on the street once a month. I stay in shape. And I always carry." He opens his jacket and shows me his shoulder holster. He is wearing a custom fitted dress shirt that shows off the inverted triangle made by his broad shoulders and narrow waist. "Street cops are the lifeblood of this organization. The street is where I started. I've never forgotten that and I don't want anyone else to."

He leans against the edge of his desk, his arms folded over his chest. "I have a rookie on scene at a suicide. Ben Gomez. He's been having trouble. Talk to his field training officer. See what you can do to help him. I've met the kid. Not my best hire, but I think he's salvageable." He lifts his index finger. "I'm putting a lot of faith in you, Dot. I've had a lot of trouble in my organization since I took over as chief. Some days I feel like Typhoid Mary. I've got four officers on stress leave and three on admin leave under investigation. No telling when any of them will come back to work. I have a small organization—seventy five officers. I can't afford to lose this rookie, too. It's bad for morale plus my overtime budget is off the charts."

He extends his hand to me. "It's one thing to study us and write books about us. It's another thing to hit the streets with us. You come highly recommended by Mark Edison. That says a lot. Most men don't have much good to say about their former wives."

He laughs a little too loudly. I wonder if he has an ex and, if he does, what she was like.

"So, welcome aboard. I know this is a tall order, but Dr. Edison said you're the one for the job. Don't disappoint me or him. Now, get in your car and get out in the field." He opens the door to his office and shows me out.

As the new department psychologist, I am in no position to protest or to tell him that I'm scared to death because I've never seen a dead body before. Not even my father's. What if I embarrass myself, faint or, God forbid, get sick to my stomach? I wonder how he expects me to suit up. Maybe I should put wheels on my couch and tow it behind my car?

The radio traffic on my scanner crackles briskly, drowning out my thumping heart. Listening to it is a guilty pleasure, like eavesdropping. This is the best of two possible worlds, close to the action but at a safe remove—the unobserved observer listening to the breathlessness of the chase, the escalating octaves that betray fear, the barked commands, the unnatural calm of the dispatcher, and the final "Code 4" signaling that the short reign of terror has given way to hours of report writing and investigation.

I drive under a cool green canopy of old oaks. Light filters through the leaves dappling the street. Fifty years ago this old northern California neighborhood was considered the ultimate in affordable, architect-designed family houses. Now the current selling prices are beyond my reach and the reach of any Kenilworth cop, fire fighter or schoolteacher. Neighbors are congregating in small worried clusters on the sidewalk in front of a uniquely shabby one story home. They watch as I park my car. I take ten slow deep breaths and step to the sidewalk. Spindly trees flank the walk that leads to the front door. The grass on either side of the cracked concrete path is brown and freckled with splotches of hard, dry dirt. The front door is open. I grit my teeth and walk in.

The air inside smells of cooked cabbage, dirty clothes and cigarette smoke. The walls are painted the color of bruised and decaying greens. I look down a long hall, dark as a tunnel. I hear voices to my front and my side, and I see movement through an arched doorway. I continue down the hall, my shoes tapping on the bare wood floor. An elderly man lies sprawled on the living room floor, wearing corduroy pants, bedroom slippers, and a gray cardigan, like the one my father wore every day of his waning life. The memory swoops in on me. How he used to button it, so that one side hung lower than the other and stuff the pockets with odds and ends until they were stretched and shapeless, driving my mother to distraction.

I force myself to look at the man on the floor. One end of a frayed rope is tied around his neck, the other end dangles from a wood ceiling beam. A dining chair lies on its side. Decaying floral drapes are pulled shut across a large window, sagging at the top where the drapery hooks have come loose. The only light in the room comes from a slide projector that sits on a coffee table playing an endless loop of family photos across a home movie screen. The slides move forward through a spent life. There is a vintage wedding portrait of two young, slim people. She wears a suit and a pillbox hat and holds a bouquet. He is in an Army uniform. Then there are baby pictures, children opening Christmas presents, a birthday party, a graduation, a teenage couple in prom clothes, a studio portrait of an older couple, and more wedding photos of a smiling young woman in a bridal gown.

The room smells musty and singed. Ben Gomez stares down at the body as photos play across his face. His face is flushed and there are beads of sweat on his upper lip. He has a thin face and body with dark, almost black hair and thick eyebrows. One eyebrow is split in two by a shiny ribbon of white scar, as though one side of his face is in perpetual surprise.

He senses my presence and looks up. His eyes are soft and black with thick eyelashes that a woman would die for. His slender face is smooth and unblemished with high cheekbones and a sharp nose. He seems barely old enough to have graduated from high school. Behind him stands an older officer, a lit cigar in his downturned mouth, fat jowls melting beneath his mustache. His gray hair is gelled into small spikes as though defying the downward pull that age and gravity have imposed on his corpulent body. He is watching the younger officer the way a scientist monitors the movements of a laboratory rat.

"C'mon Safeway," he says. "Staring at this guy won't bring him back to life. Get a move on it so we can go out and help the living."

I cough to announce myself, and the big officer comes to life. Two long steps and he's in front of me, his eyes drilling into mine. "No reporters. This is a crime scene. If you need information, talk to the PIO." He shoves a bent business card at me.

"I'm Dr. Dot Meyerhoff, the new department psychologist. Sorry you didn't know I was coming." He looks at me, taking in my green jacket and navy slacks, my glasses, my salt and pepper hair, sorting out details, looking for what doesn't fit his prescribed image of how a psychologist should look.

"I thought you'd be a man," he says, stepping back. "Come in if you want." He gestures toward the body with the top of his head. "Not much you can do for the old guy, he's dead as a door nail. Did himself, probably three days ago. Neighbors called it in, saw the newspapers piling up. Been hanging so long the rope broke. Not much to see. Knock yourself out." He sticks the cigar back in his mouth.

"And you are?"

"Eddie Rimbauer. I'm the kid's FTO, field training officer. I'll be in the kitchen if you need me. Stinks in here."

Ben's eyes are fixed on the body that lays like a discarded cornhusk doll. His lips are clamped together. He looks as though he might cry. Crying on scene is forbidden. One tear would be enough to earn him a jacket as weak, sentimental and undependable in an emergency.

"How're you doing?" I ask.

"My FTO thinks this is funny," he says, gesturing toward the kitchen. "Said the man was too cheap to buy himself a movie ticket." He looks around the room, walks to the projector and switches it off. I can hear laughter from the kitchen. Ben jerks his head toward the sound and then back to me. "Who are you again?"

"I'm the department psychologist, Doctor Dot Meyerhoff."

Ben sticks his hand out and retracts it. "Please to meet you, M'am. Sorry about the gloves." He smiles briefly. In the dim light his teeth are luminous. "I didn't know the department had a psychologist."

"It's my first day on the job."

We stare at each other for a moment. He's not sizing me up as much as looking awkward. The usual rules of etiquette don't seem to apply when there's a dead body in the room.

"What about you," I ask, "do you think this is funny?"

He frowns, his dark brows knitting together. "No way. What's funny about a lonely old man killing himself? Where was his family? Where are all those people in the pictures he was watching?"

He moves from the projector to the window to a table piled with books. He stoops to look at the titles. "History, biography. He read a lot. Must have been way smart. Why didn't he call someone for help before he hung himself?"

He continues through the room touching things lightly, as though trying to sense the dead man through the tips of his latex-gloved fingers. This is not ordinary cop behavior. Most rookies would be looking for evidence of something amiss, showing little interest in the dead man except for his profile as a potential crime victim. They would be taking an inventory of cash and checkbooks and looking for evidence of crimes beyond the bleak reality in front of them – intruders, robbers, murder made to look like suicide, clues left by predatory hired help or greedy children impatient to get their hands on their father's money.

Eddie bangs on the door frame with his baton. "Hey Doc, I need you in the kitchen. I'm having a little group therapy."

He motions me down the hall and I follow. Ben gives me a little nice-to-meet-you wave. Two firefighters are leaning against a counter that is piled high with used food containers and unwashed dishes. The place reeks with neglect.

"So Doc, these heartless S.O.B.s are telling me they could pick this house up for a song. Needs a good cleaning and a little remodeling, that's all." He flicks his fingers against a worn metal cabinet, "Guess you know all fire fighters have contractors' licenses and plenty of time off." He winks. "These guys didn't have to show up on this call. They're only here to check out the real estate."

He looks at me. "You okay? You look a little green around the gills."

"I'm fine."

"How's Mr. Safeway doing in there? That's my nickname for him. He used to work produce. Knows how to handle a cantaloupe, but he's over his head as a cop. Hey Gomez," he yells. "Don't forget to put in your report if this guy was a Q or an A."

Ben appears in the doorway, holding his clipboard to his chest like a shield. His looks worried. "Sorry, Sir. What do you mean?"

"Do I have to tell you everything?" Eddie rolls his eyes. "Q is when the tongue sticks out at an angle. A is when it sticks out straight." He uses his cigar to demonstrate.

"I don't know."

"Well go back and look."

As soon as Ben leaves the room, Eddie and the firefighters burst out laughing.

"You are so bad, man," one of the fire fighters says. It sounds like a compliment. I walk back into the living room. Ben is kneeling next to the dead man's head, looking at his face.

"I think he was joking," I say. He sinks back into his heels and curses under his breath.

"I hope I never get calloused like him."

"I hope you don't either."

"Truth is, I've never seen a dead body before. Except on television. We were supposed to watch an autopsy in the academy, but the trip got cancelled." He looks toward the kitchen. "Don't tell him that. He makes a joke out of everything I do or say."

I kneel next to him. The body smells like moldy straw. Ben smells like sweat.

"I promise not to tell if you won't. It's my first body too."

Ben looks at me astonished that someone my age, close to being a corpse myself, could have managed to avoid seeing one in the flesh.

"He told me to get used to them. Told me a story about washing someone's brains down the bathtub drain before the family got home." He shakes his head. "I don't know."

"Don't know what?" I ask.

"Hey, Gomez," Eddie calls from the kitchen. "What's taking you so long? You're not going to eat your gun are you?"

Ben raises his eyebrows and shakes his head just enough for me to see.

Eddie walks into the room. "It would be curtains for the Doc, losing a copper when she's just getting started." He turns to me. "Seen enough, Doc? Let's leave the rookie alone so he can finish his report. I want to go home today, not next week."

He takes my elbow, helps me to my feet, and moves me toward the door. His hand clamps firmly to the back of my arm. I flash back to an anti-war demonstration, the cops in riot gear, their faces hidden behind plastic shields, herding the crowd off the street, pushing us to move faster, prodding us with their batons. When we are outside, I shake him loose and pull away.

"Anything wrong?"

I want to say that I hate bullies. I don't appreciate being manhandled and I don't think humiliation is an appropriate training device. What I say instead is "Ben looks a little shook up."

"He'd better get over it. This is nothing compared to what he's gonna see. No blood, no maggots, no puke, just a little lividity. Anyhow, the guy was probably a miserable son-of-a-bitch wife beater who ran his family off and deserved to die alone." He looks at his watch. "See you later, Doc," he says. "Thanks for dropping by."

I get in my car and turn on the air conditioning. I did it. Passed my first test, looked at the body and didn't lose my cookies. My face is burning, and little rivulets of sweat are dripping down my back and under my arms. A red flush crawls up my neck and across my cheeks. They come more frequently now, these stress-induced hot flashes, heralding a premature perimenopausal hell.

My doctor tells me to stay calm. My mother tells me to find another man. She thinks that I'll have plenty of opportunities on this new job. So much for her wish to see me safely coupled again. Thus far the men I have met today are pushy, hardly old enough to date, obese and sadistic or dead. I'm not interested in meeting men. I wanted the one I had, but Mark didn't want me. He wanted space and, as it turned out, his new psych assistant, the lovely Melinda with smooth skin and a tiny waist. Then he wanted a divorce.

A horn blast startles me. Two men in black suits jump from the coroners' van and wheel a gurney into the house. The street is strangely quiet despite the number of vehicles and people moving about. The only noise is the engine on the medic van. It runs steadily, the broken heart of a failed enterprise.

I wake up before dawn, once again. The sheets are damp and my hair is soaked. The sky is the color of tarnished silver. Mornings were the time Mark and I had to ourselves. We would lie in bed talking, sometimes making love, and then linger over coffee and the newspaper, debating politics. I can fill my evenings with books, TV, and movies, but the mornings are like great, unfurnished rooms, empty and echoing. I can't bear the morning talk shows or the idea of driving through the dark to a gym to stare at myself in the mirror next to a slew of hard-bodied gym rats. Twenty years of merging my life with Mark's, and now I have to reinvent myself at 48, figure out what do with my time, what I want to eat, when I want to sleep, who I want to sleep with. I don't want to wind up like that old man I saw yesterday, dying alone with only old photos for companions.

I go downstairs to make coffee. The clock on the coffee maker reads 4:45. The aroma and steady drip of coffee are soothing. I couldn't have been the only one in the room who was picturing herself in that old man's place. I wonder how long it will take Ben Gomez to undergo a moral inversion, learn to blame victims for their own misery. I try to picture him as a grizzled, old veteran and, just to be fair, I try to imagine Eddie as a tender-hearted rookie.

Chapter Two

The Kenilworth police headquarters are housed in a drab four story concrete box surrounded on three sides by a parking lot. A chain link fence separates the public parking from the spaces reserved for official vehicles. Concrete barriers erected after the infamy of September 11th guard the front of the building, making it impossible for bomb filled vehicles or anyone else to park close to the entrance.

The wealthy residents of Kenilworth have long welcomed illegal immigrants as gardeners and maids. Since most can't tell a Hispanic day laborer from a Middle Eastern terrorist, they have apparently assuaged their guilt about imperiling the rest of us with their voracious needs for cheap labor by authorizing a capital improvement project to build concrete stanchions in front of every public building.

Kenilworth is known as a desirable place to live, a place of status, but here, in the dingy lobby of police headquarters, the misery that lies beneath the veneer of wealth and safety is on display. Posters in English and Spanish advertise for missing persons, runaways, AIDs treatment, drug treatment, ways to protect the old and the young from abuse and safe houses for the victims of domestic violence. The desk officer is sealed behind a thick wall of bulletproof glass, one eye on the clock, the other on a group of teenage boys, their skinny arms covered in homemade tattoos, who are sprawled across a row of cheap plastic chairs molded in eye assaulting colors, some sleeping, some resting with their heads on their hands.

The desk officer waves me over, glances at my security badge and presses a button that operates the elevator. A few of the boys raise their heads and watch as the doors open then close behind me. The old elevator grinds slowly upward. It smells of grease and wet metal.

Chief Baxter is trying to raise funds for a new public safety building, but it's a hard sell. The community couldn't care less that this building is overcrowded and falling apart so long as their own houses are safe and secure. The elevator shudders, stops and then starts again.

My father would have hated knowing that his carefully tutored daughter had rejected her birthright and joined forces with the enemy. Government was the enemy. Every authority figure was corrupt and, according to my father, anti-Semitic. Only working people could be trusted. My father and I used to watch old news clips of him, the college dropout, brick in hand, a defiant finger raised at the TV camera, screaming at his former fellow students to 'off the pigs'. The beautiful, wild-haired zealot being carted off to jail looked nothing like my tired, gentle, damaged father, his useless right arm dangling at his side, a memento from the police who beat him with clubs until the nerves in his shoulder were good for nothing but pain.

Sergeant Rick Lyndley and eight field training officers are in the briefing room, seated around a long rectangular table. The room is painted a non-descript beige and the floor covered with worn carpeting. Florescent light fixtures buzz like trapped flies. Two of the men are leafing through last night's beat reports. Another is looking at artists' sketches of wanted criminals and gang members. An oversized shift schedule taped to the only window is blocking the dull morning light of an overcast sky. I am the only woman in the room, certainly the only Jew and, with the exception of the sergeant and Eddie Rimbauer, I am probably the oldest. Lyndley calls the meeting to order. He is a tall, lanky man with short black hair that is turning gray at the temples.

"Heads up. Let's get going. We have a guest, Dr. Meyerhoff, our new consulting psychologist."

"Is that why she's so short, because she's a shrink?" someone asks. I laugh to be polite. It's an old joke.

There's a noise at the door.

"Alright guys, enough funny stuff." Baxter strides into the room, grinning and stands behind my chair. He bends to my ear with a mock whisper. "The more they rag on you, the more they love you. When they stop teasing, that's when you should be worried."

I'm already a bit worried. Trust doesn't come easily to cops, especially when it comes to mental health professionals.

"Gentlemen, this little lady is a powerhouse. We're lucky to have her. She's written three police psychology text books with Dr. Mark Edison, and now she's got a book of her own." He looks at me. "I have it on my desk. What's it called again?"

I can feel my face getting red. "Behind the Badge: The Police Family Lifestyle," I say.

"Can I get two copies, one for my wife and one for my girlfriend?" says a skinny, red-haired officer at the end of the table. "And can I get your autograph?"

"Settle down, guys," Baxter says. "Most of you know Dr. Edison. He's been doing our pre-employment screening and fitness evaluations for years. He thinks Dr. Meyerhoff is the best. Hated to lose her."

The truth is, my ex would have said anything to get me out of the office so that he and Melinda could play kissy-face behind closed doors. Baxter hadn't been a bit suspicious about Mark's over the top verbiage. I remember hoping, at the time, that he did a better job vetting his police applicants.

Baxter claps his big hands on my shoulders. "So take it easy on her. At least for a while."

The men around the table are hard to read. I worry that the chief's ardent stamp of approval will hurt more than it helps.

"Thanks, Chief," I say. "I appreciate your taking the time to come down here and introduce me. I'm also a little embarrassed. While I have a lot of experience and the gray hair to show for it, I still have a lot to learn, especially about field training."

"Don't worry. Sgt. Lyndley will bring you up to speed, short form," he says clapping Lyndley on the back as he leaves the room.

"Okay," Lyndley says. "Let's get started. So, Doc, we get these kids right from the academy, day or two after they graduate. The academy gives them the basics, classroom style. We give them the real world. The jump from academy to field training is like learning to scuba dive—it's one thing to do scuba in a swimming pool, it's another to dive in the ocean where there are no walls and the fish have big teeth. We keep them for 16 weeks, divided into four separate phases with three different FTOs. We write observation reports every day, and we meet every other week to discuss their progress."

He slides a paper across the table. "This is what a daily observation report looks like. Any questions?"

I shake my head.

"Let's start with Ben Gomez, that's the rookie you met about ten days ago."

Eddie gives a theatrical sigh and slaps his hand to his head, spilling cigar ashes over the thick binder in front of him. He clears his throat. "In my professional opinion, this poor slob couldn't find his ass with a search warrant. The Doc saw him in action. A simple suicide and he was acting like a puppy pooping peach pits. Unfortunately for us, Mr. Safeway doesn't know the difference between a cauliflower and a crook. Last shift we pulled over some dirt bag parolee. Gomez didn't have a clue. Didn't call in the stop. Forgot his flashlight. Turned his gun side to the perp, and then let the asshole reach into the glove box so we couldn't see his hands. I nearly shit a brick. I've told this kid a hundred times, in God we trust, everybody else better keep their hands where I can see 'em."

Lyndley looks at me. "You have to take Eddie in stride, Doc. Flew in under the radar before we had psych screening."

The other officers are looking at me out of the corners of their eyes, reading my reaction, sizing me up.

"Listen to this one. We busted a guy for stolen property. House looked like the appliance department at Wal-Mart. Benny boy got all weirded out because we hooked the guy up in front of his kids."

"What do you mean by 'weirded out'?" I ask.

"Starting bellyaching about how we were traumatizing the kids. I told him we're not social workers, we're cops. We don't take this guy to jail, he's in Mexico by tomorrow. The perp should have thought about his kids before he started selling shit out of his garage."

"Where is he compared to where he should be?" Lyndley asks.

"Lower than whale shit."

Everyone laughs. I feel compelled to smile. Humor is the coin of the realm. I remember Ben's face, how he wandered around the room touching the old man's things, like he was in mourning.

"He looked a little stressed when I saw him," I say.

"I'm the one who's stressed. Being locked up with this kid ten hours a day is going to put me in the nut hut."

"About time," someone whispers.

"The boy has no common sense. He's a nice kid, don't get me wrong, but he's not police material and never will be. There's something off about him. I can't put my finger on it. I keep thinking I know him, or know something about him."

He shakes his head as though whacking his brain against the inside of his skull would unleash the missing information. Just as quickly he regains his comic stance. "Let this be a lesson to you young guys. Stay off the sauce. It pickles your brain."

He turns to me. "Gomez is gonna get hurt or get someone else hurt. I don't mean to be disrespectful to your profession, Doc, but I could do a better job picking cops with my eyes closed. If you think you can help him, have at it, but do it before he goes under, because he's this close."

He holds out his thumb and index finger, with only a sliver of light between them.

Chapter Three

Ben looks lost in my oversized leather office chair. Between his schedule and mine, it's taken us two weeks to make an appointment.

There is a marked change in his appearance. Without the bulky padding from his Kevlar vest, his thin shoulders stick through his rumpled t-shirt like knobs. There are circles under his eyes and his skin is sallow and clammy with sweat. He smells damp.

Shift work turns life upside down. Human beings are biologically tuned to sleep at night and work in the daylight. Reverse that and it's hard to eat or sleep. On top of that, he's living in a pressure cooker without any job security. One mistake and he is out on his ear, no explanations needed. Not to mention the stress of sitting in a car with Eddie Rimbauer watching him like a hawk for ten straight hours.

We start with a little small talk. He looks over at my book case, gets up, pulls out the book I wrote for police families. "Looks good. Think I'll buy a copy for my wife. For her birthday." He walks back to the chair and sits down again.

"So," I say. "Where shall we begin?"

"Is this confidential?"

"Of course." I hand him a copy of my office policy. "Read this when you get home. It explains the limits of confidentiality. What it says is that I have to report you if you are a danger to yourself or others, unable to care for yourself, or abusing children or old people."

"But no other time? You don't have to talk to my FTO?"

"Not without your permission. You sound worried."

"You went to the FTO meeting last week. What did he say about me? Am I going to get fired?"

"I thought you got feedback every day about your job performance."

"That's why I'm worried. Does he think I'm mentally off? Is that why he wanted me to see you?"

"No. Officer Rimbauer recognizes that you're having trouble. He thought I might be able to help."

"How?"

"I don't know yet. I need you to tell me what's going on."

"You're sure this is confidential?"

"Yes."

"He hates me. He's on my case day and night. Sometimes, he just stares at me. Nothing I do is right. He rides me so hard, I forget stuff I know. And he puts me down. Mocks me. Calls me Mr. Safeway in front of everyone. You heard him. Stands there and rolls his eyes. I can't sleep. I can't eat. My stomach aches all the time. I've lost ten pounds since I started with him. I didn't expect this. I did fine with my first FTOs, and then I go to Rimbauer and I can't do anything right. I'd ask for another FTO, but I'd sound like a crybaby. Like I'm making excuses for myself. Everyone will think that I'm blaming him for my mistakes." He sits up. "Could you get me another FTO?"

"I don't think I have the authority to do that. What I can do is sit down with you and Officer Rimbauer and try to work out your conflicts. It's obvious you have very different personalities."

Ben laughs. "His way or the highway. That's how he works things out."

"Ben, we're getting a little ahead of ourselves. I might be more helpful if I knew more about you. Tell me a little about yourself."

He shrugs his shoulders as though shifting a great weight.

"What do you want to know?"

"What made you become a police officer?"

His lips twitch. I can't tell if he's smiling or grimacing.

"I always wanted to be a cop. I put myself through the academy. I was number one in my class in academics."

He looks to me. I can feel him pulling for some acknowledgement, some approval. The best I can muster is a smile and a nod. Being a good student has little to do with being a good street cop. Academic-types like to revel in nuance and collect data before making decisions. Cops need to think on their feet and think fast. What they do, they do in the dark, in the rain, often before they even know who's who and what's what. To hesitate is to get killed or get someone else killed.

"It must be quite a shock to go from first in your class to feeling like you're failing."

"Until I met Rimbauer, I never failed anything in my life."

"Do you like police work?"

He falls silent, seeming to sort out what he wants to say from what he thinks I want to hear.

"At first I thought it was awesome. I couldn't believe I could get paid for having so much fun. I would have done it for nothing if I could."

This is what young cops always say. Two years on the job and that changes. Now they own trucks, condos, ski boats, motorcycles, snowmobiles and have a mountain of debt. In a few years they'll start billing their departments for every 15 minutes of overtime.

"And now?"

He winces and shrugs his shoulders. A small tic pulses on his cheek.

"The truth is, I don't know. I wanted to be a cop to help people. All Eddie wants me to do is lock people up. We served a warrant on some guy in East Kenilworth for stolen property. He had stacks of TVs and computers in his garage. There were a bunch of little kids there. They were clinging to his legs, crying and screaming, "Daddy, don't go Daddy." I wanted to cite and release, but Eddie made me put him in cuffs in front of his kids and take him to jail. I grew up in East Kenilworth. People there are poor. They do what they can to make money. The guy wasn't violent."

Ben's cheeks redden slightly as he talks. Something about this incident has personal meaning for him. I know the part of town he's talking about. East Kenilworth is as different from Kenilworth as night from day. Most people call it Little Mexico. It's in the flatlands, separated from Kenilworth's hilly affluent neighborhoods and shopping districts by a north to south freeway that runs the length of California – one city divided into two worlds, separated by language, culture and money.

"Cops used to hassle me and my friends when I was a teenager. They liked to run us out of a park near my house for loitering. We weren't doing anything wrong. We weren't gang bangers. We didn't use drugs, didn't rob people, didn't do graffiti. The worst I ever did was drink a beer in public. We're Hispanic. I didn't like how the cops treated us. I remember thinking that I thought I could do better."

"And now?"

"Oh yeah. I can do way better than Rimbauer."

"How does your wife feel about you being a police officer?"

"She likes it okay. Pays the bills. She wishes I was around more."

"And the rest of your family?"

"My parents are dead. They died when I was ten. My grandparents raised me. They're okay with it."

"How did your parents die?"

His jaw muscles begin tensing and flexing under his skin. "In a car crash." He looks straight at me, his eyes suddenly wary as though I am a dental hygienist aiming at the soft tissue between his teeth with a sharp instrument. There's something he doesn't want me to know or something he doesn't want to deal with himself. I have no right to force him to reveal his feelings. I couldn't if I tried. I need to wait until he trusts me. Therapy takes time, and I don't have a lot of time before Rimbauer pulls the plug.

"Not a big deal. It was a long time ago. Fourteen years. It wasn't like I was neglected or anything."

"Losing both your parents when you were ten? Sounds like a big deal to me."

"My grandparents thought so too. Forced me to see some social worker with moony eyes. It was like she took classes looking sympathetic. I just went to please them. Why is everyone interested in my parents? The person who did my psych gave me a real hard time over it." He shifts in his seat. "How come you didn't do my psych?"

I make a mental note to call Mark and get Ben's pre-employment evaluation.

I change the subject. "So Ben? How long have you been married?"

He smiles broadly, rounding his face. "Just a couple of weeks, actually. We haven't even had time for a honeymoon. I kept quiet because I didn't want it to be a big deal. You know how they're always telling you not to make any big moves or buy anything while you're in FTO in case you don't make it. Maybe I should've listened." He looks at his watch. "What am I going to do, Doc? I don't think I can get through two more weeks with Rimbauer."

"He's a tough one, I'll give you that. But you can't change him. Hard enough to change yourself, let alone anyone else. Ever try to go on a diet or start an exercise program?"

We laugh together at this little joke about human frailty. "All you can do is control your own reactions, calm down when you're feeling stressed. It's a start. You can't think clearly when you're stressed, no one can. And you can't calm your mind until your body is calm. So let's start there."

I take out a folder of handouts on breathing techniques and progressive relaxation. I don't know if it will work. People spend years mastering self-soothing skills. But it is a first step. Ben is a nice kid, maybe too nice for this job. But he's had a rough start in life. He needs a break and, I hate to admit this to myself, I need to feel helpful.

"Start practicing these exercises. They're very easy. Work on them for 20 minutes a day. Just follow the instructions. They'll help your concentration. When your concentration improves, so will your performance."

He flips through the papers I hand him and flashes another smile. "Rimbauer told me you were going to hypnotize me or ask me if he reminded me of my father."

"Sorry to disappoint you." I pick up a second file and hand it to him. "This is a learning style inventory. It will take you about 30 minutes to complete. Do it at home and bring it with you for our next appointment. We all learn differently. This will give us a profile of how you organize information. I have a hunch you're a little different than most officers."

"What do you mean? Different how?"

"More sensitive, maybe. More of a people person than most. I noticed that you took a great interest in that old man who hung himself. You seemed concerned. Many cops wouldn't even notice or care."

"So, is that bad or good?"

"It can be very good. Cops need people skills because most of what they do involves talking to people."

He looks relieved though I'm only making him feel better for the moment. What he really needs is a tough skin to shed all the misery he's going to see. Instead, I fear he's covered with Velcro. Orphaned at ten, any call involving abandonment or child abuse has the potential to hit him hard and not let go.

"I'm sure I can help you and Officer Rimbauer sort things out." I don't feel as certain as I sound, but hope is all I have to offer. "We'll go over your learning inventory at our next appointment and then we'll bring Officer Rimbauer into the discussion. In the meantime, if you have any questions, feel free to call me."

He looks skeptical. "Okay, Doc, if you say so. I'm at the end of my rope." I flash back to the old man on the floor, to the endless loop of slides, and to the look on Ben's face. The unconscious works overtime. His is an interesting, though not accidental, choice of words.

I don't want to, but I call Mark and ask him to share Ben's pre-employment psych assessment. I can picture him at his desk, burnished with the glow of his new young love. He'll be glad to hear from me, eager to help, full of all the happy details of his new life. I can hardly bear to hear his voice or fend off his efforts at friendship. Most of all, I can't bear knowing he is immune to my sorrow. He answers on the third ring. I lie and tell him I have only a few minutes to talk because a client is waiting.

He doesn't remember Ben. "Getting old," he jokes. "And busy. I've done so many psychs in the last six months they all run together. Melinda's helping out, but she's studying for her licensing exam. Let me get his file. I'll call you back in five."

He calls back in ten.

"Sorry. I can't find his folder. We're in the middle of switching over to a new computerized system and things are a mess, boxes everywhere. It's costing me a fortune, but the old system can't support the volume of testing I'm doing, and the state insists I encrypt all my reports. I'll keep looking. Plus two of my clerical staff are out. One's on vacation and the other one broke her collarbone in a bike accident. Sorry, babe, I know you need it now."

I bristle at his calling me babe.

"How're you doing? Things working out at the PD?"

"I'd better go," I say. "My client's waiting."

"Anytime. My phone's always on the hook for you."

Chapter Four

Eddie Rimbauer is waiting for me in the hall the first day back after his four days off. I'm on my way to meet with the supervisor of records. Two of her employees have a cantankerous relationship. They fight over who takes the longer coffee break and does the least work. Their chronic low-grade anger is affecting the unit's morale, and though she doesn't say so, I can see the supervisor is worn down as much as anyone else having to babysit two grown women in their fifties.

"Step into my office," Eddie says and ushers me through a stairwell door into an airless, dimly lit landing. His eyes are puffy and irritated. "How'd you make out with Mr. Safeway?" He hooks his fingers behind his belt, on either side of his drooping belly, and rocks back on his feet.

"Sorry. I hope you understand, but I can't tell you much beyond the fact that he kept his appointment and that I'm going to do my best to help him. The details of our conversation are confidential."

"I don't want to know if he's screwing his mother. All I want to know is what's stressing him out."

"To be honest, I think you're being too rough on him. I know humor is an important way to defuse stress, but from what I saw at that suicide call – excuse my bluntness – but I thought your humor was over the top. You were humiliating him." I'm sweating. I can feel steam rising in my clothes. Eddie is staring at me, his gray eyes glinting like bullets. The edges of his ears are tinged with pink.

"What about his other FTOs, Eddie? Tell me what they've said about him."

"That he's the best thing since sliced bread. Everyone likes him because he tries hard. But trying hard doesn't mean he can do the job, and they don't have the balls to tell him that. So they pat him on the back and he shows up for work the next day, fat, dumb, and happy. Thinks he's acing the program until he gets to me. And then it's shock city. I give him what he deserves. They don't pay me to be a rubber stamp."

"I think you're putting too much pressure on him."

"And you know this how? From your years of experience as a cop? From all those books you wrote in your ivory tower? This is a police department. He has to take pressure. If he wants sympathy tell him to look in the dictionary between shit and syphilis." The edges of his ears are now flaming red.

"Have you ever asked him why he's so stressed out?"

"Are you kidding? He doesn't say a word all day. Clams up. Looks at his feet. Ten hours in the cruiser with a frigging corpse."

"Doesn't sound easy for either of you. Give me a couple more sessions and then I'd like you to join us, see if we can't sort out your differences."

"That's it?"

"What were you hoping for?"

"Beats me. I just wanted to cover all my bases before the chief pulls the plug on the poor schmuck." He reaches for the door, opens it a crack and lets it close again. "Let me tell you a couple of things, Doc. For your own good." The light in the stairwell is murky with dust motes. "Number one: that confidentiality crap doesn't fly with cops. We do our jobs out in the open with the ACLU on our ass. We don't have a lot of sympathy for shrinks who get to fuck up behind closed doors. Number two: learn how to make yourself useful around here. People are laughing at you behind your back. They think you're a joke. Another bullet point on the chief's resume. Or his latest punch."

He opens the door to the hall. A stream of air hits my face as the door closes behind him. I press my forehead against the cool metal. Outside in the hall, I can hear people laughing. Eddie can't be right. He's trying to intimidate me. I'm not a joke. People aren't laughing at me behind my back. Not yet. Not so soon.

I take the elevator up to Baxter's office. My hands are still trembling after my confrontation with Eddie. He's a big bully, just the kind of cop my father would hate. Throws his weight around when he doesn't need to, just to satisfy himself. My ex does the same thing, only with a gloss of concern and affection for my well being. Well I've had it being nice to men who aren't nice to me. My job description mandates me to identify sources of organizational stress and bring them to the chief's attention. No one else has dared to take Eddie on, certainly not his recruits. It's risky. If I get a reputation for being a snitch, no one will talk to me, ever again.

Baxter's office is a perfectly square room paneled in dark knotty pine and carpeted in brown shag. For forty years, nothing has changed in this office but the chief of police. There is a worn spot on the rug in front of his desk where generations of nervous officers have been literally called on the carpet. I walk to the middle of it. Baxter is leaning over his desk, studying a large map of the city that he keeps under the glass top, as though considering the possibility that he has gone to the wrong office. The large bay window behind him is opaque with fog. There are dark circles under his eyes. He senses my presence and picks up a thick sheaf of papers. "Budgets, same torture every year. Same fight over who has to make cuts. How you doing? Getting along okay?"

"I need to talk to you about something. I've been working with Ben Gomez. As you know, he isn't doing well. What you may not know is that the primary reason he isn't doing well is that he isn't getting along with his FTO, Eddie Rimbauer. Is there any possibility he could ask for another FTO?"

"Recruits always blame their FTOs when they get in trouble. Eddie is tough. If he's putting on the pressure, it's for a good reason."

"How can you be sure?"

"I spend over $100,000 dollars on recruitment and training for every rookie I hire. That's a big investment. I want them to succeed. I give them every chance I can, more time in the program if they need it, remedial training, whatever it takes. This is not boot camp. I don't let my FTOs deliberately harass recruits. That's old school. If Eddie was harassing anyone, I would know it."

"Maybe yes, maybe, no. The chief can be the last to know what goes on at the line level."

Baxter's eyes spark. "You've been here less than a month and you're telling me I don't know how my organization works?"

For the second time this morning I'm being dismissed because I'm a no-nothing civilian. "I'm only suggesting that Eddie Rimbauer may not be the person you think he is."

"And you know this how?"

"By watching him, talking to him, listening to what people say about him."

"Like who?"

"I can't say."

"If you have some specific information about Eddie, you'd better tell me." He pauses for a second and waggles his head. I can hear his neck crack. "Do you?"

I say nothing.

"So this is your intuition telling you Eddie is the problem?"

"Yes and no."

"Which is it?" He leans forward in full interrogator mode. "Look, Dot, if you have something specific to report about Eddie or Ben Gomez, I'll listen. But I'm not interested in speculation." He cracks his neck again. I don't know if this is a nervous tic or some kind of intimidation tactic. "Who, beside me, asked you to check on Ben Gomez?"

"Eddie did."

"That doesn't sound like harassment to me."

"Ben is already circling the drain. All Eddie is doing is covering his tracks. I want you to authorize me to meet with all the recruits on a weekly basis, not just when I'm asked. If I'm going to be helpful, I need to know early on who's in trouble. Make it policy so it won't look like I'm singling anyone out."

His bottom jaw juts out and he flaps his lower lip over the upper as though contemplating a question of national security. "Sure. Have at it. I have nothing to hide."

"What about giving him a new FTO?" I'm really pushing my luck.

"It's a bad precedent to switch FTOs when a rookie's not doing well. There may be other ways to handle this. Let's think outside the box." He walks next to me and clamps his meaty hand on my shoulder. There's something about him that makes me hope I never get caught alone with him in an elevator. "Give me a little time. I'm paying big bucks for your advice. I should listen."

Chapter Five

"What did you say to him?" Ben is in my office for his second appointment.

"Sit down, Ben. You look distressed."

He stays standing, a caul of red spreading across his face.

"You said this was confidential."

"It is."

"I've been extended. Two more weeks with that asshole. Did you do that?"

This is Baxter, thinking outside the box. He might have consulted with me first.

"He's been treating me like shit. Worse than ever. Making snide remarks. Asking me in front of everyone if the shrinklette is helping me with my problems."

"I never said a word to him about our conversation. Nothing."

"You must have said something."

"Sit down, Ben, please. I can't talk to you while you're standing."

He sucks in a breath as if debating with himself and then sits on the edge of my couch, his feet flat on the floor, ready to sprint.

"I asked Eddie a question. I wanted to know what your other FTOs had said about you."

"You challenged him?"

"I asked him to clarify something."

He laughs and leans back, shaking his head. "Shit. You don't ask Eddie Rimbauer to clarify anything. I stopped asking him to clarify the second day of training. It's too big a price to pay. He's going to fire me. I can feel it. I'm this close." He raises his hand, his thumb and index finger almost touching. It is the same gesture Eddie had made in the FTO meeting two weeks ago.

"Sometimes our worst enemies are our best teachers. You're learning what not to do, aren't you? Just the way you wanted to be different from the police officers you knew as a kid." It's a desperate attempt at reframing the situation and Ben isn't buying it. I'm arguing with logic and he's living with fear.

He rolls forward to the edge of his seat and jabs his finger at me. He's picking up more from Eddie than he realizes. "You're not sitting next to him ten hours a day. He doesn't have the power to fire you. Don't you get it? If he fires me, I'm toast. No one will hire me. I need this job. My wife is three months pregnant. I'm going to be a father."

He smiles for the moment and then loses it as the enormity of parenting sinks in. I'm terrible at math, but it's obvious that his wife was pregnant before they got married. What a pile-up – new wife, new baby, new job, and who knows, a shotgun wedding with pissed-off in-laws.

"I'll tell you what he wants. He wants me to quit so he can bad mouth me to every police department I apply to."

"You talk as though he has a personal vendetta against you."

"That's what it feels like."

"Why?"

"How do I know? Maybe he doesn't like the way I look."

"Ben, there are going to be more Eddies in your future. Supervisors you don't like, police chiefs who make bad decisions. You can't pick and choose your superiors, and you can't control the ones you get. It's the nature of this business."

His head recoils just lightly and he raises his split eyebrow. "Are you telling me to quit?"

"No. I'm only saying that the FTO program is the time to try this job on for size. Like you said when we first talked, this job isn't turning out the way you expected it to. Or maybe you just don't like this department and would fit better somewhere else. Cops do that all the time, go somewhere else that suits them better."

I flash to my own life. If leaving was so easy, why had I clung to Mark?

Ben shakes his head as though I haven't a clue. He chews the inside of his cheek. His eyes are bright, almost feverish. "I worked too hard to get this job. I'm not going to let that sonofabitch drive me out of here. If I go, he'll have to drag me out feet first."

"That's the spirit. Get mad. Get determined. It'll give you what you need to get through these next two weeks. You've been through a lot in your life. Think about what or who got you through the tough times. Use those same tactics again. Who's your back-up? Your go-to person when you need help."

"My wife, I guess."

"Good. Does she know what's happening?"

Cops are notorious for keeping their work life a secret at home. Their intentions are to spare their families and keep the crap they see from contaminating their family life. It rarely works out. The silence only creates distance and hurt feelings.

"She's got enough to deal with. She's throwing up a lot. And when she's not throwing up, she's sleeping."

"One of the hazards of police work is that it takes over your life. It's very important for young couples to work together so this doesn't happen. Right now is one of the most stressful times in your career, but it's temporary. You need your wife. Let her help."

"Like how?"

"Help you study, quiz you on the penal code. Listen while you blow off steam. There's lots of things she could do."

"I'm acing the tests. It's my command presence and officer safety shit that's a problem. What am I supposed to do, practice choke holds on my pregnant wife?"

"Why do you call it officer safety shit?"

"Eddie acts like there's an ax murderer behind every door. Treats old ladies like they have an Uzi up their sleeves."

The idea of old women carrying guns is actually more appealing than the frail, brittle-boned and defenseless future I imagine life has in store for me.

Ben shakes his head and says, "I don't think you have to treat people like criminals until you know they are. That's why people hate cops."

"Look, Ben, you may not like Eddie, but he has a lot more street experience than you do. Years and years. You get to be the kind of cop you want to be after you get off probation. In the meantime, your job is to imitate Eddie and get through FTO. Think of it like getting a plumbing license. Do what you need to do to get through this. You'll have plenty of time to develop your own style."

He shrugs.

"Now, back to your wife. I think it's a good idea if I sat down with the two of you. It sets a good pattern for working things out as a family and you're going to have a family pretty soon. Talk to her about coming in to see me. It couldn't hurt."

Chapter Six

I miss the next FTO meeting because it's on a Sunday, and I don't want to miss my women's group one more time. We've been meeting since grad school when we were drawn together to talk about women and psychotherapy. Did therapy help women change the patriarchal structure or did it just help them adjust to an oppressive system? Now we talk about lumps and grandchildren. I love these women like sisters. Without them, I wouldn't have survived my dissertation or my divorce. I tell Sgt. Lyndley that I'll check in on Monday for an update on Ben.

My office phone is ringing as I open the door on Monday morning. It's Eddie. "Have a nice weekend, Doc?"

"Yes, thank you."

"Nice to have a weekend off. I got to baby sit Mr. Safeway."

"So, how's he doing?"

"Like crap. Circling the drain. The guy's a window licker on a short bus."

"A what?"

"A retard. He doesn't get it. Never will. All we're doing these two weeks is going over stuff he should have got in the first phase. See for yourself. We got a Redman training day on Thursday. Defensive tactics. Four o'clock. It's his last day of extension, kind of like a graduation ceremony. I'm sure you'll want to be there."

The old Kenilworth High School is a sprawling, one-story structure composed of multiple buildings surrounded by concrete. It was long ago declared unsafe for students but apparently not for cops who have claimed the old school for a training facility. Crushed and bent traffic cones left over from a defensive driving class litter the parking lot on the west side of the complex. There is blackened refuse on the east side where some fire department has burned the dilapidated buildings for practice. Baxter's right. The department needs a new public safety building.

I drive around until I spot a pod of police cars parked behind a large flat-roofed building. I follow the grunts and shouts and the flat, thwacking sound of bodies landing on floor mats until I find the gym. The room is hot and reeks of sweat. I look for Ben and Eddie and don't see either one. Cops are yelling and swinging their batons at the instructor who is dressed in puffy red protective gear, looking like Spiderman with a bad case of edema. One at a time the Redman deflects their blows and throws them on their backs where they lay panting and groaning.

I remember my own very different kind of training, poisonously polite conversations with supervisors who would stab me in the back and smile. That all changed for the better when Mark became my supervisor and for the worse after we married. For a moment I entertain a delicious fantasy, me in the Redman suit, Mark on his back like a bug.

"You little pants shitter. Get your ass over here." I don't have to look to see who is screaming or who he's screaming at. Ben comes out from behind a wall with his baton in his hand. He's wearing a protective helmet and holding a bloody tissue to his lip. "Get the fuck in there." Eddie pushes him toward the Redman. "You don't get to vote on this. Go."

Ben drops the tissue and raises his baton over his head. For a moment I think he is going after Eddie. Then he turns and charges into the ring, shouting something I can't understand. He takes a few futile swings before the Redman lifts him off his feet and slams him into the mat face down, gasping for breath. Or crying. I can't tell which. Somebody blows a whistle and announces the training is over, time to pack up and go home.

"See what I mean?" Eddie's standing behind me. "He's a liability. We can train him 'til the cows come home, he won't be nothing but a civilian in a cop suit. You can kiss the chief's ass all you want, this kid's ready for the blue juice."

Ben is standing by his car, a non-descript white two door sedan badly in need of body work. Ben could use some body work himself. Beside his split lip, he has a large swelling welt on his cheek and multiple scrapes on his arms.

"I hate this. He made me go in four times. Nobody else had to do that many."

"He's afraid for you. Police work is dangerous. You have to be able to defend yourself. Or defend someone else. He's trying to teach you."

"Call that teaching? Throw me in the ring, kick the crap out of me and make me do it again."

"You need to be prepared for the unexpected. That's what gets cops killed."

"Tell Rimbauer about being prepared. He's so fat he can't walk 10 feet without getting out of breath."

"Eddie's not on trial here. You are."

I sound like a mother scolding a small child. It's dark and it's starting to drizzle. I want to go home. Yelling is only putting salt on his wounds. I take a deep breath. The poor kid is desperately trying to hang onto his job. He has a wife to support and a baby on the way. That's a lot more stress than being cold and getting my hair wet.

He turns suddenly and opens the door to his car. "I got to go home. The wife's waiting for me. She's pretty moody since she got pregnant." He starts to get in his car and pauses. "I'm sorry I yelled at you. I know you're trying to help. I'm trying, I really am. Rimbauer won't cut me a break, and everybody else is too afraid to stand up to him. You're the only one who tried and it didn't work. This two week extension business wasn't worth crap. I want a chance with another FTO. If I can't cut it with somebody else, then so be it, I'm out of here. Can you help me out, Doc? I don't know who else to ask."

"Here's what I'll do. I'll go back to HQ and talk to the chief, see if I can get you extended with another FTO." The muscles in his jaw relax and I hear him loose a long sigh. "In exchange, you and your wife will meet with me tomorrow at 10:00 a.m. We have a lot to talk about."

He starts to say something but changes his mind.

Baxter doesn't believe me. He's spent ten minutes lecturing me about what a good FTO Eddie Rimbauer is. "He has his problems, granted, and he's rough around the edges, but he knows his stuff. He was my training officer back in the day, and I learned a lot from him."

I am not persuaded by Baxter's testimonial or his example. "One last chance and that's it. Ben just wants the opportunity to work with another FTO. If he doesn't make it, then he's ready to quit. He has a lot of heart. If it were me, I'd have quit weeks ago. You should have seen him. He was exhausted, beaten up, humiliated, and he kept trying."

"I've already extended him two weeks. There has to be an end. We can't keep training him indefinitely. Not everybody's cut out for this work. I try to weed them out before I hire them."

"Then give me another chance. I've only met with him twice. That's not enough time to figure out what's wrong and to see if it's fixable, especially since he had already had three weeks with Eddie. By the time I saw him, his self-confidence was in the dumps."

I can see Baxter flexing under his jacket, as though his muscles and his brain were looped together. "Okay. Here's what I'm going to do. I'm going to give him a week off so he can rest up. He's probably exhausted. Then I'm going to start him with another FTO. If he doesn't measure up, he's out. I'm making an exception here because my new department psychologist is recommending it. I hope you know what you're doing, Doc."

Me too, I think to myself.

April isn't what I expected, although I'm not sure what that was. She is short and plump beyond pregnant. She is wearing black leggings and a low cut, sarong style jersey top that shows off her mother-to-be mammaries to great advantage. Apparently modesty has gone out of style for pregnant women. She appears dressed to remind everyone of how she got pregnant and what she'll be up to after she gives birth.

"Dr. Meyerhoff, this is my wife April. April, this is Dr. Meyerhoff."

Ben looks as though he hasn't slept. He seems thinner than ever and there are dark shadows under his eyes. We shake hands. April's is doughy and warm. Her nails are painted midnight blue. "Nice to meet you," she says and pulls her hand away.

"Thanks for coming in. Sit anywhere you're comfortable."

She looks around the office. Ben looks at her. Finally she chooses the big chair that sits at right angles to the couch. Ben sits at the end of the couch closest to her and reaches for her hand. She crosses her feet at the ankles. She is wearing sandals and each of her toes is painted a different fluorescent color, like tiny tropical fish. There are daisies drawn on her big toes and in the center of each daisy is a small rhinestone. I wonder if she did this herself or if she paid someone to give her a pedicure. Given their circumstances and the tenuous hold Ben has on his job, I wouldn't think there was anything left over in their budget even for little luxuries.

"Ben says you haven't been feeling well, so I appreciate your making the effort to be here this morning."

She shifts slightly in her seat, withdraws her hand from Ben's and sets it lightly over her belly. Ben's head is tilted forward. His eyes dart back and forth between April and the floor.

"Let's start with the good news," I say. Ben looks up. "Chief Baxter has agreed to give you another FTO, kind of a last chance opportunity."

Ben makes a fist and pumps it in the air. "Yes." It comes out like a hiss. He turns to April. "I told you I'd work something out." He turns back to me. "Thank you, Doc. Thank you, thank you, thank you."

"There's even more good news. He wants you to take a week off before you start with your new FTO. He thinks, and I agree, that you must be exhausted. Wouldn't be fair to you or to a new FTO if you're weren't rested up."

"Is he going to get paid for that week?" April asks.

"Jesus, April," Ben says under his breath.

"We need things for the baby."

"The baby won't be here for another six months."

They sink into sulky silence.

"Sounds like things are pretty tense between you two at the moment. No surprise, considering the stress you're both under. That's why I wanted to talk to you together."

April turns her eyes to me. She has a practiced neutrality, almost like a cop. I wonder what's behind that cool façade.

"We're okay," she says.

"No we're not." Ben's looks at me, his eyes pleading for understanding. Red blotches mar his cheeks and forehead. "We're here. We might as well be honest. We don't talk, we don't have sex, we don't do anything together anymore. All you do is sleep and play on your computer."

April's mouth knots up in a snarl. "And all you do is work. You're never home, so how can I do anything with you?" She looks at me. "And when he's home, all he wants to talk about is work. Boring." She cuts the word in two, each syllable slowly rolling off her tongue like a bolt of cloth.

"Okay," I say. "We need a break. Ordinarily, when I start working with a couple, I like to spend a little time with each of them individually. I've had a chance to talk with Ben alone, so maybe, April, you and I could talk for a few minutes while Ben waits in the lobby. Would that be okay?"

She gives me a 'whatever' look and Ben bolts for the door.

"So, April, let's back things up a little bit. Like I said, I can see that you are both under a lot of strain. I understand why. You have a lot on your plates. The trouble is, you're fighting each other, not the problem. It's not easy being a cop and it's certainly not easy being pregnant. You're probably just getting used to living together."

I wait for her to react, to wince, smile, well up with tears, anything to show me that I've hit the mark. But I get nothing. I already have rapport with Ben. I need to connect with April too or we won't get anywhere. Couples counseling is like walking a tight rope. Each partner silently keeping score, gauging the therapist's every facial tic as a mark for one side or the other. I start again with something neutral.

"Tell me, how did you and Ben meet?"

"At community college, in the library."

"Love at first sight?"

"It was for him. He said I was the most beautiful girl he had ever met."

"Wow. That's quite a compliment."

She shrugs.

"And for you? Instant attraction?"

"Not really. I mean, Ben's hot, but I know a lot of hot guys."

"But you didn't marry them."

"Because of my Dad."

"What do you mean?"

"The guys I went out with, he'd run their license plates and everything to see if they had a juvie record. Grill them about where we were going and who was driving. Most of the time guys never asked me out again. Ben was way responsible. And he wanted to be a cop."

"Is your Dad a cop?"

"Used to be. He's the district attorney of Sacramento County."

Knocking up the district attorney's daughter. Not a great start for a cop. Good thing they don't work in the same county.

"So, how do you like being married?"

"Okay, I guess."

"You and Ben are fighting a lot?"

"Same as everybody. Same as my parents."

"Different from what you expected?"

She looks at her watch. "Is this going to take much longer? I'm hungry. I eat all the time. By the time I have this baby I'm going to weigh a ton."

"I mean, if I were in your place, young, pregnant, not feeling well, and my husband was totally preoccupied with work, I might feel lonely or resentful."

"I told you before. I'm bored. And I'm bored talking to you."

"And maybe a little angry, too?"

"I don't get angry."

"Everyone gets angry."

"Not me. Can Ben come back in?"

She stands up without waiting for an answer and opens the door. Ben walks in, looking from April to me and back again. I wonder if he sees the pounding under my cheekbones or the way the muscles in the back of my neck are pulled tight as a drum. A good therapist would have more compassion for April. I just want to shake the little bitch by her shoulders. So much for therapeutic neutrality.

We look at each other, each of us waiting for the other to say something. I pick up the gauntlet. "Okay then, let's move on. Every couple has at least ten irreconcilable differences. It's not abnormal to fight, all couples do. The trick is to repair the damage after the fight. That's why I'm recommending that you go away together. The chief has given you a week off. You told me you never had a honeymoon, so why not take one now? Given all the stress in your lives, it appears that you've both lost touch with how things were between you when you first met."

A visible flush inches up Ben's neck, no doubt stirred by thoughts of rekindling their early days of hot sex. He takes a deep breath and says, "I need to study."

April rolls her eyes, making sure I notice.

"You need a break more. April's right, you can't keep going like this. And April needs a break too." I look at her for acknowledgement. She is examining her fingernails. I look back at Ben. "Being pregnant is not easy. You need to pay attention to what's going on with her as much as she needs to hear what you're going through. Treat yourselves to a change of scenery. You won't have another opportunity after you go back to work and certainly not after you have the baby. Use this time to slow down and talk. Really talk."

Ben looks at April. April looks at her toes.

"Getting your relationship back on track. Is this something you want?" I ask them.

April nods. Ben looks down, his shoulders compressing under the weight of this new task I've given him.

I go to my file and get my handout on active listening skills. "I want you to learn something we call active listening. It's a simple way to improve your communication. All it takes is learning to restate what your partner says and reflect back their emotions. Take these, too."

I give them my handout on problem solving. I feel like a grade school teacher distributing home work sheets, only without the purple ink and the smell of the mimeograph machine. I doubt that Ben or April ever heard of a mimeograph machine.

"You need to fix the problem, not the blame. Problem solving is easy when you know how. Look at these together when you get the chance."

Almost two hours have passed. I'm tired and I have to pee.

"I've given you a lot of things to think about and an unusual homework assignment – get out of town and have some fun." I'm the only one smiling. "Feel free to call me from wherever you are, if you want to. Definitely call me when you get back. We'll make another appointment before you start with your new FTO."

They stand. Ben reaches to shake my hand. "Thanks, Doc. I appreciate everything you've done. It's going to be okay. I'm going to be okay."

April walks out of my office without a word.

Chapter Seven

There's an FTO meeting this morning. Sgt. Lyndley begins with two announcements. Number one – Ben has called in sick after his week off. This is not good. Rookies would come to work with two broken legs just to prove how tough and dedicated they are. Especially Ben.

Number two is a memo from the chief. Per our conversation nearly three weeks ago, Baxter is finally getting around to officially authorizing me to meet weekly with all recruits.

"Any questions?" Lyndley asks.

Eddie stands and turns away from the table. "Yeah. Is there a target on my back?"

"I'm assessing recruits, Eddie, not FTOs," I say.

"So that's why I have a new recruit and Gomez, who should be back at Safeway polishing apples as soon as he gets over the sniffles, has been assigned to someone else?" He walks toward me. "So you won't be running to Lyndley or the chief every time my new rookie whines to you that I'm abusing him and that's why he's fucking up?"

"No I won't. What I might have are some suggestions to make about modifying your training technique to match the recruit's learning style."

"Modify my training technique? Is that all?" He clutches his hands to his chest. "Be still my heart."

"Enough, Eddie," Lyndley says. "If that's what the chief wants, that's the way it is. End of discussion. We got a lot of recruits to review. Let's start with your new guy, Manny Ochoa."

Eddie sits down, pulls a pair of reading glasses from his pocket and puts them on. The tiny glasses look comical perched on the end of his large, knobby nose. He opens a folder and glances at the top page. "It's early days, but actually, the little beaner's doing pretty good. Excuse me. I mean the little bi-lingual Hispanic Latino beaner. He doesn't say much, but I think he's got good instincts and a taste for the job. We set up in front of a Mexican bar." He turns toward me. "FYI, illegals don't use banks. They keep all their cash with them so they can drink it up and send what's left back to Mexico. All the crooks have to do is wait outside the bar until they see one of these rubes weaving home on a bicycle and they jump him. It's like shooting fish in a barrel. We made three 211 arrests and threw a few of the beaners in the drunk tank. All in all, it was a productive evening."

He takes off his glasses. "You see, Doc? I don't eat all my young."

I'll get a chance to see for myself when I meet with Manny and the other recruits.

It is an enormous task, turning a civilian into a competent police officer. Common wisdom says it takes five years to become a good street cop – a hybrid human who is part priest, judge, counselor, rescuer and enforcer. Rookies have just sixteen weeks to memorize a mountain of codes, laws and policies. Sixteen weeks to perfect using the tools of the trade – cars, radios, maps, guns, tasers, pepper spray and handcuffs. Sixteen weeks to master officer safety, command presence, defensive tactics, communication skills, report writing and investigation. Not to mention the intangibles like judgment and intuition.

The first two rookies I see seem to be managing well, nothing but compliments for the quality of the training they are receiving. Despite all the stress of being novices, they are having the time of their lives. Their world is full of novelty and they are intoxicated by their own power. Neither of them has ever been assigned to Eddie Rimbauer.

Manny is ten minutes early for our appointment. I motion for him to take a seat. He waits for me to sit down before he does. He and Eddie are a thoughtless match, one so big and boisterous, the other compact, quiet, somber and quite handsome.

"How are things going for you?"

"Good. I'm learning a lot."

"I hear you're doing well. Officer Rimbauer gave you a good report at the FTO meeting."

He looks relieved.

"You have very different personalities and styles, don't you?"

He smiles for the first time. "Way different."

"Is that a help or a hindrance?"

"Both, I guess. All the FTOs have different styles. I learn from everybody. It just takes a little time to get used to a new FTO."

"How does Officer Rimbauer compare to the other FTOs?"

"He's way more experienced." He hesitates a moment. "And tougher."

"Too tough?"

"No."

"Do you know Ben Gomez?"

"Sure. Nice guy. We study together sometimes, that kind of thing."

"How's he doing? I was supposed to meet with him today, like I'm meeting with all the recruits, but he's sick."

Manny shrugs his shoulders. There are small seeds of sweat on his upper lip. This is not the direction he expected our interview to take. "Okay, I guess."

"Officer Rimbauer has an unusual sense of humor. I've heard him call Ben 'Mr. Safeway'. Does he tease you, too, or kid around in public?"

He pauses. "No, M'am. Not a problem, M'am."

His face is unreadable. He's a fast learner, has his professional demeanor down pat. Shrouding his innermost thoughts and feelings with an impenetrable mask is an essential tool of police work. Who wants to see a cop tremble with fear? What child molester would confess to someone who obviously finds him repulsive? Stupid of me to think that Manny or any other rookie would reveal something about his training officer, especially something bad, and especially to me.

"I've been asking all the questions, Manny. Do you have any questions for me?"

"Just one," he says, turning to a framed black and white photograph of Sigmund Freud that Mark had given me when I finished grad school.

"The guy in the picture? Is that your husband?"

Chapter Eight

I call Ben at home and get his answering machine. I wait for two hours, but he never calls me back, despite April's cheery electronic assurance that they will do so as soon as possible because they are really, really sorry to have missed my call and hope I'm having a really awesome day.

Baxter stops me in the hall. He's heard about Ben calling in sick and interprets it the same way I do. He gives me a pep talk. We tried our best, these things happen, no one's to blame. Who knows, maybe Ben will find a job with a smaller department, or maybe he should aim for something less challenging, like a community service officer position. He promises to call Ben and check in.

The next day Ben's letter of resignation is posted on the bulletin board on A-level. It is brief and to the point. He is resigning for personal reasons and thanks everyone for their support. I call Ben every day for another week. He never calls me back. I hate unfinished endings. Actually I hate endings of any kind, especially when I'm not the one who wants to call it quits.

Six weeks later Ben is dead and I am in the chief's office standing on that worn spot in the carpet. It is 5:30 a.m. I can see myself reflected in the window behind Baxter's desk, dark shadows beneath my eyes. The sun is coming up, marbling the black sky outside with bloody red stripes. Baxter is staring at his computer. "This is a first for me," he says. "A suicide note by email." I walk behind his desk so that I can see the screen: "Dear Chief Baxter: Thanks for treating me like dirt. There are some things you should know. Eddie Rimbauer is an emo loser."

"What's an emo loser?" I ask.

Baxter shrugs. "Beats me."

I continue reading: "Rimbauer was on my case every day. He's a bully. He tried to force me to quit. I went to the doctor for help. She only made things worse. She told me what I said was confidential and then she told him everything. She ordered me to bring my wife in for counseling which wrecked our marriage. I had a happy marriage and now I have nothing thanks to her."

Baxter shoves his desk chair under me before my knees give way and pours me a glass of water. "Want a copy?"

The printer spits it out before I can answer.

"I don't understand. He wasn't suicidal." My heart is pounding like I've just run up a flight of stairs. "He was happy about getting a new FTO. Happy about getting some time off. He was under a lot of stress, sure, so was his wife. But he trusted me. I know he did. Why didn't he call me? Why didn't he call someone?"

Baxter hands me Ben's note and sits on the edge of his desk, facing me.

"Dot, I need to know everything that happened between you two. Everything he told you about Eddie." He jerks his head from side to side, making that crackling noise in his neck.

"I can't tell you. It's confidential."

"He's dead."

"It still applies."

The law is unclear about this. I opt for the conservative answer. The small veins around Baxter's eyes and temples bulge.

"You don't get it. An officer under my command is dead. An officer I hired. I've already started an IA. You'll be compelled to give a statement."

"An internal affairs investigation on me?"

"On everyone connected with Ben. Remember, your firm was the one who recommended him, said he was psychologically stable."

"It's not my firm anymore, and I didn't do his psych."

"Well your name's still on the letterhead. Not to mention the fact that I hired you specifically to prevent this kind of thing from happening." He stands up. "I'm going to the briefing room to tell the troops. Then I'm going out to see the wife and her family. I'm not looking forward to this. Set up a psychological debriefing for our people tomorrow. I don't want any more casualties. Now, go home and take care of yourself. You look like shit."

That night I have a nightmare. I'm at the beach at a massive police convention when huge waves rise up without warning, giant walls of ocean hover overhead, threatening to crush everyone. I race through the crowd screaming, pleading, trying to get someone to pay attention to the impending catastrophe. It is as though I am invisible and everyone there is deaf. I wake just before the waves crash, gasping and panicked, my nightgown twisted around my legs like seaweed.

I arrange the chairs for the debriefing in a circle and then go to the cafeteria for coffee, cookies and a box of tissues. By the time I return, several officers have pushed their chairs out of the circle, up against the wall. Some are wearing sunglasses or pretending to be absorbed in their newspapers. The room is totally silent except for the rustle of pages being turned. I take a seat and ask for everyone's attention. I explain the ground rules for a debriefing: you have to be here, but you don't have to talk. Anything said should stay in the room. They look skeptical.

Eddie is a no show. His absence hangs over the meeting as heavily as Ben's death. The only free flowing conversation centers on his whereabouts. He'd been seen drinking at his favorite bar the night before. Someone said he was so drunk that if he opened his eyes, he would have bled to death. Someone else reports that as of this morning, his car was still in the parking lot behind the bar. For the rest of the debriefing, they just sit, wrapped in emotional Kevlar, staring at me, answering my questions with one word sentences. There is nothing to talk about – no war stories, no one in custody, and no suspects – just a dead cop hardly anyone knew and the stench of a preventable tragedy. It doesn't help that I am the person who might have prevented it, and I am running the debriefing.

Chapter Nine

There is a near Olympic competition to police death. Dying in the line of duty while doing battle with a crook gets the gold. The silver goes to the accidental on-duty deaths. On-duty deaths from heart attacks merit bronze. Suicide ranks a pitiful fourth – no honor guard, no 21 gun salute, no missing man flyover, no black ribbons on badges, no bagpipes, no flags at half mast, no fire trucks lining the overpasses and no mile-long cavalcade of patrol cars and motorcycles, flashers blinking, to accompany the casket.

April has chosen a funeral parlor in an industrial area south of Kenilworth. The walls are made of painted cinder block. Artificial flowers, their leaves weathered to an iridescent green, fill the window boxes. Without the usual funeral benefits accorded to line of duty deaths, this is apparently all she can afford.

The funeral director stands at the front door handing out programs. His fingernails are as long as a woman's and his hair curls below his collar in lank, greasy strands.

"There will be no reception after the service," he whispers. "The Patcher family plans to lay the deceased's body to rest later in the day in a private" — he emphasizes the word 'private' — "graveside ceremony at an undisclosed location." He is profoundly solicitous of everyone's understanding as though the decision is his, not the family's, and a bad one at that. He stands too close and nods his head constantly, obliging the listener to nod back reassuringly in order to escape into the cool quiet of the chapel.

Eddie is standing in the narrow space between the last pew and the wall. He is in uniform wearing his sunglasses and holding an unlit cigar. He gives no indication that he sees me. The room is barely half full. I see Baxter sitting by himself. When he sees me, he pats the place next to him and motions for me to slide in.

Across the aisle, an older woman is sobbing softly into a white handkerchief. The man next to her rests his arm across her back and pats her rhythmically without turning to look at her face. There is something familiar about his profile and the angle of his long thin nose. I wonder if these are Ben's grandparents.

The older man's eyes fix forward on the closed metal casket draped with an American flag. An eight by twelve photo of Ben, in uniform at his academy graduation, sits on a wooden easel next to the casket. His smiling presence feels like a personal rebuke. Something twines inside my chest and squeezes. I can feel a small pulse drumming beneath my cheekbones.

The piped-in organ music gets louder. There is a rustle from the back of the room. All heads turn as the family begins their slow walk down the center aisle. April hunches against her father, clinging to him as though she is blind as well as brokenhearted. Wisps of blonde hair spill out from under a veiled hat that conceals her downturned face. She is wearing a short, sleeveless black maternity dress.

Her father steps one foot at a time, in the slow cadence of the missing honor guard. Tall and thin, his sharp features concentrate into a mask, his eyes narrow and focused straight ahead. Her mother walks behind, shorter and heavier than April, dabbing at her eyes with a tissue. She wears soft shoes that wheeze under her weight. Behind her is the chaplain. He mounts the platform. With slow, careful movements he unfolds a purple vestment, slips it over his head and opens his bible. He looks out at the sparse crowd with a practiced mournful smile. The service is brief and shorn of any details about Ben's death. The chaplain makes it seem as if Ben has just evaporated in the line of duty on the threshold of a career he loved passionately, called by a benevolent God to stand watch in Heaven.

Afterwards, we line up to pay our respects to the family. Chief Baxter motions for me to go ahead of him as the line moves slowly forward. April stands next to the guest book. Rivulets of mascara puddle under her eyes and leak over her bloated cheeks. I open my arms to her.

"April, I'm so sorry. This is beyond words."

Her jaw goes slack and she covers her mouth with her hands. Her tiny diamond wedding band glints in the low light. She turns to her father. "Daddy, it's that doctor. She's here."

He lurches out of the receiving line, his arms stretched to the side like a human shield, blocking my view. He bends down until his face is level in front of mine. His voice is a low growl. "Leave my daughter alone. Do not call, do not write, do not try to get in touch with her or I'll have a restraining order issued against you. Understand me?"

"I'm sorry, I only want to help." I feel a bump from behind as Baxter takes me by the arm and pulls me toward the door. He doesn't let go until we are in the parking lot.

My heart is thumping so loudly I wonder if he can hear it.

"Vinnie Patcher," he says. "Mercenary son-of-a-bitch. Always out for himself. We went through the academy together and then he went to law school. Now he's Chief D.A. in Sacramento County. He's an ambitious bastard. Smells big money and he's salivating."

"Don't be so cynical. Grief makes people act crazy. His son in law's dead, his daughter is suffering and his grandchild is facing life without a father. You'd probably be crazy too, in the same situation."

"Don't be naïve. Patcher's crazy like a fox. I offered the family a liaison officer, an escort to the funeral, counseling, whatever. He didn't want any of it. Wouldn't even let me speak to his daughter. He doesn't care about Ben. I'm telling you, this guy is trouble. He's always been a pain in the ass. And now he's got a good cause."

Chapter Ten

I spend the weekend beating myself up for being a lousy therapist, a failure as a wife, and a disappointment as a daughter, consorting with the enemy when I should have been happily married and having children.

My mother calls and invites me for Saturday night country line dancing, the highlight of the week at her apartment complex. But I can't face her, over eager and expectant, grilling me for signs that my life is again filled with never ending prospects for a fabulous future.

If she's heard about Ben, she gives no indication. Since my father's death, she has stopped reading newspapers and watching television news because it is too depressing. She is, once again, the perpetual optimist of her youth, seemingly unchastened by the fact that her sunny outlook was to blame for hooking up with my father in the expectation that their life together would be bursting with utopian possibilities. She made our penury seem like an adventure in simple living, and blessed my father's crappy menial jobs for giving us an ethical life, free from corporate greed.

Where he saw evil, she saw a wounded spirit. Where he saw conspiracies, she saw a network of well intentioned, but ill-informed actors. As for my own truncated social life, she calls it a time for healing, during which my true life's companion is searching for me as hard as I am looking for him. Work is only something to fill the time before he makes his appearance.

I wake up at six on Monday, shower, and put on a black suit to match my mood. My house feels like a prison. Eddie and Ben have been dogging me for two days, tramping through my mind in a never-ending loop of images. Ben, alone and desperate, staring at his gun. Eddie, drunk, driving off the road into a ditch, the sound of his head cracking the windshield. Ben, terrified, cold metal against his skin, tears pooling in his eyes, thoughts racing — yes, no, yes, no — until the final yes and the sudden spray of blood and tissue.

I leave the house and head for the police department as soon as I'm dressed. No coffee, no juice.

I find Eddie in the report-writing room with Manny.

"What's up, Doc?" He waves his cigar in the air like a carrot. "How's things in the nuthouse? You know my boy, *Mañana*."

"*Manuelo*," Manny says in a soft voice. He stands up and shakes my hand. "Nice to see you again."

"Sorry to interrupt."

"Don't worry about disturbing us. *Mañana* has got to learn to multi-task. This isn't college, college boy, where you get to do one thing at a time. This here is po-leese work."

"You weren't at the debriefing," I say.

Eddie's eyes narrow just slightly. "Hey *Mañana*, run over to the cafeteria, get me a donut and coffee. And get the Doc something too."

I decline. He shoves a five-dollar bill in Manny's hand.

"Go out the door, turn right, walk up the stairs, turn left, and go through the big double doors marked c-a-f-e-t-e-r-i-a." He spells slowly and robotically. Manny's mouth is drawn into a thin line, his lips locked together. A growing ruddiness splotches his coffee colored complexion.

"So, Doc, what can I do you for?"

"I was concerned when you didn't show up at the debriefing."

He shrugs, tilts back in the chair and puts his feet on the desk.

"Why didn't you come? It was mandatory."

"Mental masturbation is for the kids. I don't need you or anyone else picking through the turds in my head. I got my own doctor, Doctor Jack Daniels." He pats his chest as though he has a bottle underneath his uniform. "I've done this job for years without talking about it. As far as I'm concerned, that debriefing crap is just a big circle jerk where everybody cries, says their feelings and leaves feeling worse than when they started. Too bad choir practice has gone out of style. A bottle of booze, some buddies in the parking lot and you get it all off your chest. Done. Finished. Kaput."

"Somebody said you've been on a binge."

He drops his feet to the floor, sits up in his chair and wheels around to face me. "Cops gossip more than girls. What I do on my own time is my own business. Period. You saw me at the funeral. Was I drunk? Maybe you noticed I was the only one there with enough respect to wear my uniform."

He shakes his head. "Stupid fucking kid. It was dumb to do himself, like everything else he did. He would have got over it, found another job. Nothing ever stays that bad."

"Sounds like you may be speaking from experience."

He stands up, his finger pointing at my chest. "Listen to me, Florence Nightingale. You can shove your mail order Ph.D. right up your ass. Ben Gomez was never going to be a cop. Never. The fact that he ate his gun over some dipshit thing proves my point." The door opens and Manny comes through holding a paper sack and a cup of coffee.

Eddie spins around. "Out. You don't come in until I tell you to come in."

The door closes. He turns back to me, his finger still pointing.

"What do you mean proves your point? What point?" I ask.

"Get over it, Doc. You can't fix it. Not now. You had your chance. And you can't fix me, so don't try."

He moves towards the door and opens it. "Heads up, *Mañana*. Time to hit the streets."

He turns toward me, backlit by the light in the hallway and bows slightly. "*Hasta lumbago*, Doc. Have a nice day."

Chapter Eleven

Gary Morse, thin as he was in graduate school, is leaning on the door to his office wearing his old corduroy jacket and holding an unlit pipe, his once long black hair almost entirely silvered.

"I've been waiting for you, Dot." His deep baritone voice is a balm. "How you doing?"

"Not too bad."

"The gang's all here getting coffee and settling down. I thought I'd walk in with you." It is like him to know exactly what I need.

Gary and I and the other therapists in our building meet once a month in the staff room to present cases to each other for peer consultation. Everyone knows about Ben. They must – it's been headline news, including the fact that, according to his father-in-law, he had been seeing me, the department's new psychologist.

There is a slight syncopation in the conversation as we walk in. Everyone looks at me, and when I look back, they turn their heads, pretending to be looking elsewhere. Someone hands me a cup of coffee. Someone else gives me a hug. They are restrained in their curiosity. They want details, but are too polite to ask directly. I'd probably feel the same if our situations were reversed. I join the charade, pretending not to notice how eager they are to learn what I have done wrong. I watch as they silently measure their competency against mine, the so-called expert in police psychology.

Gary walks upstairs to my office after the meeting. We walk out to a breezeway that overlooks a small garden. "You were pretty quiet in there."

"I didn't have anything to say."

He bangs his pipe against his shoe. Flakes of ash drift over our feet. He refills the pipe, tamping tobacco into the bowl with a nicotine stained finger. The fragrant aroma of burning tobacco settles on us like mist.

"Look, Dot," he says, "I don't know the particulars of what happened. If you want to tell me, I'm here to listen. And if you don't want to talk, that's fine too. I've been in this business as long as you have. When a client commits suicide, the therapist suffers. I know you must be going over and over it in your mind. I would be. Just don't be too hard on yourself. We've all made mistakes, big mistakes. Myself included. Join the crowd."

"Have you ever had a patient kill himself?"

He shakes his head no.

"Then let me tell you. Some mistakes are worse than others."

He takes a long draw on his pipe, exhaling the smoke with a soft whistle. He looks hurt.

"I'm sorry. I know you're only trying to help. I appreciate it. Can we change the subject?"

"Sure." He hesitates. "So what did you do this weekend beside beat yourself up?"

"Nothing much."

"Seeing anyone?"

"You sound like my mother. No, I'm not seeing anyone. All the decent men want women way younger than me."

"Not all of them. Janice and I are the same age." He takes another draw on his pipe. "I know you. You have pretty high standards, maybe too high when it comes to men?"

"I have two standards, vertical and breathing. And no therapists. I'm through with men who'd rather talk about a relationship than have one."

Mark and I had spent months in therapy. All the time he was secretly seeing Melinda, displacing his guilt onto me while I struggled to understand what I had done to make him so distant. I was trying to patch things up. He was trying to let me down easy.

"One more thing," I add. "Whoever he is, he should be turned on by cellulite."

Gary makes a face and gives me a gentle punch on my arm. "As a matter of fact, I have an idea for you. Janice and I are remodeling our house. We like the contractor a lot. He's easy going, responsible and plenty smart. I have no idea if he likes cellulite. His name is Frank and he's single. Interested?"

"Wait 'til the dust settles."

"When will that happen?"

"Your guess is as good as mine."

Chapter Twelve

Fran's Coffee Shop is a favorite with Kenilworth cops. Fran herself is a legend. I've been asked by the cops so many times if I've eaten there, that I feel like I'm failing some basic rite of passage.

This is one failure I can fix.

Fran is behind the counter turning enormous hamburgers on a griddle using a sheet rock trowel as a spatula. Onions and garlic sizzle in a pool of cooking oil. Her face is flushed and her hair curls damply over her ears.

She sets a bowl of soup in front of me. "Start with this, hon. I'll get your dinner order in a minute."

She moves quickly for a large woman, orchestrating conversations between patrons and shouting at a small troupe of developmentally disabled men working in the kitchen. At the rate they move, I suspect she employs them more as an act of charity than efficiency.

Police memorabilia and plastic flowers decorate the wall over the griddle. In the center is a small shrine to Fran's husband, B.G., a Kenilworth cop who was killed fifteen years ago responding to a domestic violence call. There are spots of grease and tomato sauce everywhere but on B.G.'s photo.

Three young Kenilworth cops are eating at the counter. One of them looks up. "What's up, Doc?" he says, grinning, as though he had invented the joke. They laugh and simultaneously tilt their heads to their shoulder mics. They're on their feet and out the door in a minute, leaving their half-eaten meals on the counter.

"Poor kids never have time to eat, let alone digest." Fran wipes her hands on her apron. "You must be the department doctor I've been hearing about. I've been wanting to meet you, but I know you've been busy. Tragic about that Gomez boy." She hands me a menu. "What'll you have?"

I order the meatloaf. It arrives from the kitchen, big as a placemat, covered with gravy and surrounded by potatoes. Fran asks twice if I want a second helping and when I refuse, she sets a piece of pie and a cup of coffee in front of me.

"Mind if I join you?" She calls someone to come out of the back and tend to the counter. "I gotta get off these feet."

She pours herself a coffee and squeezes her bulky body onto the stool next to me. I look down at her feet. Her ankles are swollen. Ropey purple veins twine around her thick calves.

"Things settled down yet?" she asks.

I want to tell her that things have settled down so much it's like Ben never existed. Out of the room, out of mind. No one talks about him, much less mentions his name. It's only been a month, but as far as I know, no one else's heart aches at his memory. No one else wakes up in the middle of the night thinking about him and feeling sick at the stomach.

"I've heard good things about you. Even went to the library to read your book. Wish I'd had that book twenty years ago. They should give it to all the newbies and their wives." She sips her coffee. "Mind if I ask you something? It's probably none of my business, but it's been on my mind. You know Eddie Rimbauer?" She doesn't wait for an answer. "I've known Eddie since he was a skinny kid who delivered newspapers to my door hoping I'd invite him in for milk and cookies. He's still eating my food, only now he's so big I tell him he should sit on the crooks because he's too fat to chase them."

She laughs so hard coffee splashes out of her cup. She leans over the counter for a rag and then refills our cups. The smell of sweat and bacon grease hovers around her.

"He was a lonely kid. Pathetic really. His parents drank and fought, drank and fought. I'd see him wandering around the neighborhood, late at night. He was just a baby, mind you, too young to be out after dark. As soon as he was old enough, he joined the police cadets. Spent all his time at the police station. That was his real family. Them and me." She sticks a cube of sugar on a spoon, immerses it in her coffee, watches it turn brown and dissolve. "That boy has changed. In more ways than getting fat."

"Police work changes people."

"Not everyone. My B.G. was as sweet a guy when he died as he was when he started. He used to tell me how lucky we were. He saw so many awful things it made him grateful for our good fortune. He had a big heart, always felt bad he couldn't do more for people, especially kids."

"So what changed Eddie?"

There is a loud crash in the kitchen followed by a howl. A man appears in the doorway, gesturing frantically for Fran. "Not my fault. Tony burned himself. Not my fault."

Fran gets to her feet. "Tony's not supposed to go near the stove," she shouts back. "Some days this place is like a sheltered workshop. Nice to meet you, Doc. Sorry to bend your ear. I'm a worry wart. Or a busybody. Depends on who you ask."

Chapter Thirteen

I put the Styrofoam boxes full of leftovers from Fran's into my refrigerator and root around for some antacids. The light on my answering machine is blinking. I push the play button. It's Gary's contractor friend, Frank.

"Gary gave me your phone number. He said you said to wait until the dust settles. I'm in construction. We make a lot of dust, doesn't bother me at all. Maybe I can help. Call when you can."

I go upstairs to the bedroom. I am too full to sleep and my pants feel tight. I change into a pair of old pajamas with a stretchy elastic waistband and turn on the TV. The local nighttime talk show is on. The topic for the evening is "Police Suicide: Epidemic in Blue?"

My very own ex-husband, the well known police psychologist, Dr. Mark Edison, is the featured guest. This does not make my stomach feel better. I sit on the bed. Mark looks extraordinarily well, healthy and relaxed. There was a time when I thought he was the most beautiful man I had ever met and treasured the very sight of him.

"Is this an epidemic?" The bony blonde host with impossibly long legs asks. "Should the public be alarmed?"

"An epidemic of one?" I talk back to the television. I've been doing this a lot lately.

Mark responds. "Policing is a high stress occupation. Without special assistance, police officers are at risk for a host of problems – divorce, suicide and alcoholism."

"What can be done to help?" The host looks stricken with concern. Mark holds up a copy of a paperback book. For a nanosecond I think it's my book *Beside the Badge*. I have a rush of gratitude. Mark does care that he's hurt me so badly. He's trying to make it up by promoting my book.

"My wife, Melinda Edison, and I have just published a new book. The topic is very timely. It's titled *Bullet Proof Your Mind: A Survival Guide for Law Enforcement Officers and their Families*." The host looks awed.

"Tells us about the book. Where can we order it?"

"You can order directly from our website, markedisonassociates.com. That's one word, markedisonassociates."

I shut off the TV. This is not an interview, it's an infomercial. I wonder if he had to screw blondie to get this much airtime. I feel like throwing up. Not only am I the biggest fool who ever lived, I'll bet anything that Mark and his parasitic wife have plagiarized my research. My so-called scholarly ex-husband would stop at nothing in the interests of advancing his career. Years ago he started passing out stressometers instead of business cards. Press your thumb against the card for ten seconds and it changes colors. Black equals high stress and blue/green a state of calm. It was schlock science. The colors react to temperature, not stress. I could have a hot flash in the middle of a massage and the card would turn black. He thought it was a great way to promote our practice.

On the other hand, who am I to feel morally superior? I gave a suicidal man breathing exercises and a learning style inventory when I knew he wasn't sleeping or eating, classic suicidal symptoms. I gave him handouts on active listening and problem solving skills and told him and his wife to take a vacation when he must have been drowning in hopelessness. I never asked him if he was thinking about killing himself. I told him to call me if he was feeling bad, when I should have called him. I didn't empathize enough with how trapped and utterly without options he felt.

Small pulses of pain gather behind my eyes. I swing my feet over the edge of the bed. How nice it would be to have someone around to bring me an aspirin, rub my feet, and reassure me that, despite everything, I am still worth loving.

In the morning my headache is gone. Thanks to Fran, I might actually eat a proper dinner at home tonight. I take a coffee out to my tiny patio and sit at the wrought iron table. The sun is just starting to warm the air, and the sky is a clear, silky blue. Tendrils of white clouds drift slowly in the wind.

I wonder what Fran was starting to tell me about Eddie. No surprise that he had a lousy childhood and that one or both of his parents were heavy drinkers. After years of screening officers, I've come to expect that kind of history. So many cops start policing their own families when they're kids, protecting Mom from Dad, looking after their younger siblings. No one emerges unscathed from that kind of childhood. It's too late for me to help Ben, but if I can get Eddie to acknowledge his pain, stop numbing himself out with alcohol and food, then there are treatments that can alleviate his misery, even after all these years.

Chapter Fourteen

The office gardener has been at work sprucing up the lawn and weeding the flower beds in front of the building. Lobelia and impatiens bloom along the walk and cascade over the planter boxes. The loamy smell of moist dirt transports me to the garden behind our house where my mother grew vegetables and I, thrilled to have grown-up responsibilities, pushed seeds into the earth. Best of all were the moments sitting on the back stoop, a metal colander in my lap, shelling the green peas I had just picked. The memory makes me feel almost cheerful.

There is a large manila envelope from the California Board of Psychology in my mailbox, stuck between catalogs of continuing education seminars and a copy of the American Psychologist. Inside is a letter informing me that a complaint has been filed against me by April Patcher Gomez. There are three charges: 1) that the respondent, Dot Meyerhoff, Ph.D., has violated client confidentiality, 2) that the respondent has been negligent in assessing Benjamin Gomez's emotional stability to perform the job of police officer, and 3) that the respondent had been negligent in her treatment, failing to recognize the signs and symptoms of a suicidal depression. Attached is a request for the release of all records pertaining to Benjamin Gomez, signed by his wife.

There are several pages of information concerning the proceedings to follow, including my rights. I am warned not to contact the complainant. Should the Board pursue the complaint there are five possible outcomes, three of them entail losing my license to practice.

I've heard the horror stories, how the Board of Psychology is on a jihad to protect consumers against unscrupulous and incompetent psychologists, pursuing their prey with a vehemence that borders on persecution. Without my license, I'll be out of work, unable to pay the mortgage on my townhouse or my lawyer's fees, forced to wait tables at Fran's café. The details of my case will be splayed across the Board's public website. My colleagues will see it. My friends will see it. Mark will see it.

There is a couple waiting for me. It is their second appointment. I take a deep breath and greet them with a smile as though I'm not carrying the seeds of my own destruction in the envelope under my arm. They are so young and handsome. He has a mustache and buzz cut hair that stands up like the bristles on a brush. She is very pretty, despite kabuki-like make up more suited to a formal evening out than to jeans and a tank top. They sit stiffly on opposite ends of the leather couch.

"Nothing has changed," the wife says, looking at me as if I had failed her for not fixing months of misery in our one prior session. She turns to her husband. "I'm sick of this. Why do you always have to go out with the guys after shift? Why can't you just come home? Don't you see enough of them at work?"

They are Ben and April redux. This time I need to do things right, pay attention, not minimize things. What she says is true. Police work is a greedy mistress. Families play second fiddle to the demands of the work. Court appearances come before planned vacations, squad mates matter more than old friends, and shift work disrupts everything. Cops have two families, their work family and their real family. It's both a blessing and a burden.

"These are my guys. We watch each other's backs. Where they go, I go. I'm part of a team."

"What about the baby and me? I thought we were your team."

"You are."

"Then why don't you come home more often?"

"We've been over this, how many goddamn times? We need the money. You have the house you wanted, now I have to pay for it. How do you think we're going to do that if I don't put in for overtime?"

They go round and round in a repeat of their last session. Despite my resolve to pay attention, I fade out, lose focus, their angry voices dissolve into static. All I can think about is the letter from the Board and what's happening to me.

"Bullshit. You're not doing this just for the money. You want more time to play with your friends. When you're home, all you do is sleep."

"I'm tired. Don't you get it? I'm getting hammered with overtime. What the fuck do you want me to do? Wimp out? Run home to you when everyone else is pulling double shifts?"

They recoil at the intensity of their mutual disappointments and fall silent for a moment.

"I thought we agreed that I'd work so you could stay home with the baby." He is speaking softly now. "Do you want to change your mind?"

"I'm lonely. I'm by myself with the baby all day and night. I hate my life. Some days I wish we'd never had her." She reaches for the box of tissues on the coffee table in front of the couch.

Something inside me snaps to attention. "What do you mean you hate your life?" The young woman is crying, streams of tears striping her make-up, giving her a feral look. Her husband is bent over, his elbows on his knees, one hand to his forehead obscuring his face. He is shaking his head. "I have to ask. When people feel trapped by a situation they can't change, they can get desperate. Sometimes they come up with some pretty radical ways to escape the pain they're feeling."

Her eyes narrow. She looks at me as though seeing me for the first time. "Are you asking me if I'm thinking of killing myself?" She clasps her hand over her mouth. "Oh God, no. I wouldn't do that."

"You do sound depressed. Perhaps we should talk about getting you evaluated for post partum depression. Some women find anti-depressant medication very helpful."

"I can't take pills. I'm nursing."

"Your emotional health comes first. If you're depressed you won't have the energy you need to care for your baby."

Husband and wife exchange looks and inch closer until their bodies are wedged together, his arm around her shoulders, her hand on his leg.

"I'm not depressed. I'm frustrated. I would never hurt myself or the baby." She turns to him, her eyes wide with alarm. "Really, I promise."

"I think we've had enough for today, Doc," the husband says. "We should stop."

They stand up in tandem, united now, against me and my insinuations.

"I'm sorry. I didn't mean to frighten you. I just wanted to offer you and your wife an option. Sometimes I have to ask tough questions. I can see I've upset you both."

"Not a problem. I'll work something out with the guys. They'll understand. They've been through this, too."

He moves toward the door. They can't wait to leave.

"Next week, same time?"

"I'll give you a call, Doc, okay? I don't know what my schedule is yet."

He is lying, of course. And why not? I've been clumsy and tactless, overreacted like a novice at the slightest hint that another of my clients might be suicidal. Reduced the complexity of a painful situation to an insultingly simple diagnosis. I should stick with writing and testing and leave counseling to someone like Gary, who has empathy and insight, who isn't so caught up in the soap opera of his own life that he can't think straight.

They close the door behind them and I can hear their footsteps, quick and light on the stairs. I pick up the envelope from the Board and re-read the complaint. I'm not sure I should fight this. Maybe I deserve to have my license pulled.

Chapter Fifteen

After the next day's staff meeting, Baxter asks me into his office and tells his secretary to hold his calls. He shoves a sheaf of papers across his desk.

"April Gomez is suing the department for negligent hiring, negligent retention, breach of duty to care, wrongful discharge and harassment – the whole enchilada. Didn't take Patcher long to get her to do it. I'm surprised he waited a month. You're one of the named defendants. That's standard procedure. The lawyers would name Jesus if they thought he had money."

"Do they have a case?"

"I don't know. I haven't talked to the city attorney yet. He's at a conference. Sometimes these things never get to court. It's cheaper to pay people off and make them go away. Patcher knows this."

"If we have to go to court who covers my court costs?"

"Your malpractice insurance."

"Not the city?"

"You're a contractor, not an employee."

"No way. If my insurance company has to pay, they'll drop me or raise my premiums sky high. Why isn't she suing Eddie, too?"

"His name's on here. But you and I and the City are the deep pockets. Eddie Rimbauer's just a cop. Probably doesn't have a pot to piss in, spends all his money on booze and alimony. Patcher knows that. He's not going to waste his time."

"Patcher knows about Eddie's drinking?"

Baxter winces. "What a cop does off duty is his business so long as it doesn't interfere with his work."

My father would have been on his feet, yelling about the blue wall of silence, how cops are like a gang of thugs, always protecting each other, looking the other way.

I pull the envelope from the Board of Psychology out of my briefcase.

"Mrs. Gomez has been busy. She filed a complaint against me with the Board of Psychology. If the complaint is sustained, I could lose my license and if I do, I lose my ability to practice psychology. Even if her lawsuit never goes to court, the Board can pull my license."

Baxter cracks his neck, making a noise like someone crinkling a wad of cellophane. I imagine him stuck, his neck twisted, and his face permanently turned to the ceiling.

"I'll talk to the city attorney about that, too. In the meantime, don't tell anyone else."

He puts the papers in his briefcase, closes the cover and snaps the locks shut.

When I don't move, he asks, "Anything else?"

What I'd like is a little empathy, but I can see I'm not going to get it from Baxter. So I say, "I'm worried about something. Suppose Eddie screws over another recruit and I get blamed again?"

"I told you before, Eddie isn't harassing recruits. Look Dot, you need to be careful who you blame and for what. The tables could turn. Somebody might bring up the fact that we never had a cop kill himself until you came on board."

"And I was never sued or brought up on charges by the Psychology Board before I joined this department. What's next, am I going to get shot?" My voice sounds shrill, and I feel the press of tears behind my eyes. I dig my fingernails into my palms and will myself not to cry. "You can retire at 55 with a pension and get another job. I'm a consultant. I don't have a pension."

There is a tap at the door. Baxter's secretary sticks her head around the corner. "Is everything all right?"

"Fine," Baxter says. "We got a little loud. Sorry. We're finished here. Dr. Meyerhoff is just leaving. Not to worry."

He walks to the door and gently shuts it behind her. It is a small distraction, but time enough to subdue my tears.

"I'm not prepared to roll over for Eddie Rimbauer, and I'm not prepared to close the books on Ben's death until I'm satisfied that I understand what happened. I will not be the scapegoat here."

"No one is trying to make you a scapegoat. Trust me." He hands me my briefcase. "Let me give you a little advice. Every cop knows that one day he may have to kill someone. If he can't accept that, he shouldn't be a cop. Must be the same for psychologists. You have to be prepared for the possibility that one of your clients, patients, whatever you call them, could kill themselves."

I feel a moist heat rising under my suit jacket. What nerve, lecturing to me about my own profession.

"I don't know how anyone prepares to deal with suicide, Chief. You can talk about it, read about it, but the reality of it is indescribable."

Traitorous tears start building behind my eyes.

"If you can't tolerate having a patient kill himself," he says, "maybe you're in the wrong job."

Chapter Sixteen

At the end of the week, there is a message from Frank, inviting me out for a drink. The few blind dates I've had since Mark and I divorced have felt like therapy sessions, endless recitations of past heartbreaks. September 11th, Katrina, the tsunami and earthquake in Japan, nothing seems to matter to these men more than the pain and unfairness inflicted on them by their ex-wives.

I hope to God the range of what I have to talk about is more interesting than picking through the turds of my life. Middle-aged people have too much emotional baggage. Dumping it takes an entire evening that would be better spent shoving sticks under each other's fingernails. I have no plans for the weekend, and I want it that way. I delete Frank's message without responding.

Manny Ochoa comes to my office on Monday. It's a glorious spring morning. The trees are flowering. Hundreds of tiny brown birds are nesting in the tree outside my office window making a joyous racket. Manny has graduated from the field training program to probation and I'm doing his exit interview.

He's dressed for the occasion – spotless khakis, a sports shirt and a tan windbreaker. This is how things should have turned out for Ben. Manny is grinning ear to ear, proud and eager, relieved to be out on his own, driving solo, making his own decisions, without someone in the passenger seat evaluating his every move. There's still a chance he could be fired without cause until his probation is over, but given the way he sailed through field training, that's unlikely. I'd like to give him a hug, but he's so reserved that I shake his hand instead.

"Thanks, Doc. Thanks for your help."

"I didn't do anything. You sailed through the program."

"It was reassuring to know that if I had a problem I could talk to you about it."

I'm relieved to hear I contributed something, if only symbolically. Our weekly sessions had been filled with long silences. I did most of the talking.

Manny never had any problems, nothing pressing on his mind, nothing he wanted to talk about, not even Ben's suicide. "It's sad," was all he said.

"So, this is probably the last time we'll have a chance to talk in person for a while. You're going to work dogwatch. I'm rarely here that late at night or that early in the morning. If something comes up and you want to talk, give me a call, let me know when I can call you back. I don't want to wake you up."

He thanks me. Even on a happy day his default mode is silence.

"So, this is an exit interview of sorts. I want to ask you for some feedback about your experience in the FTO program. What were the high points and the low points?"

"It was all good. I learned a lot."

"That's it? Nothing else to say?"

"Not really."

"What about Ben's suicide? You've never said much about it."

"What's to say? He was a good guy. I liked him. We had some stuff in common. I don't know why he did it."

"What did you have in common?"

"We both grew up in East Kenilworth. He was Caucasian, but he understood stuff about being Mexican that a lot of white people don't get."

"He was Caucasian? With the last name of Gomez?"

"His mother was Mexican, his father was white. So I guess that makes him Caucasian, doesn't it?"

"But his father's last name was Gomez."

"That's what he told me. That his father was white."

"Not important," I say. "Go on."

"He was friendly. Like I told you, we studied together sometimes. He was a little ahead of me in FTO so he helped me out, gave me advice, that sort of thing."

"What kind of advice?"

"To stay away from Officer Rimbauer." He breaks into a smile and just as quickly settles back into seriousness.

"Manny, you may be the one person here at work who knew Ben the best. Do you have any idea why he killed himself?"

"Me? No way. Why? Is there something off about it? I didn't know him that well. I really didn't."

He flattens himself against the back of the couch, as though I had just accused him of a crime.

"If you want to know more about him, ask his grandparents. They raised him."

"How do you know that?"

"He asked me if I knew them. Everyone in East Kenilworth knows them, Lupe and Ramon Gomez. They've raised five grandchildren and some foster kids, too. They've been written up in the newspaper and been on TV. Next weekend, they're going to get some award at the Viva Mexico Festival."

He looks at his watch and stands. This is a day to celebrate, not a day to sit indoors talking to a psychologist.

"Thanks again, Doc." He shakes my hand for the second time. "Don't worry so much. You couldn't have stopped Ben. Everything happens for a reason, even if we don't know why."

Baxter was right. The tables are turned. My clients are reassuring me.

Gary and I are using our lunch break to take a walk. A dense layer of fog chills the air and blocks the sun. People who don't live in California always assume the entire state is like Southern California, palm trees and beaches. It's easy to spot the summer tourists in San Francisco, shivering in their shorts and sandals, looking as though they've been cheated.

"Don't do this, Dot. I know you feel terrible, I would too. But, it's inappropriate and intrusive for you to approach the grandparents. It would be one thing if they asked for your help, but they haven't. There is nothing to be gained from this. The young man made his own unfortunate choices. It's egotistical to think you could have stopped him, you barely knew him. Learn from this and move ahead. Talk to the consulting group. That's what we're here for."

"I can't just let this go without understanding what happened. I'm being blamed for his death. I have to defend myself."

"What about his wife and his in-laws? They're the ones you should be talking to."

"I can't talk to his wife because she's filed a complaint against me. And Ben's father-in-law threatened me at the funeral. Told me to stay away from his daughter. Reaching out to Ben's grandparents is my only option. He has no other family."

"Grief drives people to act irrationally. You're not immune to this yourself, you know."

He stops walking long enough to pound his pipe against his shoe, spilling ashes on the sidewalk. He unfolds a soft leather pouch and carefully shakes tobacco into the bowl, as if each flake was precious. He lights a match. The wind blows it out. He curses softly, tries again several more times, gives up and slides the pipe back into his jacket pocket.

"You came to me for feedback and advice. So here it is. I'm going to be blunt. You're projecting blame where it doesn't belong and seeking dispensation from people you don't know and who may not have it to give. You're the only one who can forgive yourself. Work this out in consultation or get into therapy yourself."

Later that evening, I concoct a plan that has an appealing economy of efficiency. I'm going to invite Frank to the Viva Mexico Festival. With any luck, I'll run into Ben's grandparents. It will be a chance to extend myself to them without putting any of us on the spot. I decide not to tell Gary because he's made it clear that he thinks it's the wrong thing to do. But my gut tells me, even if I can't explain it logically to him or to anyone else, that it's the *right* wrong thing.

Chapter Seventeen

So far, so good, as far as first dates are concerned. Frank is handsome.

Not like Mark who always looked like he stepped out of GQ, but shaggy with a full beard flecked with gray and short white hair that curls at his neck. I like how he's dressed – jeans, a long-sleeved shirt, a leather vest, boots and a cowboy hat. He fits right in with the festival crowd, except that he's a head taller than most and has very blue eyes. Our conversation on the ride over is easy, nothing personal and no probing.

By the time we reach Little Mexico, firecrackers and rockets are shattering the late afternoon air, spooking dogs into a chorus of frightened yelps. We begin at the church. The interior is glowing with light from hundreds of flickering votive candles. *Milagros*, tiny pieces of metal shaped like body parts, glint in the candlelight, a shimmering iconography of affliction. The air is heavy with incense. A stream of people moves noiselessly forward, fanning out to pews on the right and the left. Every third or fourth person drops to their knees and inches down the center aisle toward the altar.

Outside, a procession of people is snaking slowly around the square following a horse drawn cart. A phalanx of altar boys carry a statue of the Virgin Mary on a small flower-draped platform. People are throwing roses into the street.

"That's so the Virgin doesn't have to walk on the hard pavement," Frank explains while rolling his eyes at me and laughing.

A pale yellow sun lights the dusty air. Rockets are exploding, and a brass band is playing music that sounds more German than Mexican. Frank buys two glasses of tequila, speaking Spanish to the bartender. Its grassy flavor is strong and bitter. A small group of men gather around an open fire, poking at a huge copper pan with long wooden paddles. Inside the pan a whole pig, snout up, sizzles in its own fat.

Frank clinks my glass and says, "To Mexico. My Mexican friends invite me to the festival every year. I'd have been here even if you hadn't called, only I'd have drunk a lot more tequila and wouldn't be having such a good time."

We finish our drinks and he puts his hands on my shoulders and propels me through the crush of merrymakers towards a woman selling fried sticks of dough sprinkled with powdered sugar. I'm feeling light headed from the tequila.

"I take it you've never been here before." He has to bend over to make himself heard.

"Some people I know are getting an award today. I don't know exactly where or when."

There is a burst of music from a roving group of *mariachis* dressed in big hats and black suits resplendent with braid and metal decorations.

"This way," Frank says.

We pass a large circle of teenagers. The boys are walking arm in arm in one direction, the girls, arm in arm, in the opposite.

"That's the *peregrinacion*," he says. "Just like in Mexico. When a boy sees a girl he likes, he throws confetti at her or squirts her with liquid goo. If she likes him back, she lets him walk with her."

There is a loud squeal followed by giggles as a spray of white finds its mark on a girl in a purple dress. I want to tell her that the business of picking a mate is a lot more complicated.

The sky is growing dark. In front of us a family of four is grilling corn on a charcoal stove, then stripping the kernels into plastic cups. They greet Frank by name and shove two cups of corn into his hands.

"Their son works for me. Wonderful people. Here, have a taste." He feeds me from a cup of corn with limejuice. "Now, try this one." He tips a spoon full of corn with cream to my mouth. Our quick and easy intimacy astonishes me. A volley of popping explosions racks the air. The crowd around us shrieks.

"*Pirotecnica*," Frank shouts, pointing to a whirling pinwheel on top of a wooden tower. "We can't miss this. It's the best part. Takes a minute."

He grabs my hand and pulls me toward an open field. Fireworks explode in all directions cascading sparks on the square. One explosion triggers two more that trigger four more until dozens of pinwheels are spinning wildly, spraying the crowd with whooshing ribbons of flickering colored embers. Children run screaming and laughing as a wooden bull bursts into streaking sparklers that chase them across the field. One final ignition and an image of the Virgin of Guadalupe spins about in the flames, her halo bedazzled with glittering phosphorescent fizz. Round and round she spins, illuminating the night with her otherworldliness, shimmering and blinking until she fades into darkness.

Frank bends down and kisses me on the cheek. "That's my favorite part. Gets me every time." He strikes his fist over his heart. His eyes are moist. "Jesus, I hope I haven't made you miss your friends."

"That's okay. They don't know I'm coming."

"Are you sure?" I nod, surprised at how sure I feel.

"Good. Do you like to dance?"

I nod again. He takes my arm and guides me through the smoky air toward the bandstand.

The Gomezes and five small children are sitting at a picnic table in front of the bandstand. Balloons are tied to the slats on the benches, bobbing in the breeze. The children are so absorbed in eating cake they take no notice of the musicians unpacking their instruments. A marble figurine of a child holding hands with two adults sits on a pedestal in the center of the table.

Mrs. Gomez is wearing the same dress she had worn to Ben's funeral. Her glossy black hair is twisted into a cascade of corkscrew curls as though she was going to a prom. Tiny diamond crosses dangle from her ears. She sees me as soon as I come around the corner and freezes. Only her eyes move, tracking me as I walk past their table.

"Stop, please," she calls to me. "I know you. You were at my grandson's funeral. You were sitting with the police chief."

The children stare at me, forks in the air, frosting beards their chins.

"Are you a police officer?"

"No,"

"What are you?"

"I'm Dr. Dot Meyerhoff, the department psychologist."

Her eyebrows lift. She throws her legs over the picnic bench and scrambles to her feet. There is a run in her stocking. She moves around the table and stands so close to me that I can smell perfume in her hair. She is barely an inch taller than I am.

"I am Lupe Gomez. That is my husband, Ramon. We are Benjamin Gomez' grandparents." She pronounces his name Ben-ha-meen.

Mr. Gomez slaps the table with the flat of his hand. The noise of it, the sudden violence, shakes the children from their seats, and like a flock of startled birds, they fly to his side, crowding him, patting him on his face and back.

"Not here, Lupe, not in front of the children."

He is a miniature version of Ben, smaller, sparer and browner, but with Ben's same eyes and thick eyebrows.

"Come to our house. We need to talk to you. It is very important."

She writes their address on a paper napkin and stuffs it in my hand, without waiting for a reply. Gary was right. This is a bad idea. But before I have a chance to think about how to gently refuse their invitation, they are on their feet, packing up.

"Excuse us, please," Mr. Gomez says, looking at his wife. "We need to go now, Lupe. It's getting late. The children have school tomorrow."

On our way home Frank asks me about the Gomezes. I tell him as much of Ben's story as I ethically can. The lightness and anonymity of the afternoon, when we were free of our work mantles, evaporates with every word.

I talk. He listens. The more he listens, the more I talk.

I'm trying to impress him, although I'm not sure why.

I tell him I'm conducting a psychological autopsy. That's exactly what I'm doing, although it hadn't occurred to me until I hear myself say the words.

A small frown creases Frank's forehead. A psychological autopsy is not something most people encounter in their everyday work.

The hills to the west of us are turning from green to a dusty gold, a shade darker than the moon.

"So they weren't really your friends? You made that up," he says, not looking at me. "This wasn't really a date, was it? You were working and you needed an escort. I didn't know psychologists worked undercover."

He doesn't give me time to answer. "Let me tell you how that makes me feel, Doctor. Like a fool. There I was, showing you around, blubbering over the fireworks, introducing you to my friends. If you had told me what your agenda was, I could have gotten right down to business. Not bothered with all that other stuff."

He pulls up in front of my townhouse.

"I wasn't deliberately trying to mislead you. I had a great time. Really. I did. I guess I just needed a reason to call you and ask you out."

Our reflections look back at us from the darkened car windows as though we are double dating ourselves. "Want to come in for coffee or a glass of wine?"

"No thanks," he says. "Tomorrow's a work day."

Chapter Eighteen

I'm at the Monday morning staff meeting listening to Baxter talk about the budget when my cell phone rings. It's Eddie, demanding that I come to the report writing room, code 3, on the double. Baxter looks irritated at my being called away by some unknown emergency.

As soon as I walk in, Eddie sits me down in front of a computer. "What do you know about this?"

It's an email from the records clerk: "To: Officer Rimbauer: Re Officer Manuelo Ochoa's request for a background check on Benjamin Gomez. We don't have a case number. Is this an open case? Please advise."

"*Mañana,*" he yells over his shoulder, "Leave the frigging report and get your skinny butt over here." He turns to me. "I shoulda been out of here hours ago. Lyndley's in training, I get to baby sit the newbies."

"Yes Sir?" Manny is standing at Eddie's desk, he looks worried.

"Did you run a background on Ben Gomez?"

"Yes, sir."

"What the fuck were you looking for?"

"I'm sorry."

"That's not an answer. What were you looking for?" Three newer rookies skitter out of the report writing room and down the hall toward their lockers.

"I wanted to know more about Ben. That's all. He was my friend."

"Bull shit. Did she tell you to do this?"

"No. It was my idea. I didn't mean any harm."

"Don't lie to me, *pendejo.* Your ass is on the line. A cop who lies isn't worth shit."

Manny looks at his feet. "I'm sorry, Sir. I'll take any discipline you want to give me."

Eddie comes out of his seat with such force that his chair careens across the room and bangs into the wall. A framed copy of the department's mission statement falls to the floor, cracking the glass. "I don't need permission to discipline you, you arrogant little prick. You're on probation.

Unauthorized use of the computer is a big no-no. What has she been telling you? Do you think I had something to do with Gomez eating his gun?"

"No, Sir." He looks from Eddie to me, me to Eddie, as though he's afraid to take his eyes off either one of us. "Is the Doctor in trouble?"

"Fuck the chivalry, asshole. Take care of yourself. From now on, if you have to talk to the good doctor, you give name, rank and serial number. That's it. Nothing else. Understand? Now get the hell out of here."

Manny turns in a tight circle and walks out of the room with slow, precise steps like someone marching to his execution.

"Is he in trouble?"

"Of course he's in trouble."

"How much trouble?"

"I don't know and none of your business."

"I didn't ask him to do this. Believe me."

"If you said it was raining, I'd go outside and check. I don't know why you got a jones for me, Doc, but I'm telling you right now, call off the campaign to nail my ass to the wall and leave the rookie alone."

I take the elevator back to mahogany row, hoping my hands aren't shaking so much anyone will notice. I open the door to the staff room. It's empty, the meeting's over and everyone's gone to lunch. Just the word makes my stomach growl. I need to eat and I really want to hear what Fran started to tell me about Eddie. It's been more than two weeks since we talked.

Fran ushers me to a table in the back. When she delivers my salad, she sits down, clearly exhausted. There's a new man behind the counter.

"That's Bruce. He started yesterday working lunches. I think he's going to be okay. I just had to hire another person. I spend more time helping Tony and Sheldon than they do helping me. How's your salad?"

"Delicious. Enough for two."

"So, what's on your mind?"

"You never had a chance to finish what you were saying about Eddie. About what changed him."

She takes a sip of coffee. "He's not in any trouble, is he?"

"No. It just seemed like you had something more you wanted to say."

"I'm no psychiatrist, but between you and me, I think he never got over his wife. I probably shouldn't be telling you this, but they were high school sweethearts. Me and B.G. were at the wedding. She was a beautiful girl. Two years married, she's hooked on God knows what and so out of her mind that she can't stop, even when she got pregnant. They lost the baby. A little while later she got AIDS and died. Thank God she didn't pass it to Eddie. He's been married twice since. Rebound marriages. They don't last."

Fran stares into her cup, a slight iridescent sheen reflects the florescent lights overhead. "The reason I wanted to tell you this, Doc, is that I want you to look after him. I can feed him and be his friend. But he needs more than that. He needs professional help."

"I don't think Eddie thinks too highly of professional help."

It's the understatement of the year.

"He's bitter. He spent a fortune on detox centers, psychiatrists, you name it. None of it helped. He's wrong. I know grief. When B.G. was killed, I wanted to die too. I had friends, I had family, I had my Church. I had Eddie. They all helped, God bless them, but they wanted so bad for me to feel better that after a while I started pretending just so they'd feel better. I went to a grief counselor. She let me wail and weep until I got sick of listening to myself. I don't think Eddie's ever shed a tear. Men are different. He just shut down. Puts on a happy face when he comes in here, but he's killing himself with the eating and drinking. Work's the only thing he has going for him. The only thing he's ever had going for him. When I heard that rookie committed suicide" – she crosses herself – "and Eddie told me he was the rookie's FTO, I got scared. I thought he might get fired because of it. He's a dead man if he can't work."

"What did Eddie say about the suicide?"

"Made a joke. Like he always does. Went on a bender. I'm glad the department hired you. He needs looking after. They all do."

I go back to my office. There are now five men in my life: one is dead, one is in trouble, and the rest are angry with me. I sit at my desk and take out a yellow legal pad. At the top of the page I write 'psychological autopsy'. I haven't a clue how to proceed. My only preparation is having read Mark's chapter on psychological autopsies in the first book he wrote about police psychology. The book he asked me, still a graduate student, to help edit and then dedicated to me for my invaluable assistance and promising future.

I start by listing names and annotating them. I feel better seeing my gnarled thoughts organized into tidy lines and columns. Ben Gomez is first. He is the root of the matter. I make a note next to his name: "What/who drove him over the edge? Keep it from happening again!" I add a second exclamation mark.

Eddie Rimbauer is next. Beside his name I write, "Could be displacing unresolved issues of grief and anger onto Ben and me."

Third is Mad Dog Patcher, which is how I've come to think of him. I draw a picture of a snarling dog foaming at the mouth and baring his teeth.

Baxter is fourth. I've done nothing but stir up trouble for him. By the time this is over, I'm going to owe him, big time.

Frank is last on the list. Technically speaking, he doesn't even belong here. I'm planning to call him and apologize. Ask him out for dinner. He's right—I had used him to go to the Festival, but that isn't reason enough to go into a major sulk. On the other hand, it's refreshing to meet a man who can talk about hurt feelings instead of clamming up, getting angry and storming off. We'd had a good time together, both of us. He's worth another shot. I take a pen and put a question mark next to his name.

It's a blue pen, same as the color of his eyes.

Chapter Nineteen

It's been a busy week with a bad start. Somehow I've managed to avoid running into Eddie. By the time I get home on Friday, I'm too tired to cook. I put on a bathrobe, fix myself a bowl of popcorn, pour a large glass of red wine, and turn on a cooking show.

The TV chef is making an impossibly complicated dinner for one, which she proceeds to eat at a dining table set with silver and crystal. Totally disingenuous. If she was really single, she'd be eating over the sink. There is a knock on my door, followed by triple rings on the doorbell. I jump, spilling popcorn on the rug. I look through the peephole. Eddie is standing on the doorstep, by himself.

"Open up, it's dark out here." I brush salt off the front of my robe and open the door.

"Am I interrupting something, Doc? Heard you talking to somebody and I see you got your sexy lingerie on."

He gives me the once over. I'm barefoot, wearing a long-sleeved floor-length robe that zips up under my chin. He walks past me into the living room and looks around. "Smells good. Got any more popcorn?"

He looks up the stairs, walks into the kitchen, opens a few cabinet doors and ranges through my house like I'm a suspect in a crime. "Nice house. Lived here long?" I don't answer. "Kind of light on decorations. Not too many plants, no knick-knacks."

"What are you doing here? I don't see people without an appointment. And only in my office. You need to call me first."

"I'm having a crisis. I can't wait." He takes a fistful of popcorn and plops down in a living room chair.

"What's happened to Manny?"

"Manny is it? You must be on close terms. Sweet."

"Where is he?"

"Back at the station writing 'I will not use the computer for personal use' a thousand times."

"You need to leave, Eddie. This isn't funny."

"You're not being very hospitable."

I pick up the remote control and turn off the TV. "What do you want?"

"A beer would go down nice with the popcorn."

"You know what I mean."

He leans forward and starts counting off on his fingers. "I'll make you a list." He starts with his thumb. "What I want is for you to quit snooping around my life. What I want is for you not to intimidate the best rookie we've had in years into doing something that could get him fired. What I want is for you to understand that I had nothing to do with Gomez killing himself. What I want is for you to quit playing Nancy Drew and get-the-fuck off my case."

He shoves the remaining popcorn in his mouth. "Let me give you some advice. Don't be a wannabe cop. You'll get hurt and you'll hurt other people, like Manny."

It was the same thing he had said about Ben.

"How much trouble is Manny in?"

"Thanks to you, he'll probably get two days on the beach – that's two days with no pay – have his probation extended and have to take some dipshit class in ethics."

"I didn't ask him to do this. He did it on his own."

"No encouragement from you, huh?"

"He knows I'm concerned, that I want to understand what happened to Ben. He wants to understand, too."

At least I hope that's the case.

"In other words, you told him that I drove the kid to off himself."

"I never said that to him. Never."

"But you think it, don't you?"

"I don't know what to think." There is a momentary silence. "Look, I don't think you forced Ben Gomez to shoot himself in the head. No one can make another person do that."

"Now you're talking."

"Ben seemed to think you had some kind of vendetta against him."

"He was a wuss. Couldn't take the heat."

"If he was a wuss, why did you put so much pressure on him?"

"So now we're back to the I-didn't-pull-the-trigger-but-I-hounded-him-to-death theory? Why would I do that? He needed to be fired, not because I had a hard-on for him. He didn't have the right stuff. All he wanted to do was run traffic stops and arrest people for overdue library books. There's more to this job than that."

He pulls a cigar from his pocket.

"Please don't smoke in here."

"What? I'll kill your plants?" He flips the unlit cigar between his fingers. "So why do you think I had a vendetta against Gomez?"

Here I am, alone in my house, at night, barefoot, and in my bathrobe talking to an armed man. This is neither the time nor the place to be making psychological interpretations. "It seemed plausible, that's all."

"Really. Why?"

"Did you know his parents died when he was ten? That he was raised by his grandparents?"

Eddie raises his bushy eyebrows. There isn't much light in the room, but I can see a small tic vibrating under his cheek. "Yeah, he told some people. They told me."

"Maybe, because you knew this, you convinced yourself that there was no way he could be psychologically stable enough to be a cop."

"Don't start with that psychobabble shit. So, he had a crappy childhood. If it wasn't for crappy childhoods, we wouldn't have no cops or firefighters. I didn't condemn him for that. It was a bad fit. This isn't the job for him."

I take a deep breath. "Is it possible that you may have over identified with him? His bad childhood? The significant losses he experienced?"

"What the fuck does that mean?"

"You had a difficult childhood yourself, didn't you? And great losses as an adult. I know your wife was a heroin addict who died of AIDS. And I know she lost your baby."

His face flushes red. A narrow band of muscle in his forehead starts pulsing rapidly.

"Who told you this crap?"

"I can't say."

"You'd fucking better." He sits up and clamps his hand over his weapon.

"Or what? You'll shoot me?"

I'm teetering on the edge of the couch, hugging a throw cushion to my chest like a shield. I can see the muzzle flash, hear the zing, feel the impact.

"It was Fran, wasn't it? Some coppers told me you've been eating there. She never lets up. She's like Mother Teresa, out to save the world. Always on my back, telling me I'm killing myself with grief."

I edge away from him, toward the end of the couch, using my bare feet to push myself along. The tile is cold. I need to buy a rug.

"Scared? Think I'm going to shoot you? Ready to run for the phone?"

He exhales in a long hiss. His body goes flaccid and he sinks back into the chair, his empty gun hand flopping on the armrest. "The chief's going to shit bricks when he hears about this," he says so softly he may be talking to himself. "Call him. I don't give a fuck anymore. I should shoot you, but I won't. You're not worth going to jail for."

I stay where I am, clutching the cushion. Eddie says nothing, just stares, splattered across the chair like something dropped from a great height. Ice cubes, hard as stones, clatter into the plastic bin in my freezer, making my heart beat even faster. Outside, the blackness is broken only by the headlights of a passing car. I stand, slowly. I don't want to startle him. My legs are shaking. He hears me moving, but he doesn't look up. I clear my throat.

"This conversation, Officer Rimbauer, like all the others I have had with police officers in your agency, including Ben Gomez, is confidential."

He raises his head slowly. "You're shitting me, right? The minute I leave, you're going to call the chief, tell him I barged in here and threatened you."

"Not if you don't tell him I live like a transient and drink wine with popcorn."

He jerks his head, as though I'd slapped him. "Expect me to believe that shit? I'm a cop. As far as I'm concerned if your lips are moving, you're lying."

"Then I guess you'll have to wait and see if you can trust me."

He pushes himself out of the chair, never taking his eyes off me. Something metal jangles as he readjusts his duty belt.

"Well, fuck me," he says. "That's a stand up offer. I didn't expect that from you."

I walk to the door and open it.

"I'll take the deal," he says. "Not like I have any other choice."

The night air rushes in, cool and moist, with a promise of rain. Eddie's hair is sticking limply to his forehead, like the strings of a mop. He walks out onto the front step, turns, takes his cell phone out of his pocket, smiles broadly, and snaps a picture of me, barefoot, in my bathrobe.

"Evidence. Just in case you change your mind."

Chapter Twenty

The Patchers live in a gated community of baronial mansions and golf courses, more expensive but no less anonymous than the townhouse development where I live. There is an oppressive conformity to the houses, all light colored stucco and tile with gratuitous architectural variations. Landscaped walking paths braid through the sub-division like a river of stone. The streets are empty – no people, no dogs, no flags, no garage doors open to reveal their messy innards.

It has taken me almost a week to convince Eddie to give me the Patcher's address, and only after I swore that my sole intention was to write Mrs. Patcher a letter. He used the police computer, in direct violation of those almighty general orders. I hope this will prompt him to go easy on Manny's discipline, but I don't want to ask. Eddie's being nice to me, doesn't want to tick me off and send me running to the chief. I can tell he still doesn't believe that I won't.

Vinnie Patcher's work schedule is on his carefully scripted outgoing voice mail message. He is at court today. I park my car on the boulevard that borders his development and walk to where the wrought iron fence enclosing the property ends in greenery. I push my way through the bushes. It is a joke to think that the aged guard at the security gate or the decorative fence would keep out any determined burglars. I brush the leaves off my jacket and head down the walking path that runs behind a row of homes, darting across someone's lawn to the street.

The Patchers' cul-de-sac lies in wait for me. I walk to the front door and ring the bell.

"Just a minute, please." Belle Patcher's muffled voice comes through the closed door followed by the sound of her footsteps. "Who is it?"

A peephole in the front door clicks open. I can hear a small gasp. "Go away. My husband isn't home."

"I don't want to talk to your husband, Mrs. Patcher. I want to talk to you."

"I have nothing to say. Go away."

"I won't take much time. Please, I need your help. I'm trying to understand why your son-in-law killed himself."

There is silence.

"I don't want this to happen again, ever."

More silence.

"You wouldn't want another young woman to go through what your daughter is going through now, would you?"

"My husband told you never to contact us."

"Would you want another young woman to suffer like your daughter is suffering? Would you want another mother to hurt as much as you do watching your child in pain?" I sound like I'm channeling my father's gift for flaming oratory. "Please, help me to help others. I don't know who else to turn to."

There is silence again, but no receding footsteps.

"I don't know why my son-in-law took his own life. I had nothing to do with it."

"I know that. I'm not here to accuse you of anything."

"If I talk to you, will you leave us alone?"

"Yes, of course."

"I can't talk here. There's a small park a mile south, near the Community College. Stamper Park. I'll meet you there in a few minutes."

"Promise?"

"Only if you promise not to bother us again."

At Stamper Park, children scramble on gym bars and dig in a sand pit as though they are at the beach, not a landlocked park hours from the ocean. I pick a bench on the far side, near a gardening shed. The air is fragrant with redwood chips and newly cut grass. If and when Belle Patcher shows up, I can observe her as she gets out of her car. I'm acting like a cop, feeling edgy and smart. Self-inflation is an occupational hazard of police work. It hasn't taken me long to catch the bug.

A dark blue SUV pulls to the curb and parks. Belle Patcher swings her legs out the door and slowly takes the long step to the street, holding onto the car frame for support. She is shorter and stouter than she had appeared at the funeral, her bulkiness exaggerated by a blousy green silk jogging suit. She walks quickly across the lawn. There are dark, puffy crescents under her eyes.

"Thank you so much for coming. Please, sit down."

"My husband would kill me if he found out I was talking to you."

"He doesn't have to know."

"He'll want to know where I was this afternoon. He likes me to account for my time."

"This won't take long."

"He's been in a terrible mood. April wants to move out. She shouldn't be by herself, pregnant and all."

Mrs. Patcher tears up. She keeps looking at the street, following the passing cars with her red-rimmed eyes.

"Why is she moving out?"

"I don't know. She talks to her father more than me." She looks at her watch. Barely five minutes have passed. "This is a mistake. I shouldn't be talking to you. I have to go." She starts back to her car. I go after her.

"Do you know something or someone who can help me?"

"Please don't follow me. I can't be seen with you."

She begins running, a funny jiggly motion as though her legs are different lengths. "I can't help you," she calls over her shoulder. "I can't even help myself."

She scrambles into her car and drives off.

I drive home with nothing to show for my efforts. Mrs. Patcher is frightened and deeply troubled, barely able to keep herself together. I debate telling Eddie about my visit, but decide against it. I fill the microwave bowl with popcorn and turn on the timer.

The telephone rings.

"So, were you ever going to call me?"

"I didn't think you'd want to hear from me again."

I hadn't realized how much I feared that was true until I hear myself saying it out loud to Frank.

"Well, I was mad," he replies. "And hurt. But I'm a forgiving type, up to a point. I got to thinking about it. I had a really good time until you met the

Gomezes. Under the circumstances, it was pretty amazing that you could enjoy yourself, even a little. I don't know how I'd feel in your shoes. The worst thing that happens to me at work is that someone whines at me because the job is over budget or taking too long. Nobody ever kills themself."

Tears push at the backs of my eyeballs. I am really vulnerable these days, to even the smallest act of understanding.

"So how do we get this train back on track?" he asks

"How about I buy you dinner?"

"Works for me," he says.

It sounds like he means it.

Chapter Twenty One

The Gomezes' living room is filled to overflowing. The tops of all flat surfaces, tables, chests and bookcases are covered with family photographs in silver frames. Soccer trophies line the mantelpiece like an army of toy soldiers, their ranks doubled by the reflection in the mirror behind them. Mrs. Gomez invites me to sit with her on a velour sofa. There is a pitcher of water and three glasses on the coffee table in front of us.

"I still see him, you know. I turn a corner and there he is. I think maybe he's not really dead. Maybe they put him undercover and made a fake funeral. I keep hoping that one day he'll knock on our door and tell us about his adventures, all the arrests he made. My husband thinks I'm crazy."

"I do not." Mr. Gomez comes into the room. His black hair, wet from the shower, is shiny like onyx. He wears an ironed over-shirt and trousers. "I apologize for making you wait. I wanted to settle the children down in the back room so we could talk in private."

He sits opposite us in a flowered armchair. The television plays softly behind a closed door, some kind of cartoon with music and canned laughter.

"We have many questions."

"That's the sad legacy of suicide. Survivors are left with many unanswered questions."

A door to the living room opens slightly. A child's voice says something in Spanish. Mr. Gomez waves his hand and the door closes.

"Please continue," he says, his face earnest, expectant, like a student listening for important clues about what might show up on the final exam.

"Thank you for agreeing to talk to me. I'm hoping that you can help me understand why Ben took his own life. I only met him a few times. I know very little about his childhood. It would help if you could fill in some of the details."

They look at each other with radar born of a long partnership and silently decide that she should begin.

"After our daughter and son-in-law died, we took him in. We would have taken him long before, but my daughter refused. She was a good mother. She kept him clean, sent him to school. It was just hard, you know, for her to cook regular for him. When he came to us, he was very skinny. Remember, Ramon?"

"Like yesterday. He used to steal food from the refrigerator. We told him to eat whenever he was hungry, he didn't need to steal from us. For months, whenever Lupe cleaned his room, she would find food and candy wrappers hidden under his bed and in his shoes."

"We could hear him at night, crying. He didn't believe his parents were dead. They were cremated." She winces slightly. "That is against our religion, but my son-in-law didn't like the Church. So we didn't have a grave to show Ben. We planted a tree in our backyard in their memory but he ripped it out. He kept saying that his parents were alive, they just didn't want him anymore. We wanted to adopt him right away. Give him a new start. It took him a long time to agree, because it meant he had to accept that his parents were really dead."

"I know sadness in my life." Mr. Gomez pushes himself to the edge of his chair and plants his small feet on the floor. Outside, the afternoon light is fast fading into a gloomy pall. He switches on a table lamp, illuminating us in a circle of light. "I came to this country from Mexico. Snuck across the border with my two brothers when I was sixteen. The coyote left us in the desert and we had to drink our own urine to survive. My youngest brother died in the heat, lay on his side curled up like a pork rind cooking in fat. My older brother never got over it. He started drinking. The last time I saw him he was homeless." He stops and bends his head so that I can't see his eyes. "I told the story of my brothers to Benjamin over and over to show him that he had a choice. He could survive his parents' death, build a good life for himself like I did, or he could give up like my brother. It was up to him. Maybe I was too hard on him. I was only trying to give him hope."

"You see how we are?" Mrs. Gomez says. "We keep going over and over everything. Was it our fault? Was it something we did? Was it something we didn't do? We tried to get him help. He went to counseling for a year after he came to us, and we thought he was doing better. He smiled more and started making friends. He got involved in sports. The older he was, the better he was. His teachers liked him. He did well in school. He was very responsible, had a job on the weekends as a bag boy in the grocery to help us out. He seemed to stop grieving."

She stops, her eyes unfocused, caught somewhere between then and now. Without a word, Mr. Gomez picks up the story as though he and his wife are tied together by an invisible rope. When one flags, the other pulls forward.

"Some people say it was his job. He always wanted to be a police officer. He wanted to help people. Because he was Mexican, he thought he could help our people. The police we had, they treated people bad, Mexican people especially. He was working his way through college when he met April in one of his classes. They fell in love. We didn't want him to get married before he finished college, but he wouldn't listen. He worked hard in high school and didn't have time or money for dating. He didn't know girls. April was his first girlfriend and he was totally *enamorado*. Maybe we should have let him act like a teenager, go out on dates, have fun." He looks at his wife. "They eloped. Not even a church wedding. That hurt us deeply."

Mrs. Gomez clears her throat. "He told us taking a job with the police was to make money for college. That the police would pay for his tuition. He promised us he would finish his degree. But by then we didn't see him so much anymore. Between marriage and the police training, he didn't have time. You have to let them go, you know. What could we say?"

"Did you notice any changes in him after he started police training?"

"He was excited at first. Loved the job. But pretty soon he started to look bad. He lost weight, said he wasn't sleeping good. He told us it was much harder than he thought it would be."

"Did he have trouble with anyone at work? For instance, did he ever mention his field training officer?"

The Gomezes look at each other and shake their heads. "You have to understand Doctor, that after a while, he didn't talk to us much about anything. Not his wife, not his job. And then he stopped coming around all together. We heard about his death on the television."

Tears course over Mrs. Gomez's cheeks. She dabs at her face with a white handkerchief. "We couldn't believe it. He had been through so much, losing his parents. How could losing a job be worse than that?"

"Did he leave a note for you?"

"Nothing, no note, nothing. It's like he never knew us."

Mr. Gomez' face darkens with anger. "Do you know how we found out about the funeral? We read it in the newspaper. We didn't even know his wife was pregnant until we saw her at the chapel. You're the first person from the department to talk to us, and Benjamin has been dead two months."

"I don't care about that, Ramon. What I want to know is why? He is the only link to our daughter. Now we have nothing."

She covers her face with the handkerchief. Mr. Gomez' eyes well along with hers.

"What about Benjamin's baby?" I ask. Mrs. Gomez stiffens, her lips compressing into a hard line.

"I don't want to talk about that baby. That girl took Benjamin from us. She will take the baby too." A burble of giggles erupts behind the closed door to the family room. "I have enough grandbabies. There is no more room in my heart."

"You don't mean that, Lupe. Benjamin's child is our blood."

"Half our blood. It will be like Benjamin all over again, a child, half-ours, half a stranger. I'm too old, my heart is too hard."

Mr. Gomez starts to say something. She stops him, raising her hand in the air, the flat of her palm facing outward, her eyes narrowed to pinpoints of obsidian. "*Basta*, Ramon. *Basta*."

Her anger wells. We sit, shaken, cautious, looking over our shoulders. The balance between us tilts.

"It's getting late. I should go. I don't want to impose on you any further. I appreciate the time you've given me. I can't imagine how painful it is for you to relive all these memories."

Mrs. Gomez grabs my wrist and holds fast. Her slender fingers clamping down on my arm until my fingertips feel fuzzy from the lack of blood. "Why? Why did he kill himself? You are the psychologist. Tell me."

"I don't know."

"If you don't know, who does?"

"I don't know that either. That's what I'm trying to find out."

"When you do, you will tell us?"

"I will."

"Promise?"

"I can't guarantee—"

"Promise me. Swear it, in the name of our Lord Jesus."

And because it's the only way she'll release my arm, I do.

Chapter Twenty Two

Once again I'm up with the sun, replaying my promise to Mrs. Gomez, a promise I wonder if I can deliver. It is already muggy and warm. I drive to headquarters for a meeting with the communications supervisor to plan a stress management workshop for her staff. The communications center is housed in a poorly lit windowless room in the basement of police headquarters. The architects who built this building back in the 1950s believed that, in the event of a nuclear attack, the basement would be protected from nuclear fallout and the dispatchers could continue to work. After the collapse of the World Trade Center, the idea seems quaint, if not laughable.

An empty aquarium, its sides blotted with dried algae, sits on top of a row of metal lockers near the front door, the brainchild of someone who thought that looking at fish would trump the almost steady influx of misery that comes in over the 911 lines.

The room hums like a beehive as the dispatchers move between stations, talking to each other or to callers, tethered to their consoles by expandable wires that allow them to move but not leave the room. The glow from the circle of flat screen monitors that corral them turn their faces brackish.

The supervisor's shapeless girth spills over the sides of her chair. She extends her hand to me. She has long, painted fingernails and graceful fingers that look as though they belong on someone else's body. We move to the conference room for privacy. In one hand, she carries a notepad, in the other a mammoth tumbler of soda with a long bent straw that curls into her mouth like an oral IV bag.

She flicks on the light. The room is bare except for a fake wood table and upholstered office chairs. She selects a chair without arms. Her name is Raylene.

"In this business, Doc, you're either sworn or you're sworn at, and we're the sworn at." She looks at me to see if I get the joke. "The cops think we have it easy 'cause we stay calm on the air. They should only know."

She lists the stresses – screaming parents with choking babies in their arms, the suicidal caller who shoots himself while talking to the dispatcher, and children calling for help because Mommy isn't moving after Daddy hit her. Number one on her list of pet peeves are police officers who fail to call in their locations.

As though on cue, Eddie opens the door to the conference room and gestures for me to come out.

"I'm in the middle of something, can't this wait?"

"If it could, I wouldn't be here would I? Sorry Ray, but the shrink has an emergency of her own. If I was you, I'd reschedule. She's not coming back soon."

"What's going on?" I ask him out in the hall.

"Can't you fucking hear him?"

"Who?"

"Patcher. He's in the Chief's office screaming his bloody head off. Seems like you paid his wife a little unauthorized visit. He wants you arrested and he wants Baxter to fire my ass for helping you."

"That's why I didn't tell you. To keep you out of trouble."

"Didn't work. The chief had someone look at my computer. I did a search for Patcher's home address. They think I was the one who gave you the go-ahead."

"Oh, for Heaven's sake. I'll straighten it out."

He raises both hands. "Don't try to help me. You'll only make things worse."

I can hear Patcher yelling as we get off the elevator. A moment later he storms out of the chief's office, his face florid, little globules of spit dotting his lips. Baxter is right behind him. When Patcher sees me, he stops.

"You meddling bitch, you had no right to come into my home and intimidate my wife. What are you doing, Rimbauer? Boning the good doctor in exchange for my address?"

I can feel Eddie brace behind me, I hear the soft slap of his hand against the leather of his gun belt.

"I did not enter your house, Mr. Patcher," I say. "Never set foot inside. Your wife agreed to speak to me on her own volition."

"My wife has no volition. She's a sick woman, under a doctor's care, on anti-depressants. You lured her out of the house and forced her to drive while under the influence."

He is breathing hard and sweating. Stains cascade down the sides of his shirt almost to his belt. He leans forward, placing his hands on his knees as though he's going to be sick to his stomach.

"Vinnie," Baxter pleads. "Come back into my office. You're in no shape to drive. You look like you're going to have a heart attack. Let me call the medics. We'll work something out. I'll take care of things, don't worry." He grasps Patcher by the shoulders until he straightens up and guides him down the hall, one hand at his back.

I look around. Cops are everywhere, standing silently in doorways and behind the water fountain, drawn by the commotion, ready to take action. Baxter stops at the door to his office, his hand still on Vinnie Patcher's back.

"I have things under control. Thanks everyone. You can stand down." He looks to Eddie. "Officer Rimbauer. Escort the doctor out of the building. Now."

"I am in the middle of a meeting," I say.

"I don't care if you're in the middle of giving the Sermon on the Mount. Until you hear from me personally, you're on administrative leave. With no pay. Rimbauer, confiscate her security key and report back to me. We need to talk."

Eddie is silent during the long wait for the ancient elevator and the walk to my car.

"What does he think I'm going to do? Bomb the place?" I look at Eddie out of the corner of my eye. "He'll get over it. Give him a day. I put him and you in a tough position by going to see Mrs. Patcher. I apologize. It was stupid."

"Spare me the fucking hindsight, will you?"

"Baxter's scared of a law suit and more bad publicity. When people are scared they lash out."

"Explaining something doesn't fix it. You've just been canned, and I'm about to be."

"Canned? I'm on administrative leave. It's not the same thing."

"It is in my book."

"I really hope I haven't done you any damage. I thought we were getting along better."

"Yeah? Well friends don't let friends bullshit themselves." He opens the door to my car. "I hope this baby's paid for Doc. You're out of work."

Three days pass with no word from Baxter. I'm giving him time to cool off. I have never before felt so rejected, unless, of course, I want to count Mark asking for a divorce.

Large drops of rain splatter against my office window. I've been sitting so long my feet are asleep. I rotate my ankles until pinpricks of feeling return and then hobble across the room to turn on the lights against the gloom. I go out for a sandwich and when I return there are five messages on my phone.

The first two are hang-ups. The next is a call from Gary inviting me to lunch, his smoky voice reproaching me for not having called him to let him know what's going on. The fourth is a chillingly efficient message from Baxter's secretary admonishing me to cancel all department appointments until the chief's investigation is completed and I have settled the complaint with the Board of Psychology.

The final message is an officious female voice informing me that I have been given an appointment with a professional conduct investigator from the Board of Psychology in Sacramento. If I am unable to make this appointment I can reschedule, but doing so would delay adjudicating my case for as long as 60 days. If I am more than 15 minutes late, the appointment will be automatically cancelled. I am expected to bring all records pertaining to the client Benjamin Gomez and warned that modifying these documents is a criminal offense.

Gary leaves a two-day-old copy of the local newspaper in front of my office door with a note attached. "Did you see this? Nice work."

The headline reads: Police Department Psychologist Placed on Administrative Leave. My name and picture are underneath the headline, top left corner, above the fold. I shouldn't be shocked, but I am. Baxter put me on leave in front of Vinnie Patcher and half a dozen police officers.

Someone, probably Vinnie himself, leaked it to the press. There is a short interview with Baxter who confirms that his department psychologist and another unnamed employee are under investigation for improper use of department records and misuse of their authority. Protocol keeps officers' names out of the press. Psychologists have no such protection. Because this is an open investigation, Baxter declines to comment further, although he appreciates that there is public concern. He reports that Dr. Mark Edison has offered his services, *pro bono,* during this crisis and acknowledges that the board of supervisors is considering terminating my contract and hiring Dr. Edison.

Who, I wonder, leaked the story to Mark?

Chapter Twenty Three

I get to Sacramento just as the ragged shrouds of ground fog that lay across the highway are starting to evaporate in the super hot air. The Board of Psychology is located along a row of forlorn Victorian houses. A sand-filled stone urn crammed with cigarette butts and crushed soda cans stands at the door. I can see that not a single penny of my hard earned tax dollars has been squandered on aesthetics. The receptionist directs me to sit on a molded plastic chair. I am rumpled from the short walk. Ben's file lies on my lap, warming my already warm thighs.

"Dr. Meyerhoff?" A door opens to my left and a tall, thin woman wearing a fitted red suit with a short pleated skirt leans into the lobby propping the door open with her elbow, a germ freak or maybe she's just finished polishing her nails.

"Follow me, please."

She spins around and walks briskly down a narrow corridor on spiked red heels. I follow behind, drab by comparison, in a tan suit and my teal green good-luck sweater.

"In here, please," she gestures to an open door that leads to a small office. "Have a seat."

I sit on one of two ancient wooden chairs that face a gray metal desk.

"I'm Marsha Hudson, professional conduct investigator." Her dry ringless hand skims mine in a perfunctory handshake. She has an angular face with deep set eyes, a wide flat mouth and a sharp chin. Her glossy, straight brown hair swings like a heavy curtain. Small age lines cobweb around her mouth and at the corners of her eyes.

"Are you a psychologist?"

"I'm a trained professional conduct investigator. The interview today is only a first step. After talking to you and examining your files, I will make a recommendation about pursuing or dropping your case. You have the right to appeal my recommendation."

I wonder how someone who has never been a therapist can sit in judgment of me. Ms. Hudson pulls a piece of paper from her desk, looks at it and slides it across the desk. "This is a copy of the complaint and your rights and responsibilities. Please make sure all your information is correct."

"My given name is Dot, not Dorothy. It's a family joke. My parents started calling me that in utero when their doctor told them I was no bigger than a dot. When I was born, they kept the name."

Ms. Hudson is not amused by this family anecdote. She corrects her copy of the paper and asks me to initial the correction.

"Since you're here by yourself, I presume you have elected not to have legal representation."

"Do I need legal representation? I thought this was a fact finding interview."

"That's entirely up to you." Ms. Hudson's mouth settles into a hard thin line. "If there are no further questions or corrections, let's get started. May I see your files, please?"

"I have only one file."

She removes a pair of red framed reading glasses from the top drawer of her desk. She opens the file folder, slowing moving the bony index finger of her left hand across the page. Expect no mercy, I warn myself. The spare, color-coordinated Ms. Hudson is as contemptuous of flaws in other people as she is of her own.

"Is this all?"

The file contains handwritten notes from my meetings with Ben and copies of the handouts I gave him. She squints and slides a paper back across the desk, marking a place in the margin with a long red fingernail.

"What does this say? I can't read your handwriting."

I turn the paper around."Fabric softener, eggs and Diet Coke."

"Is this part of your clinical notes?"

"No. Of course not. I must have written it before I started the interview, or after."

Ms. Hudson writes in her notebook.

"I want to clarify something. Mr. Gomez wasn't my client, not in the usual sense. The Kenilworth Police Department is my client."

Ms. Hudson peers over the top of her reading glasses. "You saw him three times, once with his wife and then he killed himself. What was he if he wasn't a client?"

"Those were educational sessions. I was teaching him stress management techniques. He was having trouble in the FTO program."

"FTO?"

"Field training. Don't professional conduct investigators go through field training?"

"I'll ask the questions, if you don't mind. Is this the total record of the services you provided to Mr. Gomez while he was under your care?"

"I did more. I just didn't document it in writing."

"What else was it that you did?"

"I had ancillary interviews with his training officer. I was trying to assist him in modifying his training techniques in order to help reduce Mr. Gomez' stress. I also voiced my concerns about this particular training officer to the police chief, and I observed Mr. Gomez in training. After Mr. Gomez died, I interviewed his wife's family and his grandparents, who raised him."

My voice rises an octave with every sentence. It doesn't matter what I say. Without documentation, there is no proof that I have done anything to help Ben except hand him a piece of paper with the kind of advice available in any popular magazine sold at supermarket checkout stands.

"There is nothing in your notes to suggest that you made any attempt to assess your client's potential for suicide. Or that you sought peer consultation. I find this particularly egregious considering the high rate of suicide amongst police officers."

"That's a myth. There are studies that show that the suicide rate among police officers is no higher than the general population. In fact, some of those studies indicate that it's lower."

"Do not lecture me, please Doctor. Just answer my question. Did you or did you not assess your client for suicidal intent?"

"He was frustrated and scared because he thought he was about to be fired, but he wasn't suicidal. Lots of people get fired and don't kill themselves. Me, for instance. I'm about to get fired and I'm not suicidal."

"I don't appreciate sarcasm either. How do you know Mr. Gomez wasn't suicidal if you didn't do an assessment?"

The alarm on her watch starts beeping softly. "Our time is up, Dr. Meyerhoff. I'll return your file after I make my recommendation. Is there anything you want to add?"

"Are you going to talk to anyone else about him?"

"I don't have the time to do field interviews."

"So you accept his wife's complaints about me at face value, but you won't believe me when I tell you I acted according to professional standards?"

"I didn't say I didn't believe you. Please don't misquote me or second guess what I'm thinking."

"Obviously, Mr. Gomez's wife wants to make someone else responsible for her husband's suicide. That's why she's pointing her finger at me."

"Let me remind you that Board of Psychology rules forbid you to have any contact with the complainant. These are not my rules, Dr. Meyerhoff. These are the rules of the State of California." She stands up. "As I said earlier, if you disagree with my recommendation, you can always appeal the decision."

"What do I do in the meantime? I've been off work for three weeks."

"I'm sure I don't know. My job is to protect the public from unethical and incompetent psychologists. Not to protect psychologists from their clients."

She opens the door and walks out. Her heels make tiny triumphant drumbeats down the hall.

Chapter Twenty Four

The summer heat is unrelenting. So is my anxiety. I can't stand waiting for something to happen. There's no word from Baxter or the Board of Psychology. My women friends try to cheer me up and it works, but only when we're together, which usually involves food and several bottles of good wine. I make excuses to avoid my mother and her abrasive optimism. There are plenty of things I should be doing. I should call Frank and take him to dinner as promised. I should check in with Mr. and Mrs. Gomez. I should use this time to unpack the boxes sitting in my garage or plant flowers in my yard. But the only thing I'm capable of is worry and scaring myself to death.

I drive to where the Patchers live. This is crazy, but it's better than being penned up at home while other people decide my fate. I look at my watch. Vinnie Patcher will still be at work. I think Belle knows something that's she's afraid to tell me. Ms. Hudson made it clear that I'm not to contact the complainant, but she said nothing about talking to the complainant's mother. So what if Vinnie Patcher throws another tantrum? There isn't much else he can do to me, short of physical violence. My father's voice rises in my ear, "Never back down from a bully, baby girl. Stand up for yourself. Because if you don't, nobody else will."

The guardhouse is empty and the gate to the complex hangs open. I drive into the Patchers' cul-de-sac and park diagonally across the street from their house with the nose of my car facing toward the freeway. The Patchers' garage door is up and there is a small white car in the driveway. All its doors are open and the trunk is a jumble of boxes and black plastic bags. April is rushing in and out of the garage, throwing bundles of clothes into the car. Her face is flushed and sweaty. She moves awkwardly, as though trying to walk around her protruding stomach. Long damp strands of hair keep falling over her face. She is wearing rubber flip-flops, shorts and a sleeveless maternity top. Her bare arms and legs are pink from the sun.

A car screeches past me and turns into the driveway, coming to a halt with its nose on the rear fender of April's car. The smell of burning rubber singes the air. Patcher jumps out, grabs the keys from the ignition of April's car and stuffs them in his pocket. His face is crimson. He pounds on the car roof. April screams at him. He screams back. She pulls open the passenger door, grabs her purse, and strides down the driveway, her face fixed with savage determination. Patcher starts after her as Belle bursts out of the front door with her wobbly run, grabs his arm, and holds him back. He looks from mother to daughter in a fury of indecision.

I start my car. In a moment I am next to April shouting at her to get in. Tears and sweat mix on her face. Her sandals are slapping against the scorching pavement. I slow the car. She tumbles through the passenger door and collapses on the seat. Patcher is on us in a flash, charging up the street, yelling at the top of his lungs, his wife lumbering behind. I lock the doors. He races past us toward the open gate. I slow down.

"Keep going," April shouts, "Run the fucker over."

She leans toward the steering wheel and mashes her foot on top of mine pushing the accelerator pedal to the floor. There is a thud. Patcher spins off the hood of my car into the bushes and bounces to his feet like a trained gymnast, screaming in rage. I can see him in my rear view mirror, bent double, sweat running off him in rivulets.

"Are you crazy? You just tried to kill your father."

"So what. He had it coming." She is gasping for breath. Her hands pressed against her belly.

I pull out into the street.

"Where are we going?" she asks.

"To jail."

"No way. He won't do anything against me."

"Then to the nearest women's shelter."

"No. He knows where all the shelters are. Your house. Take me to your house."

"My house?" A siren keens behind me. "I could lose my license. You filed a complaint against me. I'm not even supposed to talk to you."

There is a self-serve car wash on the opposite side of the road. I turn abruptly in front of the ongoing traffic and aim for an empty stall, my tires squealing. As I pull in, a police car speeds by, heading for the freeway entrance. We sit in silence, listening to each other's labored breathing.

"He made me file the complaint. I didn't want to."

"Just now, where were you planning to go?"

"To get my own apartment."

"You and Ben didn't have your own apartment?"

"We couldn't afford first and last month's rent."

"How are you going to afford it now?"

"I don't know." She starts to cry. "I can't stay there anymore."

"Don't you have any friends or family you could stay with?"

"No." She shakes her head spraying droplets of sweat and tears across the dashboard.

"Well you can't stay with me."

She pushes open the door. "Then I'll kill myself. Like Ben did."

She grabs her purse and starts running toward the busy street. I'm pretty sure a suicidal woman doesn't need her purse when she throws herself in front of a car, but I'm not so sure I understand anymore who is or isn't going to kill themselves. I don't want to be wrong again. I lean on the horn and gesture for her to get back in the car.

My phone is unlisted and my only published address is my office. Still, I know it won't take Patcher long to find my house. April is sullen on the way to my house, her fist to her mouth like a child.

"One night," I say, "you can stay here one night because it's late. Tomorrow you're going to a shelter."

I heat some canned soup in the microwave and we sit side by side at the kitchen counter, eating in silence.

"Any dessert?" she asks.

We move into the living room with separate bowls of popcorn. It is her favorite food in the whole world, although lately it has been giving her indigestion.

"What happened back there with your father?"

"He wants to control my whole life. Thinks because I'm pregnant, I should stay home all the time and not go out with my friends."

"I thought you said you don't have any friends."

"How can I make friends sitting home? I'm lonely." Her eyes gloss with tears. "Either my parents aren't talking to each other or they're fighting. My mother never goes anywhere or does anything. Just looks at me and cries."

"What are you going to do?"

"I can't raise a baby by myself. I don't even have a job. I'm thinking of giving it up for adoption."

She looks at me, assessing my reaction. I think of Mrs. Gomezes' prediction.

"Your parents would help you, wouldn't they?"

"Only if I live with them. I can't live with them, they're crazy."

"How would Ben feel about adoption?"

"He doesn't have to raise it. I do. If he cared about me or the baby as much as he said, he'd still be here." She picks pieces of unpopped popcorn out of the bowl. "I'll get a good home for it. Open adoption. I'll meet the parents and I can visit the baby anytime I want. If it's a boy, I'll name it Ben."

"Have you talked this over with anyone?"

"I'm nineteen. I can make my own decisions."

"Sometimes it's best not to make important decisions while you're in a crisis. You're still grieving. Adoption is irreversible. You should think it through very carefully."

She pats her bulging stomach. "I don't have a lot of time." She sets the bowl of popcorn on the floor and stands up. "I'm tired, I want to sleep."

I take her upstairs to the empty guest room and we make up the bed. I give her an old t-shirt that used to belong to Mark.

"Whose was this?"

"A friend's."

"You married?"

"Divorced."

"Any children?"

"No."

"So why are you lecturing me about adoption?"

"I wasn't lecturing you. I was just trying to help you think about it."

April gets into bed, her stomach sloping under the blanket. I sit down on the foot of the bed and rest my hand on her ankle. At times, I regret not having children. It had been a constant tension between Mark and me. But when push came to shove, publication deadlines won out over pregnancy. Instead of babies, we made books. Looking at April's swollen, sullen face, I feel lucky, at least for the moment, to have escaped the pain of watching a loving child turn into a scornful stranger.

"Ben wanted a family, didn't he?"

"He was wicked happy that we were going to have a baby." She rolls to her side, still facing me, her eyes open. "He'd have been a good father, better than me as a mother. He was so straight. Didn't drink or do dope because his parents were stone junkies. Didn't want to do that to his own kid."

"What did you say about his parents?"

She frowns. "They were junkies. Didn't you know that? I thought you were his shrink and he told you everything." She rolls on her back again. "I can't get comfortable."

I hand her another pillow. She moves back on her side and wedges it under her stomach.

"How do you know this?" I ask, thinking if Ben's parents were drug addicts, why didn't his grandparents say something to me about it?

"He told me. How do you think? Duh."

She opens her eyes wide and twists her mouth into a moronic grin. Once again, I have an overwhelming urge to slap her. I don't know what kind of training or saintliness a therapist needs to treat adolescents, but I'm certain I don't have whatever it takes.

"He didn't want to tell me at first because he was ashamed. I thought it was funny. He was so straight and his parents were speedball artists. My parents are total nerds, and I want to party all the time."

"Does your father know about Ben's parents?"

"No way. He'd have busted us up in a minute."

"Really?"

April pulls herself up to a sitting position. Her baby-fat face shifts into sharpness. "Are you kidding? When my father wants something he gets it. Ever see my mother walk? Notice her limp? My father did that."

"What do you mean?"

She turns away from me. "Can we talk about something else? Or watch TV?"

Off comes the mantle of therapy. I grab her shoulder and turn her towards me. "I'm not playing this game with you. Ben is dead and everyone is holding me responsible. When I ask you a question, you answer."

"He knocked her down the stairs and she broke her hip. Happy?"

She tries to shrug my hand off her shoulder. I don't let go. "I came home late from a date. My mother told me it was okay to stay out. He told me the next time I disobeyed him, he'd break her arm. My mother said that she fell down, but I don't believe her. She always defends him. Says his job makes him over-protective because he sees so much bad stuff. Tells me I should understand that he is the way he is because he loves me. Bullshit."

She flings my arm off, scoots down and pulls the covers up to her chin. "You ask too many questions. I want to go to sleep."

"I'm not finished. Not by a long shot. Why did Ben kill himself? And where were you when he did?"

She squints her eyes closed and stuffs her hands over her ears like a child.

"Did your father really force you to file a complaint against me or did you do that on your own?"

She pulls the blanket over her head and starts kicking me off the bed with her feet. Assault and battery on a pregnant woman isn't my style, although it's appealing. Instead, I stand up, shouting at the lumpy figure under the covers.

"Tomorrow, young woman. We have a lot to talk about. Get ready."

First thing in the morning, I call Eddie at the department. The automatic voice mail system routes me to Sgt. Lyndley's extension. "You didn't know? The Chief put Eddie on admin leave. I don't know where he is. Maybe he went fishing."

I call Eddie at home. It's just past 7:00 and he's drunk.

"Hey Doc. Funny thing, I was going to call you. Tell you about my idea. I've got a little vacation time coming. Think I'll go up to the Sierras. I have a fishing buddy up there. While I'm there, I'll check around, see what I can find out about our boy, Ben."

"Do you think that's a good idea?"

"What else I gotta do with my time? The chief thinks I did it. You think I did it. Maybe I did. I should check it out for myself."

He hangs up before I can ask him what exactly he thinks he did.

April is not happy when I wake her to say I'm going out to get us something for breakfast. I tell her to stay inside and keep the blinds closed.

"Don't call anyone, don't go anywhere. The minute I get back we're going to have that talk."

Fran is turning flapjacks with her trowel. Sausages sizzle on the griddle. "I've been looking for you. Are you in hiding?"

"Sorry, I don't have any time to talk. Can I get two pancake breakfasts to go?"

She yells for some help at the stove and grabs my arm, steering me through the steamy kitchen and out the back door to a concrete patio. A small picnic table with a lopsided umbrella stands between a row of garbage bins and an assortment of scraggly plants growing in old metal cans.

"Coffee?" she asks. I shake my head.

"Eddie's gone. He came by here to tell me he had time off, courtesy of the chief, and he was going to Mexico where the beer is cold and cheap. He's thinking he might as well retire down there."

"Really? That's not what he told me this morning."

"He's not going to Mexico to retire, Dot. He's going somewhere he can drink himself to death or worse. He hates traveling. Thinks everywhere but America is dirty and dangerous. I know him. Without his job, he's a dead man. There's no way I can leave the restaurant to look for him." She grabs my arm. "Stop him, Dot, before he does something terrible to himself. Promise me you'll try."

I lift her hand off my arm and hold it between my own two hands. She's a dear woman, but this is one promise I'm not going to make.

When I get home there is a note on my kitchen counter. "Thanks a lot. I'll be in touch. P.S. I borrowed your t-shirt and some make-up. XOXOXO, April."

I'm not feeling the slightest bit XOXOXO. I have just committed professional suicide by violating a psychology board regulation. Eddie Rimbauer is maybe going to kill himself because of me. And the unstable and immature daughter of an unstable, powerful man, a girl I have voluntarily taken into my home, has disappeared, pregnant and penniless, into a strange city.

Chapter Twenty Five

Better late than never, I call Frank and invite him out for dinner. He sounds surprised to hear from me after all this time. He hems and haws a little bit, trying to decide if he wants to accept my invitation. It takes two or three apologies cum explanations to persuade him that I'm not a total flake before he agrees to meet me at Sabrosa, a Mexican restaurant in East Kenilworth.

The walls are covered with tiny *milagros* and large colorful masks. Tin framed mirrors sparkle in the candlelight. The waiter seats us in a booth next to a small alcove displaying the smiling ceramic skeleton of a pregnant female dressed in a brightly painted clay skirt and sunbonnet. She is holding a ruffled parasol in her bony hand. I can't help but think that this is an ominous portent of April Gomez' future, which I have just linked to my own.

Technically speaking, this is Frank's and my first real date. The food we shared at the festival we had eaten standing up in the midst of a crowd. Here, alone in this booth, we fumble at the chips and salsa, trying not to touch.

"How are things going?" he asks.

"So, so."

"Working hard?"

"Taking a little time off." I make it sound like my idea. If he's read about my mandatory leave in the newspaper, he doesn't mention it.

"How'd it go with that family you met in the park?"

"I'm afraid that's confidential. I can't talk about it."

"Sorry."

The waiter delivers us from the awkward moment by arriving with our meal. We eat in partial silence, commenting on the food. Frank is an amateur cook with a particular interest in ethnic cuisine. He orders a beer. I have a second Margarita.

"I was thinking on the way over here that I don't know much about you. I've been divorced five years. How about you?"

"One year."

"The first year is the hardest."

"I don't want to talk about that either," I say and regret it the moment the words leave my mouth. He takes a swig of his beer. I sip my margarita. The waiter asks if everything is okay. There is a burst of laughter from an adjoining booth, mocking our discomfort.

"You don't have to do this you know," Frank says. "No pressure. We can just finish our dinner and say Adios. It takes time to get back in the swing of things. I hate dating. Eventually, I want someone in my life, but in the meanwhile, I'm perfectly content by myself."

"Sorry, I'm not much fun to be around these days."

"I thought you were a lot of fun at the festival."

"Things have gotten worse since then."

"This is probably your line, but talking does help."

I blame it on the two margaritas, but I tell him a little about my marriage. How Mark had encouraged my writing, pushed me to work with him on three books, and then pushed me to write one of my own. I talk about my divorce settlement and explain that Mark had bought out my half of our testing and consulting practice and, in exchange, I took over the full-time contract at Kenilworth P.D.

I leave out the part about Melinda. What man wouldn't wonder about the wifely failings that had pushed my husband into another woman's arms?

Frank asks me about Ben and the ethics complaint. I am too embarrassed to tell him about kidnapping April, which is how I have come to think about it. I only say that I think the Patcher family is highly dysfunctional, and I'm baffled about how a nice kid like Ben got mixed up with them.

"I don't know that many cops, but Ben doesn't sound like a typical officer. How'd he get hired in the first place?"

"My ex recommended him."

"Sounds like a poor decision."

"Mark is a crackerjack psychologist. He doesn't make mistakes."

Frank's face suddenly looks like a closed door. I've shot my mouth off once again, this time defending my ex for no good reason. I reach across the table and lightly touch Frank's hand.

"Thanks for your concern. I know you're trying to help. It's just that it's always best to start with an easy case."

My dinner with Frank seems neither a success nor a failure. It hovers somewhere around the pleasant side of neutral, about three on a scale of one to five. Still it got me out of the house.

By the time I drive home, most of my neighbors' lights are out. I don't know my neighbors. Our interactions are limited to a brief wave as we zip in and out of our garages. The homeowner's association maintains the landscaping, eliminating any opportunity I have to socialize while watering the lawn. My tiny backyard is hemmed in on three sides by vine-covered stucco walls. Only the neighbor's cat breeches the divide to visit me.

There is an SUV parked under the shadows of a large oak tree at the end of my cul de sac. It looks familiar. I can't tell if there's anyone in it. I start to shiver in the warm air. I think about parking in my driveway and ringing my own doorbell, a tactic recommended by the crime prevention unit to frighten off burglars.

Then I remember how Vinnie Patcher had blocked April's car with his own. I turn off my headlights and slowly cruise the cul de sac. In the dark, I can't tell if the SUV is blue, black or green. A porch light goes on and someone unceremoniously pushes a black cat out the front door. It shakes itself and sits on the doormat looking at me with yellow eyes as though questioning why I'm skulking around my own neighborhood in the dark.

This is ridiculous. I drive into my garage, shut the door behind me and sit in my car listening to my heart until it slows. The SUV probably belongs to a neighbor. People around here are always buying new cars. The overhead light goes out and I feel a streak of terror, until I remember it is on a timer. In the dark, I can see packing boxes, my garbage can and the recycling bins I have piled against a wall. Nothing else. I feel my way to the kitchen door and let myself in.

The refrigerator is open, spilling light into the room. Eggs, milk, and juice puddle together in a congealing mess on the floor. Tributaries of coffee ooze down one wall. Kitchen stools lie at odd angles. I flatten against the wall and listen to the open refrigerator straining to stay cold.

Patcher's in the house, waiting for me. I edge around the corner to the living room. My only plant is upended on the carpet and the television is lying on its side, the glass screen fractured into tiny shards. My one painting hangs crookedly, pieces of ripped canvas dangling over the frame. Sofa cushions are strewn around the room.

My heart is pulsing furiously. I back into the kitchen and call 911. "Help," I whisper into my cell phone. "Please, someone help."

Manny arrives first. Sgt. Lyndley pulls up seconds later and orders me to stay on the sidewalk while he and Manny go inside, guns drawn. Lights are popping on in the neighborhood.

I look down the cul de sac. It is empty.

They come out in less than five minutes, declaring that the house is secure. Lyndley informs me that I have been burglarized, to state the obvious, probably by some neighborhood kids. He isn't persuaded to think differently when I tell him that this is an adults only development.

"Nothing's missing. Aren't burglars looking for TVs and electronics?"

"You don't know that yet. Your place is a mess. You won't know if something's missing until you put everything back."

"I'm telling you, this is personal. Whoever did this is furious with me."

"Kids these days are spoiled rotten. Their parents buy them everything they want. They have no respect for anything. They get loaded and trash stuff."

I tell him about Patcher and how he is blaming me, first for his son-in-law's suicide and now for his daughter's running away from home.

"If Patcher wanted to hurt you, he wouldn't do it like this." He doesn't elaborate on the alternatives. "Officer Ochoa can dust for prints if you want, but he won't find any."

He looks at Manny. "When you're done with your report, leave it in my box." He turns back to me. "Sorry for your trouble, Doc. If it wasn't neighborhood kids, maybe a former patient? If I were you, I'd change the locks a.s.a.p. And from now on, make sure all your windows are closed when you go out."

"Is there someone I can call for you?" Manny asks. There are sooty smudges all over my kitchen where he has dusted for fingerprints. "You shouldn't be alone after something like this."

"Thank you, no. There's no one I want to call."

He looks puzzled. People think psychologists qualify to counsel others because their own lives are so together. I am sorry to disappoint him.

"Let me walk you upstairs," he says. "There's something you should see."

My bedroom looks like a homeless encampment. I can smell sweat, pungent and coarse, like an animal in rut. My clothes are trampled on the floor. Dresser drawers have been pulled open and upended. Jewelry is strewn everywhere.

The only things of real value I own are a diamond tennis bracelet Mark gave me after our first book was published – it still boggles my mind that he thought I would wear something so ostentatious – and the gold locket my father bought for my sixteenth birthday. Lord knows how many overtime shifts he had to work at the print shop to pay for it.

Manny puts his hand on my shoulder and turns me gently toward the back of the bedroom door. My good luck sweater, the one I had worn to the interview with Ms. Hudson, is pinned to the door by a kitchen knife that has pierced it through the center, right where my heart should have been.

I sleep, barely, on my living room couch, with all the lights on. As soon as the sun comes up, I call the chief. He starts work at the crack of dawn.

"Someone broke into my house last night. I think it was Vinnie Patcher. Trashed everything in sight. He wants to hurt me. He stuck a knife through one of my sweaters and pinned it to the door. You don't have to be a psychologist to see the symbolism. Can you assign somebody to keep a watch on my house?"

"What a coincidence. I was just about to send an officer to your house to bring you into the station. Vinnie Patcher claims you kidnapped his daughter and ran him over with your car."

"I did not kidnap his daughter. She was trying to get away from him and he was restraining her. She got in my car voluntarily. She's over eighteen. She has the right to go where she wants to."

"You don't have the right to run people over with your car. That's assault with a deadly weapon."

"I did not run him over. He deliberately stepped in front of my car, trying to stop us."

"That's not what he says."

"He's a liar. You told me so yourself. Anyhow, I have a witness. His daughter can tell you what happened."

"Where is she?"

"I don't know."

"Patcher thinks you do. He thinks you put her up in a hotel."

"I haven't got the money to do that. I've been on administrative leave for six weeks with no pay, waiting for you to finish my IA. Remember?"

"Actually, your status has changed. As of today, your contract is terminated. You don't work here anymore."

Chapter Twenty Six

I leave four messages for Mark, all urgent. When he finally calls back I'm outside, hauling a garbage can full of broken dishes to the curb. I sit down to listen to his message.

"Sorry, babe. I should have called you earlier. I don't know where the time went." There's a pause. I can hear him breathing. "I really wanted to tell you this in person but I guess that's not going to happen. Melinda's pregnant. We're thrilled." He coughs. "About covering for you at the PD? Think of me as Mark the bookmark, holding your place until you get back." Evidently he doesn't know I've been fired. "I can't believe I just said that. I know this isn't funny. My point is, chin up, this will all blow over soon. Try not to worry, okay? Talk soon. I gotta go. Oh jeez, I almost forgot about Ben's psych screen. We finally found it, but under the circumstances, my lawyer thinks I should keep it strictly confidential. Sorry about that. Well, I guess that's all. Talk soon, babe. Stay strong. Melinda says hi."

Mark's offices are on the top two floors of a Victorian house that he had bought and renovated when we first started the practice. I love this building, the burnished mahogany banisters and wainscoting, the stained glass windows with prisms that splinter light over the walls. Even now, in the dark, the colored glass panes sparkle with light from the street.

I peer through the etched glass window in the front door looking for tell tale lights indicating that Mark has installed an alarm system. I don't see any. A large white board with the words 'in' and 'out' stenciled across the top rests on our antique oak credenza. Staff names are written down the side and there is a small round magnet for each. All the magnets have been moved to the 'out' column.

I walk around to the back entrance, sneaking like a thief. I can see a small nightlight through the coffee room window. I rattle the door and hold my breath waiting for an alarm to blare. There's a light rustle in the backyard garden and a flutter of birds choruses briefly, irritated by the disturbance. I take out my key. Mark had never thought to ask for it back.

The old brass lockset is still the same. I insert my key and turn it. The door opens with a familiar creak and I am inside.

The locked file room is on the top floor. I go upstairs, sliding my hand along the banister, savoring the silken feel of worn wood on my palm. Mark had always hidden the file room keys in a secret drawer in his roll top desk. I turn the doorknob to his office. Nothing happens. A glow of light comes through the frosted glass pane. I give it a little push and it opens slowly, dragging across the nap of newly installed carpeting. I step inside.

Everything is changed. The old Persian rugs are gone and the beautiful bare oak floors are covered wall to wall with off-white carpet. A cordovan leather sofa, matching chairs and a steel and glass coffee table stand where the old antique sofa and overstuffed chair once stood. In place of the roll top desk and oak banker's chair is a long metal table and an ergonomically designed mesh chair with a gnarly thicket of knobs and levers under the seat. A photo of Mark and Melinda on vacation in some tropical resort sits next to the computer. I turn it face down on the table.

I am perspiring. My heart thuds in my chest. Where is the damn key to the file cabinet? I find the roll top desk in the second floor waiting room, pushed against a wall, the crown jewel in a ring of identical black leather office chairs with chrome frames. There are worn spots on the carpet, where anxious applicants sit on the edges of their seats, waiting to be called for their interviews. The roll top opens with a clatter and I feel underneath the cubbyholes for the secret drawer. It pops open easily. The keys are inside.

Twelve file cabinets jam the small room. Mark wasn't just boasting. The practice has grown. He now employs two office staff, two part time psychologists and Melinda, the consort intern and soon-to-be-mother of his child.

The file drawer groans heavily on its sliders. There are nearly one hundred buff colored files in this one drawer, alphabetically arranged behind plastic tabs. I find Ben's folder and, in my eagerness to read it, I slam the drawer shut. The sound reverberates through the house with a shudder. I am transfixed by my own recklessness, frozen to the spot with fear until silence settles back into the room. I return to Mark's office. It is after midnight. Lights play across the fluted glass window as a police car drives slowly down the street on a lonely prowl. This is the time of night when normal people sleep and criminals are just starting to work.

There is a copy machine on the back wall. A digital sign warns me to wait until the copier warms up. I walk back to the desk and right the picture of Mark and Melinda. They look healthy and adoring. Even their names link harmoniously. I wonder if she makes him happy or if she is also destined to be tossed aside for someone younger and more beautiful.

The copier beeps in readiness. I open the file. There is a copy of the letter confirming Ben's appointment and a signed consent form indicating that he understood the process and made no claim to confidentiality. All boilerplate. There are no protocols, no reports, no letter of recommendation.

I can't face walking into my dark house, alone, in the middle of the night. I drive to Gary's house and park in front. I don't want to ring his doorbell at this hour. The weather is balmy. A light breeze carries the fragrance of roses. I crawl into the back seat, cover myself with a blanket, and fall into a deep, dreamless sleep.

Someone is talking to me, tapping his fingers on the window glass. "Go away," I say. "I'm sleeping."

"I see that."

I shake myself awake, my feet tangled in the unfamiliar blanket. I sit up. I'm stiff and my left hand is pulsing painfully. Frank is staring at me through the rear driver's side window.

"What are you doing here, Frank?"

"I'm working on Gary's house, remember?"

He waves a thermos and a coffee cup in the air. I unlock the door and he slides in the back seat with me. I pat my hair. My breath is atrocious. He hands me a cup of coffee.

"What time is it?"

"6:30 a.m. Contractors get started early. What are you doing here?"

"I need to talk to Gary."

"At 6:30 in the morning?"

"It's important."

"Must be, if you slept here all night."

"I haven't been here all night, just a few hours."

"Why aren't you sleeping at your house?"

"This is my car. I can sleep in it if I want."

Frank sighs. "Answer my question, please."

"I was scared to be home alone."

"Why?"

"Someone broke into my house."

He takes a swig of coffee from the thermos. "Who?"

"I don't know."

"Don't know or don't want to say?"

"Don't know."

"Were you home?"

"I was having dinner with you, remember?"

He opens his mouth and then closes it again. His hands tighten around the thermos. The unshaven parts of his face are turning red. "What did they take?"

"Nothing. They just trashed the place. Look, I need to get going."

Frank opens the car door and starts to get out.

"Don't tell Gary I slept in front of his house."

"Are you kidding? That's the first thing I'm going to tell him."

Gary is dressed in jeans and a t-shirt. Janice is still in her bathrobe.

"It's not what it looks like," Frank says. "I found Dot sleeping in her car in front of your house when I got here. I'm going out back to work on the addition. Maybe you can figure out what's going on."

He tromps off, his work boots thumping through the kitchen. I hear a door slam.

I shove Ben's folder at Gary.

"Where did you get this?"

"From Mark's office."

"Did Mark give it to you?"

"No, I asked him, but he refused."

"So, how did you get it?"

"Better you shouldn't know. I've got a lot riding on this. I'll do what I have to, to protect myself."

"Give me that." He snatches the folder out of my hand and sits down. "There's coffee in the kitchen. Help yourself."

The muffled sound of Frank's drilling drones in the background. When I come back from the kitchen, Gary gives me a puzzled look.

"There's nothing in here, no protocols, no scoring sheets."

"No inkblots?" Frank's voice is behind me.

He pulls out a chair and sits down, coffee in hand. "I'm taking a break, Boss."

"At least you bring your own coffee." Gary closes the folder. "Our girl here is working up a rap sheet. Like they say, hell hath no fury like a woman scorned."

"Remember what the Buddha said." Frank sets his coffee cup down and places both hands on the table. "Before you seek revenge, first dig two graves."

Gary and I look at him.

"I mess around with philosophy. Contractors can read, you know."

Gary lights his pipe with all the precision of a Japanese tea ceremony. "I keep two sets of folders, one clinical and one process oriented."

"How's that?" Frank asks.

"Clinical folders contain progress notes, topics I discuss with the client, medication notes, changes in mental status, et cetera. They're basically checklists. My process notes have all the gory details. I might check off that a client discussed relations with his mother and in my process notes I'd write that she forced him to eat spoiled food when he was a child. My clinical files can be subpoenaed, but process notes are my property."

Gary turns to me. "Sorry to say, Dot, you went to a lot of trouble for nothing. Let's hope you don't also go to jail. You got the wrong folder. The real folder must be somewhere else."

Gary has a patient waiting, so Frank takes me home to collect some clothes and bring them back to Gary and Janice's house. I protest, but the two of them inform me that I have no vote on the matter. I was not to spend another night alone until whoever had broken in was caught. I could have told them how infrequently the police ever solve a cold case, but I don't.

This is the first time Frank has been inside my house. It's still pretty trashed from the break-in. We go up to the bedroom. I had turned the mattress over, slashed side down and made the bed. Given my current state of unemployment, I don't dare spend money on a new mattress. I start packing a suitcase.

"What's this?" Frank asks. He is holding my good luck sweater with the hole in the middle. I had draped it over a chair as a reminder to take it to a tailor and ask if it could be repaired.

"I tore it on something. Isn't that awful? It's my favorite sweater."

"Damn it, Dot. I'm not an idiot. Somebody stuck a knife through the middle of this." He holds the sweater up in the air, pulling the slit apart so that light shows through. "Is this ex-husband of yours crazy? Maybe you need a protection order."

Before I can tell him that I can take care of myself, thank you, he reaches for me and kisses me, not an air kiss, not a kiss on the cheek, but a full-on frontal kiss. I pull away, acutely discomfited by the nearness of my bed and the sudden rush of hormones storming my body.

We sit across from each other at the kitchen counter. I am tempted to tell him that Mark isn't the one who broke into my house. The person who is stalking me is far more dangerous and deeply damaged than Mark could ever be.

"I think you need a lawyer. You're going to wind up hurt or in a worse position than you're already in. If I understand what's going on, you just broke into your ex-husband's office and took a confidential file. Isn't that against the law?"

"I didn't break in, I had a key."

"You don't belong there. It's not yours anymore, key or no key. You're not thinking straight."

"When did you get a license to practice psychology?"

"Anybody could see that you're in trouble."

"Stick to hammering nails, Frank. Please."

He winces and stands up.

"Get what you need," he says. "I'll wait for you in the car."

First kiss, first fight. Things are speeding up. We drive in silence back to Gary and Janice's house. Gary, Baxter, Patcher, the missing Eddie, even poor Ben from his grave are buffeting my life into a whorl of tangles and snarls. Meeting Frank complicates things even further.

Chapter Twenty Seven

I'm too antsy to spend the day sitting alone in Gary and Janice's house, twiddling my thumbs and watching daytime TV.

Not to mention that sharing an empty house with Frank, as he works bare-chested in the heat, is very distracting and not much company. He's been noticeably frosty to me since our little spat.

Gary and Janice, on the other hand, are really worried about me, always telling me to be careful.

I feel a stab of irritation at their possessiveness. Being careful is what got me into this situation. Why had I been so cautious with Ben? If I had been more gutsy, I would have dug deeper, gone to his house when he didn't return to work, asked him outright, are you thinking of killing yourself?

I second guess myself all the way from Gary's to Fran's restaurant. Fran is rhythmically flipping eggs and flattening rashers of bacon under an iron press, moving her bulky body from griddle to counter with the grace of a ballerina. When she bends over, the fleshy folds around her waist pop from between her t-shirt and the elastic waistband on her pants. She doesn't seem to care what she looks like. Doesn't even try to tug her shirt down. Despite all the sexual banter and innuendo she exchanges with her customers, it strikes me that Fran never again expects to be seen naked by a man.

I sit down on a stool. She shoves a mug of coffee at me, its porcelain edge worn with age. "There's still no answer on Eddie's home phone. Has he called you? I've been to his apartment three times. He's not there, and his neighbors don't know where he went. I called you last night. Why haven't you called me back?"

"No, he hasn't called me. And I wasn't home last night."

"He's going to kill himself, I know it."

"Eddie isn't going to kill himself, Fran." I say this like I haven't been worried about him myself. "He's probably just somewhere drinking beer."

"I don't think you're in a position to judge who is or isn't suicidal." She freezes, spatula in the air. "That was a terrible thing to say. Forgive me? I'm so worried about Eddie, I don't know what I'm saying half the time. If he turns up alive, I'm going to kill him with my bare hands." She reaches over the counter and hugs me. "I didn't mean what I said. What can I do to make it up to you? Are you hungry?"

"Give me a job."

"That's ridiculous."

"I need something to do or I'll go crazy."

"Tell your friends that you need clients. "

"I'm under investigation and being sued. That makes me more of a liability than a hot prospect for referrals."

"Then look for Eddie."

"I'm not a cop, Fran. I wouldn't know where to start."

"Have you ever cooked or waited tables?"

"No, but you could teach me."

"Do you really want people to know you're working here?"

I don't know the answer. On the one hand, it's embarrassing. On the other, I'd feel a lot safer surrounded by cops.

Fran peers over the counter looking at my feet. I am wearing boots with stacked heels. "Lesson number one, comfortable shoes. Come back when you get some."

I go home to get the new walking shoes I had stowed in the back of my closet. My yard needs watering and the house could use a good airing out. Before we had our little argument, Frank offered to install a fancy monitored alarm system in my house, one that automatically rings down the police and has motion activated lights in the front and back yards and panic buttons in the garage and in my bedroom. He may have changed his mind about me, but I hope he hasn't changed his mind about the alarm. I told him I couldn't pay him and the way he said he'd find a way to collect made me go weak at the knees. I open several windows and go upstairs. My good luck sweater is still draped over the chair where Frank left it. The memory of our kiss leaves me feeling spongy and soft. I lie down on the bed and close my eyes. Outside my window, a mocking bird engages in noisy discourse with itself.

Something wakes me – I'm not sure if I've been sleeping for a minute or an hour – a noise, unfamiliar and out of place, a scraping sound like someone pushing open a sticky window. I lay frozen with fright, listening to the creak of feet padding softly across the bare floorboards in the dining room and then up the carpeted stairs.

I drop my feet over the edge of the bed and stand. My heart is pounding, and I can hear the rush of blood in my ears. There is an open window about six feet away. I could scream for help but my neighbors are all at work. I pick up the cordless phone. The dial tone sounds like a klaxon. The soft steps stop. I move toward the open closet door. There is a set of unused hand weights on the floor. A little collection of unfulfilled promises I made to myself and then abandoned in a miasma of post-divorce melancholy. I elbow my way into the hot airless space behind my winter clothes and raise the weight. Plastic storage bags stick to my sweaty skin. I have never before hit another human being in malice, and I'm not sure I can do it now.

A shadow falls into the room. I hesitate, then lunge forward, swinging the weight in a downward arc like a hatchet. A large hand stops me in mid-air, tears the weight away and turns me around, yanking my hand behind my back and up between my shoulder blades. Pain streaks down my arm.

"Are you fucking trying to kill me?"

Eddie throws the weight across the room, splintering the baseboard with a loud crack. My legs collapse, I fall on him, and he catches me as I hit the floor and leans me against the wall. My whole body is shaking.

"What are you doing sneaking around my house?" I barely have enough breath to speak. "Why didn't you ring the doorbell?"

"There's a fucking window wide open downstairs. I thought maybe you were being burglarized. What did you want me to do, ring the bell and announce myself to the crook?" I'm cradling my arm. "Hurt? Probably a little strain. Nothing serious."

He helps me to my feet and we walk downstairs into the living room. My heart is still pounding in my ears. He goes into the kitchen, pours me a glass of ice water and brings it back with a bottle of aspirin that was sitting on the counter.

"Take two. Call me in the morning. I always wanted to say that."

"Fran's going out of her mind worrying about you. We both were. We thought you were off somewhere drinking yourself to death."

"You were worried about me? Five minutes ago you were ready to knock me into the next century." He looks around. "Where's all your stuff?"

"Spring cleaning. I'm going to buy some new furniture." Now is the perfect time to tell him about Patcher breaking into my house and trashing everything. But then I would have to tell him about the incident in Sacramento and about April.

"You're shitting me, right?"

He makes a pot of coffee and we move outside to my tiny patio. The sun is warm and the air smells of freshly cut grass. Hummingbirds dart through the shrubs, their iridescent ruby throats glinting in the sunlight, their wings droning softly.

Eddie swipes at the air. "Fucking birds sound like bullets."

His face has lost the fluorescent pallor that comes with years of working midnights. I can barely see the netting of broken capillaries that cover his nose and cheeks like a caul.

"I told you I was going to the Sierras. I got a friend at the Sheriff's department." He draws quotation marks in the air around the word 'friend'. "Owes me big time. Stopped him for DUI a couple of years ago. He was down here in the big city taking his girlfriend out to dinner while his wife stayed home with the kids. I remember because the girlfriend had a face like forty miles of bad road. I let him off because he was a cop. Perks of the job. He pulled the case file on Ben. Usual procedure is to investigate an unattended death, make sure somebody didn't off the vic and make it look like suicide."

He takes a swig of coffee and wipes his shirt sleeve over his mouth. "No surprise, they did a shitty investigation, didn't look for prints, hair, fibers, nothing. The motel room's been repainted and back in service. Anything they might have overlooked is gone."

"I don't understand. Are you saying Ben was murdered and someone covered it up?"

"You've seen too many movies. All I'm saying is that the S.O. did a shitty job. I read the coroner's report. It's a 1000 to one that Ben did himself. No one could've forced him into bed and make him shoot himself in the head. He wasn't much of a fighter, but the survival instinct would have taken over. Even a wuss like him would have put up a helluva fight. Made such a mess those Keystone cops couldn't have missed it if they tried." He waits for a response. "So, what do you think?"

"Frankly, I'm flabbergasted. I can't believe you went to all this trouble for me."

"I didn't do it for you, I did it for me." He shifts forward on the little wrought iron patio chair, looking like Horton the elephant balancing on a flower. "I haven't had this much fun in years. Beats rolling up on a couple of crack heads who beat the crap out of each other every night. Wish Baxter had given me more time on the beach, so I could nose around a little more."

"For what."

"I never did get to talk to the motel owner, only his wife, and she was pretty fucked up, nipping at a thermos. Wasn't coffee, I can tell you that. Takes one to know one." He raises his eyebrows. "She said she and her old man were in the back watching TV and boozing. They never heard the shot. When she went up to clean the room she found his body. Nasty shock. My hunch is she traded it in for a three day drunk."

"Did she say anything else?"

"Yeah, she had an interesting observation. Said if she was married to, and I quote, 'that little bitch', she'd be more inclined to commit homicide than suicide. Seems April came banging into the office demanding more bottles of shampoo or some shit like that. Caused a big commotion. Not that she disturbed the other patrons of this flea bag. There weren't any others. Not exactly your four-star hotel."

"April was with him?"

"Unless he's fooling around with another short, blonde, pregnant woman. The motel owners never saw her after the shampoo rampage and don't know what time she left. She wasn't around when the wife found Ben's body and neither was their car."

"So what should I do now?" I can hardly believe I'm asking Eddie Rimbauer for advice.

"Why ask me? I barely made it out of high school. You're the one with the Ph.D." He leans forward suddenly, his face barely ten inches from mine. His breath coffee warm. "What's up with you? Something's not right. You're not going to off yourself too, are you?"

"Just the opposite. I'm trying to find a way to live with myself. I've never had a client commit suicide before, and I'm not coping with it too well." I take a sip of coffee. It's gone cold. "How do you cope?"

"Me? Booze, sex and a lot of overtime. I don't recommend it." He runs his fingers around the rim of his empty cup. "I always wondered what shrinks do when they need help. Talk to yourself in the mirror?"

"Talk to friends, colleagues, family. Same as everyone else."

"Bullshit. If you did, you wouldn't be talking to me."

"I feel responsible for his death. I missed something. And I'm not the only one who thinks so. I need to know what happened. He was mad at both of us, but, unless I'm absolutely deaf, dumb and blind, he wasn't suicidal. "

"Get over yourself, Doc. What's done is done. You can't fix it. When I was a young copper I thought I was going to stop the tide of crime. Fucking fantasy. Most crimes are cold and the crook is history. Doesn't stop the victim from thinking this is TV, and I'm going to start dusting everything for fingerprints and running shit through a computer."

I think about Manny and the smudges he left on my kitchen counter. Was he the eager rookie hoping to identify the person who broke into my house or was it a placebo designed to comfort me and make him look good?

"People bring on their own misery," he says. "Leave their garage doors open, their windows unlocked, then moan and cry because some perp helped himself to their jewelry and their TVs."

"And your wife? Did she bring on her own misery?"

He blows a long whistle of air out through his lips. Then picks up his empty coffee cup and pretends to drink. "I don't think that's any of your business."

"God, that was stupid of me. I'm really sorry."

"For christsake, quit that. I hate it when women cry."

He shifts in his seat and looks away. Suddenly, he gets up, coffee cup in hand, and walks the short distance to my rear garden wall, where he stands, his back to me, looking at something off in the distance. "I don't know why I'm telling you this, but I had to come to terms with the fact that I could fix problems on the street that I couldn't fix at home. I put my wife in an armlock once and hauled her off to the hospital like some street corner hype, and all it did was make her cringe every time I came near her again."

His voice breaks and he coughs to cover it. "Took me a while before I realized that if I could change myself I would've quit eating and boozing years ago. So how in hell was I going to change my wife? As far as blaming myself? Sure. I whined 'poor me' for a couple of years. I sounded like the shit heads I see on the streets."

He turns around, his eyes unnaturally bright and glossy. "There ought to be a statute of limitations on whining. Daddy beat you up when you were a kid? You get five years to be an irresponsible jerk and then forget it, it's over. The wife leaves you for a syringe full of heroin? Kills your baby and then gets sick and dies? Ten years tops and then you have to quit blaming all the crap in your life on her. After a while you have to shove the shit that happens to you out of your mind and move on. You have to get tough with yourself before you can be tough on anyone else."

I think of my father, his useless arm, his conspiracy theories. How he wore his broken life like a badge of honor, the brilliant student leader, clerking in a print shop for thirty years, clinging with pathological certainty to his own sad story in the belief that he was a hero.

"Maybe I'm just looking for someone else to blame," I say. "One of my colleagues thinks that's what I'm doing. So does Baxter."

Eddie walks back to me and leans on the table, his big hands nearly cover the surface. "Listen to me, Doc. On the one hand, you should stick to what you know, whack jobs and whiners. On the other, I'm going to tell you what I tell my rookies. Follow your gut. Never listen to anyone else – especially the police chief. He don't know jack. If he does anything, it has to be spelled out in the general orders and blessed by the fucking Pope. Frankly, I think you could use a shrink of your own, but if your gut tells you that you need to stick your nose into this, then that's what you should do. Do what's right, not what's going to get you a letter of commendation."

He looks at his watch. "And another thing before I go. Don't go near Patcher by yourself. The sheriff in Sierra and him are buddies. Ben almost went to work there, but they turned him down at the last minute. Patcher's doing his own little investigation. He knows I've been sniffing around and his back is up. Don't try any of your shrink voodoo on him. He's a cruel son-of-a-bitch. He'll have you for dinner."

"He's already started on the appetizers. He's suing me."

"You're getting off light. He's capable of a lot worse."

We walk together to the front door. His eyes dart through my living room and into the kitchen. "Your place sure looks empty to me. Is there something else you should be telling me?"

"Yes." I put my hand on his arm. "I'm really sorry I tried to hit you over the head with a ten pound weight."

He laughs, steps towards me as though he's going give me a hug and then stops, giving me a cocky salute instead.

"No apology needed, little lady. When a man comes into your bedroom uninvited, he's up to no good. Next time, if there is a next time, don't hesitate and for godsakes, don't miss."

Chapter Twenty Eight

Fran lets me work the lighter dinner shift. I tell her it's not the money I'm after. I need something to do, something else to think about except Ben, Frank and the end of my career.

I'm hopelessly clumsy and unteachable. She puts me behind the cash register with a warning not to move. I don't do well at making change either. At the end of the evening, she invites me to eat dinner there every night for free, but asks me to please find something else to do with my time.

That night I dream about Ben. I've had this dream or ones like it before. He is calling me, his disembodied voice blowing across a deserted landscape ringed with low mountains. I crawl up a scree-covered slope, trying to get to him. As soon as I near the top, I slide down, scraping my arms and hands until they bleed. I do this again and again. The sound of my own whimpering wakes me.

Early morning air from a partially open window cools my cheeks. I switch on the light next to my bed and record the fragmented images of my dreamed incompetence in a notebook. For years, I kept a dream journal but stopped because Mark used to deride dream interpretation as one step removed from horoscope reading. It is only since Ben's death that I have started making entries again, trying to capture, in the few seconds before they disappear into wakefulness, the camouflaged and coded contents of these nighttime journeys. And then I try to extract the essence of the dream, drawing it out like a delicate filament and writing it down.

This morning's message is clear. Do not lose Ben twice.

A car rolls by and the morning newspaper hits the sidewalk with a soft thwack that repeats all the way down to the end of the cul de sac, rousing a few high pitched barks from the neighborhood dogs, all of whom are purse sized because condominium association rules don't allow for any pets that weigh more than 15 pounds. There is a thin light in the sky, enough to keep me awake. I pull on a pair of sweatpants, a baggy t-shirt and flip-flops and head out to the curb for the newspaper. There is a dark blue SUV parked across the street two houses down. My heart begins racing. I turn back toward my house and stop. I am safer outside in full view of two early rising neighbors who are backing out of their driveways heading for work. I pick up the paper, wave at my imaginary friends and begin to read with feigned concentration.

When I look up, Belle Patcher is walking across the road with her funny little hobble.

"I hope I didn't frighten you."

There are dark circles around her eyes and hollows in her cheeks. She is wearing a green-collared jersey and baggy white pants. The shirt hangs loosely, and I can see deep creases around and under her neck.

"May I come in? I have something important to tell you. About Ben."

I'm not sure I want her in my house. On the other hand, I've known in my gut that she's been hiding something, and I'm curious why she's finally decided to talk to me. Curiosity and intuition are good traits to have if you're a therapist or a cop. She starts down the path as though I've already said yes. I shove past her to the open door and direct her into the kitchen. She sits at the counter, her legs barely reaching the lower rung of the stool, chirping about what a nice house this is. Could she just have a look around?

"No, you may not. April isn't here and I don't know where she is."

I pour myself a cup of coffee and don't offer her any.

"What are you doing here, Mrs. Patcher? Why have you suddenly changed your mind and decided to talk to me? Aren't you still afraid of your husband?"

"He doesn't know I'm here. He'll check the odometer, but I don't care. I'll just tell him I went shopping at the big mall in Freeston."

"What do you want?"

"I found an address in the car. In my husband's handwriting. I took a guess that it was yours. We don't know too many people who live in Kenilworth."

"So?"

"I was worried that he came here and forced you to tell him where April is. Did you? Did you tell him where April is?"

"I haven't talked to your husband since that day at your house. Someone broke in here and trashed everything. I presume it was him. That's probably why he has my address in his car."

She looks around. "He can be violent. Believe me, I know."

She relaxes now, lowers her voice and leans in. She is half-smiling, her cheeks rouged with the pleasure of sharing a confidence, woman to woman. "One time he pushed me down the stairs because he was mad at April when she wouldn't listen to him. He blames it on his job. Says it makes him over protective. See? That's why I don't want him to know where April is. He might hurt her."

I want to sit down, but I don't want to collude with the fiction that this is a social call between friends.

"Where is she, Dr. Meyerhoff? Tell me, please. I'll do whatever you ask."

"I told you, I don't know where she is. I brought her home with me for that one night. I went out the next morning to buy some food. When I got back, she was gone. She left a note, but she didn't say where she was going."

"He drives them all away – my family, my friends, and now April." She settles her elbows on the counter, getting ready, I suppose, to tell me the long sad story of her life.

"You said you wanted to tell me something about Ben, Mrs. Patcher. What is it? I haven't got all day."

Her eyebrows shoot up in surprise, as though she had expected me to be so engrossed in the drama of her life that I would have forgotten that she had bargained her way into my house with a promise to tell me something important about Ben.

"This is what I couldn't tell you before, only now I don't care. Ben was a nice boy and Vinnie tried to break him. We knew that he flunked out of FTO, that he didn't just resign. Vinnie threatened to force April to leave him. I pleaded with Vinnie to let Ben go back to his old job. Who cares where he works? But Vinnie wouldn't listen. Ben had to be a cop or else. That's why Ben killed himself."

She sits back, looking immensely pleased with herself for having defied the Gods to deliver a secret of monumental importance.

"That's it? That's what you had to tell me that was so important that you were lying in wait for me at the crack of dawn? You need to leave. Now."

I head for the front door. She jumps off the stool and runs after me, her face twisted with a sudden surge of panic.

"That's not all. There's more. You have to help me. Please."

She puts her hand on my arm. I shake it off.

"I'm afraid April is going to put her baby up for adoption. That's why I need to know where she is. If her father finds her first, he'll encourage her. He doesn't want her to keep it. That's my grandchild. One day she wants it, and the next day she doesn't. If she gives it away, she'll regret it for the rest of her life. I can't let that happen. That's why I'm here, Doctor. Don't you understand? How could I live knowing that my own flesh and blood is being raised by strangers? I'll look at every baby I see and wonder if that's my grandchild. I told April I'd leave her father and we could raise the baby together."

"What did she say?"

Belle gives a small yelp as tears cascade down her cheeks in glistening streaks. "She told me she'd rather drown it."

She collapses against the wall, the fleshy part of her upper arms shaking with every sob. I steer her to the couch in my living room and go back into the kitchen to get her a glass of water. Just in case she is telling me the truth about her husband pushing her down the stairs, I look up the number to the women's shelter nearest her house and return to the living room, glass and phone number in hand. She swigs the water in noisy gulps, but when I hand her the phone number, her face fuses into a bitter mash, and she refuses to take it.

Chapter Twenty Nine

The days drag forward. I greet the mail carrier in hopes of having a short conversation, but he is clearly on a schedule that doesn't give him time to console the lonely with idle conversation. He hands me a sheaf of supermarket circulars fastened with a rubber band. Folded in between the throwaways are two bills and a letter from the Board of Psychology signed by "Marsha Hudson, professional conduct investigator." Ms. Hudson wants to inform me that she has temporarily halted her investigation because the complainant is not responding to letters or telephone calls. I am to understand that this is a postponement, not a dismissal. It is Ms. Hudson's opinion that there is sufficient information to warrant a sustained complaint and that the investigation will continue when the complainant can be located.

On the one hand, this is good news. Only the other hand, dragging this out just adds to the agony of waiting. I can't stand sitting around doing nothing while people I barely know are deciding my fate. Something small and irritating has been bothering me all week. Eddie told me that Ben almost went to work for the Sierra Sheriff's office, but they turned him down at the last minute. Why would a small rural department that probably paid next to nothing not want Ben, especially in the middle of a national recruitment crisis when agencies are offering signing bonuses and interest free home loans to attract new officers?

I call the business number at the Sierra S.O. and get a recorded message. An abrasively cheerful female voice thanks me for calling, assures me my call is important and asks me to leave a message. And in case I am an idiot, she instructs me to call 911 if my call is urgent. I push the redial number repeatedly until a real person answers.

"Good afternoon," I say. "My name is Marsha Hudson. I'm a professional conduct investigator with the California State Board of Psychology. May I speak to the person in charge of personnel and hiring?"

"That would be me. My name is Doris Johnson, administrative assistant to Sheriff Collier. How may I assist you?"

"I'm investigating a psychologist by the name of Dr. Dot Meyerhoff. Dr. Meyerhoff has been implicated in the suicide of an officer who had applied to your department but was rejected. The officer's name is Benjamin Gomez. I would like to know why your department rejected him."

"I'm sorry. I can't disclose that information without a signed release from the officer in question."

"The officer in question is dead."

She puts me on hold and the phone switches to a radio station. The announcer is in the midst of a manic episode. A logging truck has just jack knifed in the middle of the freeway, blocking traffic in all directions, and Windy's Furniture is having a parking lot sale on the weekend. He announces both events with the same frenetic intensity. There is a crackle on the phone.

"Sheriff Collier here. How can I help?"

I repeat my story.

"Yeah, I know. He killed himself right here in my jurisdiction. I heard he got dumped by his department and couldn't face telling his wife. It's a damn shame, if you ask me. He would have got himself another job." His deep basso voice rolls over the phone with an easy cadence.

"Why didn't you hire him?"

"The psych. My psychologist gave him a D+ rating. I don't hire D+ people anymore. I used to take my chances with them, but they cause too much trouble. They drink or they're way too badge heavy. We got a lot of rich folks and tourists come through here on their way skiing. They don't take well to the good old boy style of policing."

"Your psychologist gave Mr. Gomez a D+ rating because he was too aggressive?"

"Hold on. Let me pull the file." I can hear him shuffling papers. "I'll be damned. Looks like he had the opposite problem. He was too timid. The Doc said he would make a better community service officer than a cop, but we don't have CSOs here anymore. Had to cut the program cause of the budget." He laughs. "I got to get a new psychologist. He makes recommendations and doesn't even know how my department works. Anything else, Ms. Hudson?"

"Did you ever meet Mr. Gomez?"

"Indeed I did. As you know, the law says I have to interview him and give him a conditional job offer before I can send him to a psychologist. Struck me as a one-thing-at-a-time kind of guy. You know, take the box to the shelf, put it down, go back and get another box. Police work isn't like that. You've got be able to multi-task in this job or you'll get hurt. Even if I assigned him to the jail, he'd have to be watching ten things at once. He was a nice enough kid, but I didn't think he had his head in the game, know what I mean? I'm looking for someone who's got the eye of the tiger. Someone who's going to have fun putting bad guys in jail. Not that he wasn't trying real hard. Must have had applications in all over the place. What's the sudden interest in this guy? I heard there was some cop nosing around about him too."

"One other question. Do you know the decedent's father-in-law, Mr. Vincent Patcher?"

There is a pause.

"Yeah, I know Vinnie. We were in some training classes together years ago and occasionally we go hunting, maybe once a year, if that. Who did you say you were representing, Ms. Hudson?"

I hang up.

I take a chance and call the Sacramento Police Department. It would have been a lousy fit, working for a department in the same county where your fruitcake father-in-law is the DA. On the other hand, it was a logical choice because it would have kept April close to home, something both her parents seem intent on doing.

This time I get the run around. The department is so large they have their own behavioral science unit. It takes me nearly an hour of transfers and disconnects to reach the head of the unit, who tells me in no uncertain terms that, according to department policy and state law, he cannot disclose any information over the telephone without a signed release. I ask if I could fax the request for records signed by the deceased's wife and mail the original later. I explain that I am in a hurry.

"Your offices are here in Sacramento, Ms. Hudson," he says. "Just bring the originals in person."

I draw my lips out in a thin line, like a method actor, trying to capture the essence of Marsha Hudson sitting at her desk, rigid with contained impatience. "My offices are here, but I'm not. I'm in the field as part of this investigation. I plan on being here several days. I need your cooperation. I assure you, time is of the essence. It is in your interest to assist in these matters. Incompetent and unethical psychologists cast a pall on the entire profession."

He gives up. Too many reports to write in too little time apparently leaves him without the energy to fight a bigger, more pernicious bureaucracy than the one he works for. Not to mention that having someone on the Board of Psychology mad at you might not be career enhancing.

I receive the return fax within minutes. The applicant, Benjamin Gomez, had low yet acceptable ratings up to and including his chief's interview. He was dropped from the hiring process after he failed his pre-employment psychological screening, just as he had been for the Sierra S.O.

If two psychologists had found him unsuitable, why hadn't Mark?

I walk out into the garden and sit on my back step. My neighbor's cat, Oedipus, is walking gingerly on the fence between our two houses. He drops soundlessly into my yard, rubs against my legs and curls up next to me in the sun, purring. After Mark and I separated, one of my friends told me that all I needed was a cat and a vibrator. At the time, I didn't take kindly to her suggestion.

I stroke Oedipus' soft fur and consider that I have just added impersonating a professional conduct investigator to breaking and entering, stealing confidential information, kidnapping, breach of confidentiality and incompetence. I've been a law abiding citizen all my life, except for a few acts of civil disobedience, a good girl who did what she was told, and now I have a rap sheet the equal of a career criminal.

What I don't have any longer is a career. Oedipus stretches languorously and climbs onto my lap sandpapering my arm with his tongue. His namesake is the tortured icon of one of the world's most infamous dysfunctional families. A tingling sensation starts at the back of my neck, an electric buzzing, that rolls through me, raising the hair on my arms. Vinnie Patcher may not have murdered Ben, but he had motive enough to drive him to suicide. Ben wasn't good enough for April. No one has ever been good enough for April, except perhaps, Vinnie himself. Classic Oedipal family dynamics run in reverse. Father forces son-in-law to kill himself so that he can claim his daughter for his own. Who knows what has been going on in that family? Or who the father of April's child really is?

My phone rings.

"Fuck you, Meyerhoff."

"Eddie? Had a bad shift last night?"

"Actually I had a great shift until the chief hauled me into his office, fat, dumb and happy, and dimed you out."

"What do you mean?"

"I never would have figured you for kidnapping."

"Are you talking about April Gomez?"

"No, I'm talking about Charles Lindbergh."

"She was trying to get away from her father. I gave her a ride, that's all."

"Bullshit. You let her stay in your house."

"Did Baxter also tell you that Vinnie Patcher broke into my house and trashed it? Savagely. Put a knife through one of my sweaters? That's why you thought my place looked empty."

"No. And neither did you. I chase my tail around some God forsaken mountains trying to help you out and you don't tell me shit."

"I didn't want to get you in trouble."

"I'm already in trouble, thanks to you. Baxter's taking me out of FTO and putting me on the front desk. Permanently. Fucker expects me to take complaints and make nice with Brownie troops for the rest of my life. And then he gave me the speech."

"What speech?"

"The you-don't-have-much-of-a-future-here-think-about-retiring one. Fuck it. Maybe he's right. Everything hurts, my knees, my back, my shoulder. The only rush I get is putting bad guys in jail. And now that's gone."

"I'll talk to him."

"You coulda told me what was going on. Then I could of thought of something to say, instead of standing there with my jaw hanging open."

"I'm really sorry. I thought I was doing the right thing, not getting you involved. Now that you know, let me tell you everything."

Not that it makes any difference, at this point, but I want to tell him what April said about Ben's parents being dope addicts.

"That spineless motherfucker Baxter has known me forever, and he's throwing me under the bus to save his own ass."

"Do you want to hear what I have to tell you?"

"No fucking way. *Hasta lumbago,* Doc. You're on your own."

He hangs up. I push the call back button. No answer.

Chapter Thirty

I raise my voice and three applicants look up from their clipboards, their pens frozen in mid-air. Mark is telling me to come back later. The lovely Melinda, her fecundity hidden beneath a gauzy top, opens the door to her office, formerly my office, looks out, sees me, and steps back inside without a word.

"Now, Mark. I need to talk to you now."

"I have appointments all afternoon."

"I don't think you want me to say what I need to say here in the waiting room."

He points at me and then at his office door like he was directing traffic. I can hear him behind me, apologizing to the waiting applicants, telling them that he has an emergency and will be with them as soon as possible. He closes the door.

"Those are law enforcement candidates. It only takes one to complain that he couldn't concentrate because of a disruption, and I'll have to redo everyone's evaluation."

He is wearing a leather jacket and a black t-shirt. His hair, wavy and curling over his collar, is silvering gently. The stress of our divorce looks good on him.

I gained weight and manufactured more wrinkles.

"Where is Ben Gomez's file? I want to see his protocols."

"Under lock and key. State law. Let me remind you that my lawyer told me not to show it to anyone without a subpoena."

"Stop lying. There are no protocols. His file is empty."

Mark looks at me over the top of his glasses. It is his signature move, therapeutic astonishment.

"How do you know that?"

"Don't you want to check?"

"The only way you could know that is to have snuck in here without permission. Tell me you didn't do that."

"Maybe I did, maybe I didn't. Maybe I bribed your secretary. Or maybe I told Melinda, the innocent, how you are going to leave her the way you left me and she showed me the file rather than stab you in the heart with an ice pick."

He flashes a lopsided smile.

"I need those protocols, Mark. My career is on the line."

"I never meant to hurt you. Things happen. I thought we'd worked everything through, walked away from each other with no animus." He reaches for me. "I hate to see you suffering."

I swat his arm away. "Pedal your psychobabble somewhere else. I'm not leaving without that folder. And, by the way, I'm really pissed that you gave away all the antiques I refinished."

He walks behind his desk and sits down. "Why is it so important for you to see his test results?" The therapeutic silkiness in his voice has dried to a crisp.

"Why do you think? To ease my conscience. To help me defend myself to the Board of Psychology."

"And if I refuse to give them to you?"

"I'll go to the newspaper. You passed an applicant two other psychologists found unsuitable. I bet some reporter out there will find that interesting. The press will be on you like white on rice. So will his family."

"They'll be on you too."

"They already are. Haven't you noticed? Give me his file."

"We're going paperless. Everything's been converted to electronic transmission. Unfortunately, my computer guy accidentally deleted a bunch of records, including Ben's. I might be able to get him to retrieve it, but that's expensive and time consuming."

"I don't believe you. You wouldn't lose Ben's file, not with a pending lawsuit. Melinda will know where it is."

I open the door and start down the hall toward Melinda's office. Mark catches up to me and grabs my arm. The applicants raise their heads in alarm like a family of prairie dogs.

"Stop, he says, "I'll talk to my lawyer about letting you see the file. Leave Melinda alone."

As soon as I get back to my car, my cell phone goes off, jangling like a live thing in my hand. It's April.

"The baby came early. My blood pressure was way high and there was a whole lot of other stuff wrong. So they induced. I was freaked."

"Where are you?"

"I hate it here. It's like prison. Hang on a minute." I can hear conversation in the background, several people talking at once. "Someone's here. I gotta get off the phone."

She hangs up. I get the number from my cell phone and call back. It rings several times before a woman answers. "Good Shepherd Home, may I help you?"

I Google Good Shepherd home. It's in East Kenilworth, part of Churches United, a place of caring and respite for unmarried mothers. I didn't think such places existed anymore. I call Belle Patcher. She answers on the first ring.

"I know where April is."

"Where?"

"Not on the phone. Come to Kenilworth. You and your husband. Do you know where Fran's café is? Meet me there at 7:00 p.m."

I wasn't going to let either one of them back in my house.

"Meet with me alone," she says. "I don't know if I can get in touch with Vinnie. He'll just be angry. You know how he is. It's better if I come alone."

"No. I want to talk to your husband face to face."

I call Eddie. He's right. I need to keep him informed, not just for my sake but for his too. The technology of voice mail can't disguise the slurry thickness in his voice. "Not home. Don't leave a message. Got a problem? Call 911."

Chapter Thirty One

Fran gives me the V.I.P. booth in the back. The restaurant is almost empty. Her main business, except for a few cops and senior citizens, is breakfast and lunch.

She isn't happy with me.

"You're meeting Vinnie Patcher here? The man's a lunatic. Leave him alone."

"I'll pay for any damages."

"That's not what I mean and you know it."

She sets the table and bangs down a carafe of coffee, rattling the cups and saucers.

"Something to eat?"

I haven't eaten since breakfast. I can't, my stomach is in knots. Just the thought of food makes me bilious. A blue SUV cruises slowly by the front window and pulls into the parking lot across the street. I watch as Patcher makes a beeline for Fran's and Belle shambles behind, just barely catching the screen door as it bangs shut. He slides into the booth. Belle sits next to him. She is sweating and her cheeks are flushed.

Fran hovers at the table's edge, jabbing at her order pad with a pencil. "Dinner's over. Care for dessert? I got peach, apple, Boston cream, and custard pie, chocolate or coconut layer cake and ice cream."

"No thank you, coffee's fine," Belle says.

Fran turns on a squeaky rubber heel and walks away.

"Where is my daughter?" Patcher looks at me and through me at the same time.

"First things first. I have some questions for you."

He narrows his eyes and purses his lips, drawing his face into an arrow pointed at the middle of my forehead. "What do you want to know?"

"Why are you investigating Ben's death, and what have you found out?"

He raises a shaggy eyebrow. Long hairs curl toward his forehead. "My daughter's husband killed himself. I owe it to her to find out what happened. For your information, I didn't find anything to make me think it wasn't suicide. Now, tell me where my daughter is."

"I think you had reason to want Ben dead. He didn't fit what you wanted in a son-in-law."

Belle shrinks back in her seat. Vinnie stiffens. "Your insinuation is both insulting and libelous. I'd urge you to be careful with what you say."

"If you did have something to do with Ben's suicide, you could have easily covered your tracks with the help of your friend, Sheriff Collier, whose deputies, I understand from my sources, did a less than stellar investigation into Ben's death."

"Your sources? Eddie Rimbauer is a souse, not a source." His face splinters into tiny laugh lines. Just as quickly he clamps his lips back together. "I didn't like my daughter's husband, for your information, but I didn't kill him or make him kill himself. April deserved better than him. Only she got herself pregnant."

"It was an accident. She didn't do it on purpose," Belle says.

"Didn't she? She knew exactly what she was doing. Make no mistake. She was manipulating him so she could get away from you."

He looks at me, not at Belle, as he talks. "April is headstrong. It's never been easy to get her to see reason. She pushes my wife around. I can't be there all the time to supervise. Now, if you have no more conspiracy theories to present, take me to my daughter."

"Did you know Ben's parents were drug addicts? Did April tell you?"

"As a matter of fact, I told April. She thought his parents died in a car accident. The truth is they overdosed on some bad heroin in a low-rent motel in East Kenilworth. The cops found poor little Ben wandering around in the parking lot crying for his Mommy and Daddy." He turns to his wife. "And you thought Ben was such a nice boy from a good family."

He laughs, a mirthless, barking sound that startles Belle into spilling her coffee.

"He is a nice boy. He was," Belle says. She is macerating her coffee soaked napkin, pushing the pieces into a soggy pile. I can feel her leg jiggling under the table. "His parents' problems aren't his problems. She loved him, and you did everything you could to break them up. It didn't work."

"Didn't it?"

She doesn't answer and he turns to me. "I have a question for you, Doctor." The way he says it, doctor sounds like a dirty word. "Did you know he was adopted?"

"Yes. His grandparents adopted him."

"So what was his name before they adopted him?"

I feel like I'm on the losing end of a cross-examination "I don't know. Why does it matter?"

"I didn't think so. My investigators are pros, not like the half-dead retired cops Baxter hires on the cheap to do his backgrounds."

"Tell her, Vinnie, for God's sake, so she can take us to April."

"His birth name is Benjamin Sturgis. When my investigators ran a check on the Sturgis family, they got the whole story."

He turns to Belle. "Your nice boy was a manipulative little shit. Lied to everyone. Never told anyone he was adopted because he'd have to admit he was related to felons. Doesn't look good on an application for a police officer's job."

He turns back to me. "Know what's really funny? Your pal, Eddie Rimbauer, was there when they found Ben's parents. His name is on the police report. He's so pickled in alcohol, I'll bet he doesn't remember. Unless, of course, he recognized my son-in-law and persecuted him until he killed himself."

He cocks his head to one side. "Makes a compelling case for a law suit, doesn't it?"

He pushes Belle out of the booth and stands. "I'm finished talking. Now, take me to my daughter."

He grabs my arm and pulls me toward the door. "As soon as I see April, you can go."

Fran comes out of the kitchen with her sheet rock trowel turned spatula in hand. "You need me to call the cops?"

"No," I say. "I'll be fine, just fine."

Chapter Thirty Two

We drive, without speaking, through Kenilworth, across the freeway, into the flats of East Kenilworth. Belle and Vinnie Patcher are in the front seat. I'm hunkered down in the back.

The Good Shepherd Home is a faded two story Victorian, so gray it appears to melt into the concrete industrial buildings on either side. Curtains are drawn over every window.

We knock. The peephole scrapes open and the door widens as far as the security chain will stretch, then closes again. The chain clicks and a woman with short gray hair opens the door. She is dressed in the habit of modern nuns, a dark blue skirt and cardigan with a white blouse and flat heeled shoes. Her only jewelry is a large gold crucifix.

"I'm Vincent Patcher. This is my wife. My daughter, April Gomez is a resident here."

She looks at me. "And who might you be?"

"A family friend."

She checks her watch. "Come in, please." She motions us into a large, dimly lit foyer. A carving of Christ on the Cross hangs on one wall.

"I'm Sister Kathryn. It never rains but it pours. Until today, April's had no visitors." She looks at us with disdain for having neglected our familial obligations. "Will you be taking April home tonight?"

"Can we?" Belle's face lights up in anticipation.

"There's paperwork to complete." Sister Kathryn looks at her watch again. "Please be quick about it. Our girls go to bed early."

We climb to the second floor. The nuns have worked hard to make the residence homey and personal. Only a slight whiff of disinfectant in the air betrays the lurking presence of institutional life. April is alone in her room, dressed in jeans and a pullover. Her body has snapped back to a girlish post-partum plumpness. A partially packed suitcase lays open on the bed. Belle pushes past her husband, her arms open to embrace her daughter. April looks up from her packing and retreats as though something poisonous has just slithered into the room.

Belle looks around the room. There is no bassinet, no baby clothes. "Where's my grandbaby?"

"How did you know where I was?"

She turns to me. "Bitch," she mouths silently.

Belle is opening closets and drawers. Patcher is standing stock still.

Sister Kathryn speaks from the doorway. "Haven't you told them?"

"Told us what?" Belle asks.

"I gave the baby to a couple from Ohio. Nice people. They couldn't have any of their own. They came and got her today. She was three days early. I didn't think they would get here so quick, but they did. They left a couple of hours ago."

She turns back to her packing. "I need to get out of this place." She looks at Sister Kathryn. "The sisters are okay, but there's nothing to do unless you're going to keep your baby and then there's classes and stuff."

Belle sinks to the bed. "You gave our baby away?"

"My baby, Mother, not our baby."

"You gave her to strangers? Our own flesh and blood?"

"Get off it, will you?" April's face is purple and splotchy. "I don't know whose flesh and blood it is, and I don't fucking care. I'd have hoovered it if there was time."

"Ben isn't the baby's father?" I ask.

She shrugs. Belle covers her face with her hands, whimpering softly. Patcher turns away and walks toward the door.

I walk after him. "Are you the father? Did you get your daughter pregnant?"

Before he has a chance to answer, April turns on me. "That's disgusting. I hate my father. I don't even let him hug me. You are sick. Get out of my room."

"Not until I know who got you pregnant."

She rolls her eyes. "I was knocking boots with a bunch of guys. I let Ben think he was the father so we'd get married. After he got fired, I didn't care what he thought. I told him I was going to give the kid away and split." She starts pushing clothes into her suitcase. "Why are you ragging on me about Ben? I'm the one who got pregnant and almost died."

Belle leaps from the bed. "You slut. You selfish little slut. Do you know what I did for you?" She is slapping at April's face, tearing at her hair. "Do you know how much money you cost us?"

Patcher grabs Belle by the arms and pulls her off April. "What do you mean? What money? What are you talking about?"

Then he slaps her hard enough to leave a red blaze on her cheek. For a moment, we all freeze. Then Belle shakes herself loose. Her lips are curled up over her teeth, her hands balled into little fists.

"I bought Ben's job for him. Paid money so our grandbaby would have a decent home with two parents."

A coterie of wide eyed, big-bellied teen age girls has collected around the door, clutching each other.

"You and your insane ambitions. Without my help, he would never have been hired." Belle breaks free and runs out of the room, pushing her way through the crowd of girls and over the stair railing. There is a collective gasp and a moment of stunned silence as her body thuds down the steps. Then shrieking and crying and hysteria.

Patcher races out of the room. April sinks to the floor in tears. She looks up at me, her face scratched and bleeding. "You see? It would never have worked. The best thing I could do for my baby was to get her as far away from me and my family as I could."

Our eyes meet for a second as I leave the room, making way for the other residents who push inside in a rush to comfort their stricken friend. I can hear sirens wailing. Patcher is kneeling at the bottom of the stairs, next to his wife's crumpled form. She isn't moving. He looks up. I am surprised to see that his eyes are filled with tears.

Chapter Thirty Three

The Taxi drops me at Fran's. The restaurant is closed and the parking lot across from the restaurant is empty except for my car and Vinnie Patcher's car. I drive to the Kenilworth Community hospital. I'm not sure why I'm doing this. It's not as though I pushed Belle Patcher over that railing, but I feel that somehow my pushing for answers is part of the chain of events that drove her to jump. I'm not a disinterested bystander. Whether I've been drawn into their lives or they've been drawn into mine is of no consequence and little solace.

Vinnie Patcher is slumped on a couch in the empty ER waiting room, like a puppet whose strings have been cut. He sees me and doesn't move. I sit on a chair across from him and wait. April's suitcase and a pile of her clothes is on the seat next to him.

"She hates me. I love her more than life and she hates me. All I ever wanted to do was protect her, make her happy. Everything I've done is for her."

"Is she badly hurt? What does the doctor say?"

He jerks upright, his flaccid spine now straight as a ruler. "I'm not talking about my wife. I'm talking about April."

"Where is she?"

He gestures at a sign pointing to the ladies bathroom and collapses back into the couch. I run around the corner and bang open the swinging door. April is looking in the mirror, a mascara wand in her hand. Her cosmetics are spread out on the small metal shelf over the sink.

"What do you want?"

"Answers."

I swipe my arm over the shelf and knock everything on the floor.

"Bitch" April hisses as she drops to her knees, reaching for the rolling tubes and brushes.

I grab her by the back of her sweater, haul her to her feet and shove her into a stall and down onto the toilet seat. I reach behind and push the lock into place.

"What is it with you? You just gave away your baby, your mother tried to kill herself, your father is sitting out there looking like a broken man and you're in here putting on makeup?" I shake her shoulders. "Answer me."

"I don't know." She starts to cry and hold her stomach. "My stomach hurts. I need a doctor."

"Quit your play acting. I'm all the doctor you're going to get until you answer my questions. What were you and Ben doing in the Sierras when he killed himself."

"It was your idea. 'Take some time off', you said. 'Have the honeymoon you never had'." Her voice is a girlish sing song. "We didn't go when you told us to. Ben wanted to stay home and study. All we did was fight. I told him I couldn't stay cooped up in my house any longer. I told him to quit before he got fired. Go back to Safeway, make some money so we could move out. But no, he had to do better for his baby. So I told him."

"Told him what?"

"That the baby wasn't his. That I didn't know who the father was. That I hated him and I hated the baby. I told him I was sorry I married him, and as soon as I gave the baby up, I was going to file for divorce."

"What did he do?"

"Started to cry. Begged me not to leave him. Said he didn't believe the baby wasn't his. Promised he would get his old job back. All sorts of stuff. Only Safeway wasn't hiring, so he took some temp job in a warehouse." I lean away from the stall door. The door handle has left a painful indentation in my back.

"That's why we went to the Sierras. To the Hide-Away Motel. The only thing they hid away was the shampoo and the clean sheets. Ben wanted to make it up to me. Have some fun. Only staying in a shitty motel in the middle of nowhere isn't my idea of fun. Anyhow, I met someone else online and told Ben I was leaving, no matter what. He didn't believe me then either, so I showed him on my computer."

"Showed him what?"

"The pictures I posted on Facebook, the sexting I sent this other guy. Actually, there was more than one, but I only really liked this one guy. Even though I was pregnant, he thought I was way sexy."

"I don't want to hear this."

"First you want me to talk and now you don't. You are freaking crazy."

She stands up and tries to push past me to get at the lock. I push her back onto the seat."Did you shoot Ben?"

"You are so fucked up. How can you be a psychologist? I did not shoot him. He started playing around with his gun. Said if I left him he'd kill himself. I told him, 'go ahead, I don't care'. And then I left. Took the car. So I guess that's when he did it. Now can I go?"

"You didn't call the police or try to get help?"

"I was afraid he'd kill me, too, if I tried to stop him. Anyhow, if he wants to off himself, that's his choice. It's a free world."

I sit in my car, shaking. I should write this up. A teenage Jezebel. A family of psychopaths. Poor Ben, what agony. Everything he hoped for torn away.

I'm exhausted, but I drive to headquarters in the dark and park my car. I can see Eddie behind the glass window at the front desk. He's slumped over, sleeping. The lobby is empty. I tap on the glass and he jerks upright. It takes him a minute to figure out where he is.

"What the fuck are you doing here? You're not supposed to be in this building."

"So arrest me for trespassing."

"What do you want?"

"I guess turnaround's fair play."

"What the hell are you talking about?"

"I didn't tell you about taking April home or about Vinnie Patcher breaking into my house, because I was trying to protect you. But you knew all along who Ben was and you didn't tell me. You just kept on hounding him until he broke."

He raises up out of his chair and leans forward, breathing small clouds of moisture on the thick glass window. "I repeat. What the fuck are you talking about?"

"Ben Gomez, a.k.a. Ben Sturgis? His parents overdosed on some bad heroin in a motel. Someone found him wandering around the parking lot crying and called the police. His grandparents adopted him and changed his name to theirs." Eddie scowls. "You were there, apparently. Don't you remember or have you totally pickled your brain with alcohol?"

He takes a long wheezy gulp of air and then pounds his fist on the desk. "Sonofabitch. Sonofabitch. I knew it. That fucking eyebrow. I knew I knew him. Sturgis. The goddamn Sturgis case." He looks up at me. "He tried to run away, fell and split his head open, right through the eyebrow. Screaming for his parents, 'the police are here, the police are here'. Fuckers used him as a lookout while they shot up in that rat trap motel. I held that kid with my hand over his bloody head until the social workers got there. It was the longest 30 minutes of my life. I saw him a few weeks later during the inquest. The scar was already beginning to show. God, I'm a worthless cop. I should have recognized that scar."

"Would you have done anything different if you had."

"I don't know. Jesus fucking Christ, how could I miss this? I thought about that stupid little kid everyday for years, wondered where he wound up. Foster home? Jail? And he's right under my fucking nose. Christ, I got to get off the sauce. I couldn't find a bowling ball in a bathtub."

He drops his head and grips the desk as though he is going to fall over. I tap on the glass.

"Well if it's any consolation. It wasn't just you tormenting him. He's got the wife from hell."

"At least we had something in common – bad taste in women."

I start to say something consoling and stop myself. I'm finished making people feel better. It certainly didn't help Ben.

Eddie walks around his desk and comes through a door into the lobby. Now that he's out from behind the reflection of the glass window, I can see that his face is mottled with red splotches.

"Come to think of it, Mr. Safeway and I got more than one thing in common. We're both lying sacks of shit. I looked at his background packet one time, none of your business how I got my hands on it. He never said jack to the backgrounder about his parents or about being adopted and changing his name. You supposed to say if you've ever had another name. Swore he never knew nobody who got arrested. Bullshit. His parents had a rap sheet as long as my arm. Lying on your application is a no-no. He played us. All of us. That bumbling sucker was one crafty sonofabitch."

"We can all be fooled."

"I'm a cop. I get fooled, I get killed. Maybe the chief is right. Maybe I should hang it up."

Chapter Thirty Four

Home at last. I sit in my living room with a glass of wine. I can still hear the contempt in April's voice. The sound of Belle's body hitting the steps. Poor Ben. Nothing left to live for, no relationship, no family and no job. Betrayed. His dreams shredded into worthless bits by a heartless child. It was too much to bear. Under the circumstances, I couldn't have done much for him. That should make me feel better, but it doesn't.

April betrayed Ben because it's in her nature to do so. I now doubt she was sexually abused by her father. Still, she is a selfish, immature girl with a serious character disorder and parents even more dysfunctional than she is.

But how did Mark get drawn into this drama? What had he to gain? I try to imagine him and Belle discussing money. How long had it taken him to figure out how much to ask for? Did she give it right away or did they dicker over the price, haggling back and forth until they settled on some mutually acceptable amount?

My phone rings. It's Frank calling to tell me the alarm system he ordered for my house has arrived. I'm happy to hear his voice, eager to tell someone about the evening's events. He wants to know if I still want him to install it or would I rather get someone else to do it.

"What do you mean? Do you want me to ask someone else?"

"I don't know. You are the most interesting woman I've met in a long time, but every time we get together I manage to say something to tick you off. I'm a pretty easy going guy. I'm attracted to you in a number of ways, but I don't want a relationship that's filled with drama. I want to be able to say what's on my mind without you getting mad. I don't know if you can do that. You get pissed off every time I say something you don't want to hear."

There's a muffled ringing in my ears and my face is suddenly hot. "Busted," I say. "Guilty as charged." This is a man half the women I know would love to meet. Which is why I haven't told anyone about him, especially my mother, because she'd be on me, telling me I was crazy not to jump into this relationship with both feet.

"You're right. I've been bitchy. I feel so shitty about Ben and everything else, I can't take any more bad news about myself. You've been great. You don't deserve to be treated like this. I just wish our timing had been different."

"So maybe we should just cool it for a while. I'll come over and put in the alarm. You take care of what you need to take care of, and we'll see how things go. If they go."

"Can I tell you something?"

"What?"

"I've had a terrible day." I start to cry and make stupid slurpy noises. I describe meeting the Patchers, the blow-up at the Good Shepherd Home and my confrontation with April.

"Your ex took a bribe to falsify his psych report? What are you going to do?" He doesn't wait for an answer. "I know what I'd do. I'd blow the whistle on him. Call the newspapers. Tell the chief."

"I want to talk to him first, hear his side of the story before I do anything like that. I've never known him to be unethical. Something must be wrong."

"Cheating on you doesn't count as unethical? Gary told me about his affair."

"So much for confidentiality as a professional courtesy."

"C'mon, Dot. Gary's your friend. He thought you got a raw deal." He exhales slowly. "Am I missing something here?"

I flash with anger. We're back in that same territory. He's saying something I don't want to hear, and I want to let him have it between the eyes even though he's right. I should be furious with Mark. And I am. But for some reason, I don't want to admit that to Frank or myself.

"I appreciate your concern and your help, Frank. I really do. And at the risk of totally using up any goodwill you still have for me, I have one more favor to ask."

"What's that?"

"Don't give up on me, Frank. Please."

I ask Mark to come to my house for dinner so we can talk things over. I want to get him away from his office, out of his comfort zone and away from Melinda's prying eyes. I want him in my space, where I'm in control.

And since he's reluctant to discuss Ben's case with me, I have to disguise the invitation as a way to get our friendship back on track after the confrontation in his office. He's delighted to hear from me and remorseful about how badly things have gone between us recently, though apparently not remorseful enough to have called me or given me an update on Ben's missing file.

Gary helps me put together some assemble-it-yourself furniture to replace what Patcher smashed. He's sorting through a pile of tiny plastic bags containing screws and dowels. He's not happy with me. "I don't get you. Frank is a really decent guy. Most women would give their right arm to meet a man like him."

I hand him a Phillips-head screwdriver. "Don't start with me, please. I have enough trouble as it is."

He clamps down on the stem of his pipe and works the rest of the morning in silence.

Fran isn't too happy with me either. I order two chicken casserole dinners to go and have her write down detailed instructions about how long to heat everything without burning the meal to a crisp. She doesn't ask who is coming for dinner.

"How's Eddie doing?" I ask her.

"Terrible. He's been on a binge. It's killing him, working the desk. I try to go to his house to clean, when he lets me in. The place stinks."

She glares at me.

"He's had problems with alcohol for a long time, Fran. I didn't cause him to drink."

She shoves the packages across the counter and accepts my money without protest.

I drive home, put the food in the oven, unpack the china, silver, and crystal, most of it wedding presents that Mark didn't want. Too fancy for what I have in mind, but after the break-in, it's either these or paper plates and plastic glasses. I go upstairs to dress. My good luck sweater still has a rent over the heart.

Mark is standing at the door with his crooked smile, a bottle of wine in each hand. For a moment only, the old longing tugs at me like a bad habit.

We go into the kitchen. Fran's casserole is sputtering softly, perfuming the kitchen with the smell of onions, garlic and cinnamon. He sniffs the air. "Something smells great. You been taking cooking lessons? Let's open the wine and let it breathe."

I open a drawer, looking for the corkscrew. Something catches and the drawer sticks halfway open. I pull on the handle with one hand and push against the clutter with the other. A sharp pain slices across my fingers as I brush against a wire cheese grater. Blood drips into the drawer and on the counter. Mark is at my side in an instant, holding a roll of paper towels.

"Let me," he says, starting to blot the blood.

I pull my hand away. I don't want him to touch me.

"Back in a minute," I say and go upstairs. I can barely get the band-aid out of its wrapper to lay over the cut. The rusty smell of blood sticks in my nose and I feel nauseated. I splash cold water on my face. The woman looking back at me in the mirror is tense and frightened. I tell her to calm down. I remind her what this evening is about, that she is a grown woman, not a love-sick graduate student, that for all his charms, Mark will be no match for Marsha Hudson, professional conduct investigator. I do a short visualization, Mark, on his knees, begging the disdainful Marsha Hudson for mercy. It is both cheering and instructive.

By the time I come downstairs, Mark has opened both bottles and fixed the stuck drawer. He inspects my hand, pronounces me fit and gives me a glass of wine.

"You like pinot noir. I think you'll love this one." He raises his glass to mine. "I want us to be friends, Dot. And colleagues. I even have some hope that one day we could write another book together. We were a good team. We helped a lot of people."

He clinks his glass against mine. "I hurt you and I think I never understood until recently how deeply."

He swirls the wine in his glass, sniffs at it, takes a sip, and swishes it in his mouth, closing his eyes as he swallows and savors.

"Primo," he says and looks at me, his eyes intent and serious. "We needed to go our separate ways and I took the plunge. I wish I had done it differently, but at least I saved you from having to be the one to pull the plug."

I smile at this creative rendering of our history. "I have a somewhat different recollection, Mark. I remember that we split up when I found out about your affair with Melinda."

"*Touché*. I deserve that." He takes another sip of wine. "The thing is, Melinda might have been a passing attraction, an infatuation. I wanted to be sure of my feelings before I told you about her."

"How is the lovely Melinda, by the way? I'm curious. Did she ask why I was in your office last week? I know she saw me. What did you tell her?"

"That you wanted to consult about an officer I had screened."

I open the oven to check on the chicken.

"God, that smells delicious," he says. "I'm starving."

I take the salad out of the refrigerator and he takes it out of my hands.

"I make great salad dressing, remember? Oil and vinegar, a bowl and a whisk. Mustard, too, if you have it." He starts opening cabinet doors. "Feels like old times, doesn't it, drinking wine and cooking together?"

I want to stab him with the sharpest kitchen knife I own. He looks so pleased with himself, smiling, happy in the moment. The moment is all that matters to him. The past is open to revision and the future doesn't count because it isn't here yet.

We carry the food to the dining table and sit down. Mark refills our glasses. I'm already a little lightheaded.

"*Bon appétit*," he says and makes a show of bending over his plate and inhaling Fran's fragrant gravy.

"I want to talk about Ben Gomez. I still need his file."

Mark's eyebrows knit together in disapproval. "Later. Let's enjoy our meal and talk about something else, something pleasant."

"Okay. Does Melinda know you're here?"

He purses his lips. "No."

"Where does she think you are?"

"Working late. She gets tired and goes home early these days."

"What if she needs you?"

"She calls my cell. Why?"

"Last week you were afraid to upset her."

He sighs. I know that sound. I'm trying his patience He wants to have fun, and I'm being serious.

"I told you. She's had trouble with the pregnancy. I'm trying to protect her from unnecessary stress." He butters two rolls and puts one on my plate.

"She's going to be pretty stressed out when she finds out that you accepted money from Belle Patcher to falsify Ben Gomez' psych assessment. That's against the law."

His fork clatters against the plate. "Who told you that?"

"Belle Patcher."

"The woman's a borderline. A drama queen. She makes things up. She showed up at my office one day, out of the blue, hysterical, babbling that Ben had gotten her daughter pregnant and her husband wouldn't let them get married unless he got a police job. Begged me to recommend him. I thought I'd never get her to leave." He stabs at a piece of chicken with his fork and dips it in the gravy.

"Have you met Vinnie Patcher?" I ask. "Diagnostically, I'd say he is an intermittent explosive disorder. Gets extremely angry. He actually broke in here and trashed the place, stuck a knife though the heart of one of my sweaters. Not terribly subtle. Watch out for him. He's dangerous." I take a sip of wine. "So, what made you take the money? Gambling debts? Cocaine? Back ordered for stressometers?"

Mark grips his knife and fork so tightly his knuckles are bloodless. "How long have you known me? Outside of a little pot and an affinity for fine wine, I don't use drugs. Never have. And I don't gamble."

"Supporting a mistress?"

"For Christ sakes."

"You cheated on me, why not Melinda?"

"She's pregnant."

"So was I once. Remember?"

He looks shocked, though no more than I am at the old rage that rushes out of me. "What were you doing while I was having the abortion? Skiing, sailing? Presenting a paper? Screwing another woman?"

"Goddamn it, you told me not to stay. You said you could handle it. That it was no worse than having your wisdom teeth extracted."

"I lied." I slam my glass on the table. Wine splatters over my food, staining the rice crimson. "I was terrified of losing you. Turns out, you were even more terrified of being tied down. I guess things have changed."

"We were on a roll. Working, writing, building the practice. It took two of us, Dot. I couldn't do it alone. It wasn't the right time to share you with a child. And then it got too late." He sits still as a stone, his lips drawn into a tight crease across his face. "I think I should leave."

"I'm curious. How much was I worth?"

"Where are you going with this, Dot?"

"To the press, the police, the Board of Psychology."

"This is about you resenting me for being happy, for having a family. You should move on."

He pushes his chair back and stands up. So do I.

"Get a life, Dot. Find a man. Leave me and Melinda alone."

I slap him, really hard. A ghostly imprint of my hand blooms on his cheek and then fades. He clenches his fist and raises it reflexively. I watch it move through the air in slow motion and then drop to his side.

"What do you want?" he asks.

"I want to know why you set that boy up. Why you accepted Belle Patcher's money."

"Jesus, what's wrong with you?"

He grabs my arm and pulls me forward. I reach for the wine bottle with my free hand and swing it, catching him in the temple and sending him to his knees. He grabs my ankles and pulls me to the floor, rolling me on my back.

"What are you trying to do? Get me to leave Melinda and come back to you? Is that what you want?"

He lifts my shoulders and slams me into the floor. Jagged white lines and sparks explode behind my eyes. I bring my knee up between his legs and crush it against his groin. He gasps and bends over himself. I scramble up the stairs and into my bedroom. I can hear him retching. I slam the bedroom door and hit the silent alarm with the flat of my palm. My heart is pounding. I'm out of breath. He comes up the steps and stops outside my bedroom door.

"This is ludicrous, Dot. Open the door." He pants between words. "It's the wine. We've never been violent before, never, not even during the worst of it."

Surge after surge of adrenalin has sobered me into survival mode. Eddie Rimbauer's warning infiltrates the pounding in my ears. "When a man comes into your bedroom uninvited, he's up to no good. Next time, if there is a next time, don't hesitate and for godsakes, don't miss."

"Come out, Dot. Please. I'm not going to hurt you. I promise."

"Like you promised to love me forever? Like you promised to be faithful?"

"Open the door. I have to tell you something. I won't do it unless we're face to face."

I wipe away my tears and crack open the door. Mark is sitting on the floor with his head in his hands.

"Go on. But talk fast. I pushed the alarm. The police will be here in a minute."

He looks up. "I'm asking you to set aside your feelings toward me and open your heart. What I have to say is very delicate. You cannot go to the press with this. You can't tell anybody." He pauses for a moment. "I didn't do Ben Gomez's evaluation. Melinda did and I signed it. She's been asking for more responsibility. I was behind schedule and had a pile of reports to write, so I said yes. It was just this one assessment."

"You risked both our reputations because you couldn't say no to your trophy wife? This is unbelievable."

"Melinda's terrified. If this gets out, the Psychology Examining Committee won't let her sit for her license. Her career is over, everything she's worked for."

"How about everything I've worked for?"

"She is so upset she almost had a miscarriage. I can't risk exposing her to more stress. I'm afraid she'll lose our baby."

"You bastard. First you throw me down to protect Melinda, and now you're throwing her down to protect yourself. I don't believe you. She didn't do the report, you did. I'm going to call her and tell her what you said."

"Don't do that, please."

"Then tell me the truth."

"I am." He starts to cry. Except for when his father died, I don't think I have ever seen Mark in tears. "It won't help you to talk to Melinda. It won't change what's happened. Don't do this, please. Find another way."

"Then you go to the chief and the press. Tell them what happened. Tell them about the bribe. About the phony psych eval that you signed, done by an unqualified, unlicensed non-psychologist."

"I can't."

"Why not?"

"Because the part about the bribe isn't true." He looks up at me and holds out his hand, like a beggar. I notice the hair on the top of his head is getting thin.

"I'll be honest with you, Doc." Manny lays his clipboard down on my new coffee table. "This is a 'he said, she said' kind of situation."

"He threatened me, Manny. I was afraid."

"That doesn't change the fact that you hit him with a bottle, and he has a gash on the side of his head. The medics just called from the hospital. The doctors want to keep him overnight to see if he has a concussion. You don't have any injuries. There aren't any witnesses, so it's just his word against yours."

My bruised shoulders are days away from declaring themselves. "He's a foot taller than I am and seventy pounds heavier."

"He has no priors for d.v."

"Neither do I."

"Has he ever tried to hurt you before?"

I shake my head. My neck hurts.

"So why now?"

I tell him that Mark had taken a bribe to fake Ben's psych report, and that he thought I was going to expose him.

"That's civil, not criminal. Domestic violence is criminal. You might want to take out a restraining order first thing in the morning. It's the D.A.'s decision about whether or not to file charges against you. This is serious, this is felony d.v. If your ex wasn't safe in the hospital right now, I'd have to take you to jail."

When I call the hospital the next morning, Mark has been released. That means he doesn't have a concussion. I'm relieved. The lesser his injuries, the lighter my sentence. Bluish marks are beginning to bloom on my arms and shoulders. My neck aches with whiplash.

I start with the California Code for Mental Health Professionals and move on to the internet. By the time the telephone rings, my eyes are blurry. It is Mark's attorney. He informs me in a somber and sonorous voice, that he is about to file a criminal complaint against me. However, in light of my long relationship with his client, he would recommend negotiating out of court. *Quid pro quo.* Mark won't pursue his complaint if I agree, in writing, not to pursue what the attorney calls an unfortunate professional misunderstanding. He tells me I have twenty-four hours to think about it.

I tell him to do whatever he needs to do for his client. I am not going to negotiate or settle.

Mark is still pretending that Melinda did Ben's testing. With the code propped open in front of me, I tell Mark's attorney that I am going to file charges in civil court for healthcare fraud, billing for services rendered by a lesser qualified person, failure to properly supervise a psychological assistant and ensure that the extent, kind and quality of the functions performed by said assistant are consistent with his, in this case her, training and experience, and failure to inform the client in writing that said assistant was unlicensed. I advise the attorney that Mark is also in violation of Section 1032 of the California Government Code that explicitly states that any psychologist conducting pre-employment screening of peace officer applicants be licensed and have at least the equivalent of five full-time years of experience in the diagnosis and treatment of emotional and mental disorders, three of which must be accrued postdoctorate.

Then I call Vinnie Patcher at his office. His secretary tells me he is taking leave for a family emergency. I call him at home and he answers on the first ring.

"What do you want?"

"I want April to drop her complaint against me. I doubt she knew to file the complaint without your help, so I want you to tell her to drop it."

"Why would I do that?"

"Breaking up with Ben, lying about the baby, threatening to give it away, that's what pushed him over the edge. There were almost half a dozen witnesses who heard her brag about how cruel she was to him, including a nun. I can see the headlines. Sacramento county D.A.'s sadistic daughter drives husband to suicide."

"I don't care what people think about me."

"Don't you? You're an elected official. This kind of publicity will be like a gift from heaven for whoever runs against you. I may not be able to prove you broke into my house, but I saw you slap your wife across the face. So did the nun and all of April's friends. The D.A. is supposed to enforce domestic violence laws not break them."

"My wife was hysterical, I was trying to calm her down. I told you before. Belle is emotionally unstable. She's thrown herself down the stairs before. That's why she limps."

Chapter Thirty Five

"I want my job back." I am standing in front of Baxter on that worn spot in the carpet, my heart trampolining in my chest. He looks up from what he's reading and jumps to his feet, alert, ready for battle.

"How did you get in here? You're not permitted in the building."

"Five minutes. That's all I want, five minutes of your time."

His eyes dart around the room, looking for the secretary who deserted her post to go to the bathroom, allowing me to sneak into the inner sanctum. She is still gone. He takes off his watch, places it on the desk in front of him, and remains standing.

"Five minutes," he says, holding up the five fingers of his right hand, "not a second longer."

"I'm not responsible for Ben's death, not in any direct way. Neither is Eddie. Neither are you."

I tell him about April, her threats and her taunts.

"So he didn't kill himself because of the job. That's what I've been saying all along."

"It's not a simple cause and effect relationship. He never should have been a cop in the first place. He just wasn't tough enough, he didn't have the stamina. He had a terrible childhood. His parents were drug addicts with long criminal histories. He lied about them to your backgrounder who apparently didn't dig very hard. Imagine the pressure he was under. His marriage was falling apart and he must have been living in constant fear of being exposed as an imposter. Getting fired was the last straw."

"He resigned, I didn't fire him. How many times do I have to tell you that?"

"If he hadn't resigned, you would have had to fire him. You didn't have a choice. He couldn't do the job. And that's my point. You, Ben, Eddie, me, we were all put in a terrible position. And the person who put us there is Mark Edison. For one thing, Mark didn't do Ben's psych assessment himself. He let an unqualified psychological assistant do it. Secondly, Ben was lying to everyone about his background. A more experienced psychologist would have picked that up during the assessment. Thirdly, and this is the worst of it, Mark accepted money from Ben's mother-in-law to say Ben was qualified."

The blood in Baxter's face drains down the veins in his thick neck. His forehead gleams with yellowish sweat.

"Do you understand what I'm saying? Mark took a bribe to manufacture test results and he signed his name to a report he didn't write. That's healthcare fraud. Who knows how many other times he's done this? Every suspect who's been arrested in this town is going to want to reopen his case and look into the background of the arresting officer. Every person who ever filed a citizen's complaint is going to do the same. You can shoot the messenger with the bad news or you can get out in front of this and make it right."

"I don't believe you. You'd say anything to get your contract back. It's not going to happen, not on my watch."

"I'm reporting fraud and misconduct that is a direct threat to the public interest. In case you don't know, I'm protected by the whistle blower law. Any retaliation, loss of income, or damage to my professional reputation is your responsibility." By now I've got the law committed to memory.

"You're a contractor, the whistle blower law doesn't apply to you."

"Maybe so, but by the time a court decides whether or not to hear my case, I will have blown my little whistle all over town. I don't want to do this, but I will if you force me."

A small muscle in his chin moves up and down, tightening the corners of his mouth.

"I'm giving you an option," I say. "You're a victim. You trusted Mark, just like I did. Work with me on this. If you fight me, we'll both lose."

He bends over and looks at his watch. "I need time to think about this."

"I don't have any time. Mark lied, knowingly, purposively. He put Ben in a treacherous situation, placed your officers in jeopardy, put the department's reputation on the line and put you at risk for a slew of lawsuits." A muscle beneath his left eye twitches once, then twice. "You and I made mistakes, so did Eddie, none of us are without blame, but for God's sake, we didn't do it intentionally. We certainly didn't do it for money. Can't you see the difference?"

"So what you're saying is that if I give you back your contract, you'll drop this? And if I don't, you'll go to the press?"

"I just want the chance to make things right again."

"That's blackmail." He scoops his watch off the desk, slips it over his wrist and snaps the clasp closed. "And extortion. You're lucky I don't arrest you on the spot. If you come back into this building again, I will. Am I making myself clear?"

"You can't do that. It's a public building."

"Try me," he says.

I go back to my office. Gary's working downstairs, although he's not particularly friendly these days. I might as well enjoy the sunset of my career among the trappings of my profession – books, diplomas and leather furniture that still smells like the inside of a new car.

There is a soft knock at my door. I get up from my chair as the door opens slowly. The lovely Melinda stands in the doorway, her stomach rounding with new life. She is ethereally beautiful as though created from a medieval wall tapestry, long, slender arms and legs, glossy light brown hair that sheets down to her shoulders. There are small drops of sweat on her forehead and upper lip. She leans with one hand against the door frame. The other holds a canvas tote bag.

"I'm not so good at stairs these days," she says. She is breathing hard. "May I come in? I need to sit down."

She goes immediately to the couch, settling heavily into the low seat. I offer her a glass of water which she accepts. She pulls a tissue from the holder, folds it carefully and puts the glass down on top of it. She is wearing a maternity dress with long flowing sleeves, rose colored with purple and green accents. She lifts her hair and blots the back of her neck with another tissue, finding little pieces of business to fill the time while she figures out how to start whatever she's come here to say. I hadn't noticed before that her eyes are so green or that she is so truly beautiful. I never stood a chance.

"I wanted to talk to you earlier, but I was afraid. God, this is so uncomfortable. I really don't know what to say. I want to apologize and then I don't. I didn't intend for Mark and me to fall in love, but I don't want to take back what happened. I just wish we hadn't caused you so much suffering."

She lifts her hair again and mops the back of her neck. She is wearing a delicate gold wedding band set with tiny diamonds. "On the one hand, I feel awful about what we've done. On the other, I've never been happier. I could never imagine a life this good for myself. Never."

She reports this uptick in her fortune without hesitation, as though expecting me to share in her delightful surprise. I want to tell her that she's a day late and a dollar short. If she had wanted to apologize for seducing my husband she should have done it two years ago. The waning afternoon light forms a gloomy coil around us.

"Why now?" I ask. "Why today?"

"I'm here to ask you to stop pushing this business about Ben Gomez. I'm asking you, please, please, stop. You'll ruin us."

She is frowning, tiny little lines sprout in the space between her eyebrows. Her bottom lip pushes forward in a pout. It is a command performance. She fluctuates from one emotion to another with the fluidity of a concert pianist running her fingers along a keyboard.

"I don't owe you or Mark a thing."

"He doesn't deserve to be in trouble. It's half my fault."

"So Mark has said."

"Mark didn't ask me to come here. He doesn't even know about it. I'm supposed to be at home on bed rest." She arches her back, grimacing with the effort. "He is telling you the truth. I really did do Ben's evaluation. I've been helping out because Mark's so busy." Her green eyes muddy with tears. "I've spent five years getting my doctorate. I owe thousands of dollars in student loans. I have to be able to sit for my license to practice. Mark has to be able to work to support us." She sniffles and wipes her hand under her nose. She presses the other to her belly.

"I don't believe you," I say. "Mark did the evaluation and then he took money to change the results."

"You *won't* believe me, that's what you mean, isn't it? You hate me so much you don't want to know the truth. You're jealous that Mark and I are so happy."

Her upper lip pulls into a sneer. There is a gap between her teeth, and one incisor has grown in crookedly, a small glitch in her otherwise stunning face. I wonder why she's never had it fixed.

She asks, "How do you think I feel seeing your name and his linked together on the books you wrote? I'll tell you. It feels like no matter what I do, I'll never catch up to you and you'll never go away. You're there wherever I look, in the library, in his office, on his resume."

Suddenly she crumples over, panting, wrapping both her arms over her stomach. In a second she sits up again, sucking at the air in long, audible inhalations and exhalations. I reach for the telephone to call 911.

"No." She tilts over, half laying, half sitting as though she's going to give birth on my couch. She reaches for her tote bag. "I failed him."

"For God's sake, Mark loves you. I'm calling 911."

"Not Mark," she wheezes, "Ben Gomez. I failed him. He was unsuitable."

She tosses the tote bag toward me and then rolls to the floor at the start of another painful surge. I reach for the phone and sit down next to her. Her back is against the sofa, her legs wide. She is groaning and sweating, fanning herself with both hands. The sleeves of her dress fall to her elbows and I see that she's wearing a diamond tennis bracelet, just like the one Mark gave me, the one I haven't found since the break-in.

I briefly consider the guilty pleasure I would savor if Mark's young bride turns out to be a thief, but for now she is just a woman in pain. I put my arm around her shoulder to steady her. We sit that way, breathing together, until the ambulance whines around the corner and stops. Melinda gives a sharp yelp as the medics load her onto the gurney and carry her down the stairs and out the front door.

Her tote bag is lying on the floor. I grab it and run after them as they are lifting her into the back of the ambulance.

"For you," she says and pushes my arm away. "Read everything."

Gary greets me at the door to his office, frowning. I tell him about my visit from Melinda and her insistence that she, not Mark, did Ben's evaluation. The air in his office smells pleasantly of pipe tobacco. The white noise machine emits a steady hum. Street lights filter in through the bay window and glint off the glassed-in shelves crammed with books and journals. I sink into the cushions of his couch. A patient would feel safe and protected in this room.

We spread the contents of Melinda's tote bag on the floor. There is a bio-data sheet, a copy of the background investigation, and a packet of standard assessment tools, two more than the state requires, all marked with Ben's name. It is a person-in-a-bag, a psychometric avatar.

"Have a look, Gary. I need a second pair of eyes."

"What am I looking for? Give me the Cliff notes on cops."

"We screen only after a candidate has been given a conditional offer of employment and they've completed the background, the medical exam and the chief's interview. We're looking for emotional stability, judgment, coping skills, assertiveness, impulse control, flexibility, stress tolerance, integrity, and social competence. We're not trying to predict who will make a good cop, just who has the emotional stability to do the job."

I pick up the MMPI-2. It's hand-scored the way Mark taught me to do as a student, the way Melinda would do it. She's drawn a line through all the omitted and double-marked items and placed a dot next to all the deviant responses. The totals are tallied at the bottom in small, crisp lettering. I check the addition. There are no mistakes. Another line connects the dots on the validity scales and the clinical scales. The totals have been transferred to Ben's profile page and from the raw score to the graph. I check the K-correction, too. Everything is in order. I hand the profile sheet to Gary.

He bends his head to the paper. In this light, his hair is almost entirely white. Gary and my father had both warned me against marrying Mark. My once liberal, inclusive father told me never to trust a goy. Gary thought Mark was in love with the sound of his own voice. "Have an affair," he said, "but don't marry him. He won't let you grow up and if you do, he won't want you anymore. Don't confuse lust for something more abiding."

Gary fills his pipe, draws deeply and exhales a long plume of gray smoke as he traces the stem of his pipe over the profile page. He shakes his head. "I'm no expert but, in my humble opinion, this kid doesn't have the right protoplasm to be a police officer. He broods a lot, doesn't have a lot of self-confidence, and look at this elevation on scale 4." He passes the profile to me. "He wouldn't be adverse to bending the rules a little or to selectively reporting the truth. Not good qualities for a cop." He shuffles through the other results. "Looks like he was hoping that being a cop would give him a sense of identity he didn't have."

I hold up a copy of a letter addressed to Chief Baxter and read it aloud. "Based on the standard psychological screening data, I find that the applicant, Benjamin Gomez, does not meet the psychological qualifications required by Government Code 1031 (f)."

It is signed by Mark Edison, Ph.D. My name is still on the letterhead. My hands are trembling. I give the letter to Gary.

He frowns and says, "Mark turned him down and the chief still hired him?"

"He couldn't have. It's against the law to hire someone who hasn't got the requisite psychological qualifications."

"Could someone have changed the recommendation?"

"Mark told me he upgraded his entire computer system, that all his reports are encrypted. Someone would need a password to unscramble the code and change the recommendation."

Suddenly I feel drained, exhausted. The smoke from Gary's pipe is making me nauseous. I haven't eaten all day. I lean against Gary's couch. All I want to do is sleep.

"How in hell am I going to find out who did this, Gary? I'm not even allowed in the building."

Chapter Thirty Six

Eddie Rimbauer's apartment house in East Kenilworth is behind a shopping center. It has all the architectural charm of a cheap motel. The balconies are crammed with bicycles, boxes, baby carriages and weightlifting benches. Laundry hangs over the railings. Windows are covered with bedspreads and sheets. The occasional hanging curtain is knotted at the bottom to let in air. Wrecked and rusting shopping carts stand sentinel in the overgrown yard. The air is redolent with garbage and dirty diapers. A cacophony of sounds creates the illusion of village life – the clatter of pots, children crying and laughing, the brassy blare of *Norteño* music and the soft murmur of conversation.

I don't really want to see him, but I have no other choice. The door to his apartment is partially ajar. I knock. There's no response. I push the door open into the tiny living room. Eddie is passed out in a recliner in front of the TV, watching a basketball game with the sound off. There's a can of beer in his hand. His face is more bloated than it was a week ago. Broken capillaries spread across his nose like fine netting. It's a waste of time to talk to him in this condition. The door squeaks as I pull it closed. Eddie blasts awake like a soldier who has fallen asleep in the middle of a battle.

He looks wildly around the room until his eyes settle on me. "What the fuck? Where am I?"

"In your apartment. Your living room."

"What the fuck are you doing here? I ain't going to no rehab place. I told Fran, I'm not going."

He pushes himself off the recliner without retracting the footrest and falls on the floor. His t-shirt is soiled and his belly spills over his pants. His hair is matted with sleep.

"I need to piss." He turns over, pushes himself to his hands and knees and pulls himself up by hanging onto the chair. He wobbles down a short hall, opens a door and unzips his pants.

"What the fuck?" he says, slams the door and opens another.

I hear him urinating, a long, heavy stream. I go down the hall and open the first door. It's a clothes closet and from the smell, this isn't the first time he's mistaken it for the bathroom. I scoot back into the living room. He comes back and drops onto the chair. It bounces under his weight, the legs scraping the bare floor.

"Do you have any coffee?"

"In the kitchen." He nods to a pair of louvered doors. There are holes in the walls on either side of the doors where the knobs have splintered the paint and dented the sheetrock. His tiny kitchen is bare except for three small cactus plants shriveling on the window ledge over the sink and a salt and pepper set of comical ceramic pigs. There's a cheap coffee pot and a can of generic coffee on the counter. It's the only thing in the kitchen that looks used. While the coffee is brewing, I open the door to the refrigerator. It's filled with beer. There are packaged dinners from Fran's in the freezer. I remember when Eddie showed up at my place unannounced and mocked me for living in a barren house. Compared to his, I live in a castle. There's a full set of restaurant style plates and a drawer full of silverware, more gifts from Fran. I pour the coffee and go back into the living room. Eddie is sitting, slack-jawed, in his recliner. There's a cooler on the floor next to his chair and he reaches for another beer. I hand him the coffee.

"Sorry about the mess. I wasn't expecting company. You shoulda made an appointment." His words are slurry. "Didn't know you made house calls." He swigs the coffee like it was a beer and spews it out. "Fucking hot."

"It's coffee, it's supposed to be hot," I say. He looks confused.

"I need to talk to you. But I need you to be sober."

"I'm on my four day. I'll be shit faced until my Monday. Have a seat. You take the couch for a change."

He laughs at his joke. Beside the ancient recliner and the couch, there's only a phony wood coffee table with a chipped corner and the television. Newspapers and paperback books are stacked in corners. The walls are bare. He watches me looking around.

"Not exactly House and Garden, but it's all I can get for what I have after alimony payments."

"You don't look well. Things rough at work?"

"Not at all." He makes an elaborate sweeping gesture with his arm and spills more coffee. "Everything's peachy. I love the front desk. Helping the upstanding citizens of Kenilworth with their traffic tickets – the ones they don't deserve, of course. Beats the hell out of working the street."

"How much are you drinking?"

"Don't start on me. I got Fran crawling up my ass every other day."

"I need your help, and you can't help me if you're drunk."

"I can't help you if I'm sober. I don't know shit. Remember? I'm the guy who sat next to Gomez for ten hours a day and didn't recognize him." He drains his coffee cup and hands it to me. "Refill," he says. I pour him a second cup. "What do you want?"

I tell him about the encrypted report and my suspicions that someone at the P.D. changed the report from fail to pass. He looks at me with puzzled eyes. "Crips in Kenilworth? What kinda Crips you talking about? Crips and Bloods?"

I explain encryption the best I can. Eddie puts his coffee down, reaches for a beer and pops the lid.

"I don't know fucking-A about computers. I'm a fucking dinosaur. To me, a computer is a glorified typewriter. Took me fucking forever to learn how to use the one in the cruiser."

"I'm not allowed in the building, Eddie. The chief's threatened to have me arrested if he sees me again. I need somebody on the inside to help me."

"Talk to *Mañana*. He's a computer whiz. Grew up with all that stuff. I think his mother had computer cables for tits."

He laughs and then suddenly throws himself forward in his chair, slamming his feet and legs down on the footrest. It snaps back with a groan. For the moment he looks sober. "Don't get the little beaner in trouble. I'm warning you, Doc. He's a good kid. Don't do a Gomez on him."

'Gomez'. That's a verb made out of a noun made out of a once living human being.

There's a message from Mark on my cell phone. I call him back. Without waiting for me to ask he tells me that Melinda is home from the hospital. The contractions have stopped, but she's on bed rest until her due date.

"I want to clear something up, Dot. I didn't send her to see you. She did that on her own."

"So she said."

"She told me she showed you the disqualifying recommendation she wrote for Ben Gomez."

"She did. But what's to prove that it's the same recommendation you actually sent to the chief? You haven't been exactly honest about things with me."

"I'm not trying to hurt you. I'm trying to protect Melinda." He denies changing anything and invites me to bring my own computer consultant to examine the hard drives on every computer in his office and his home.

"So, if you didn't change it, who did?"

"I send the report to the chief. I doubt he reads them. I think he sends them on to his secretary, Barbara what's-her-name, and the lieutenant in charge of personnel and training. They have passwords too." There's a pause. "Anything else?"

I'm tempted to ask if he ever gave Melinda a tennis bracelet like the one he gave me, but I don't. If she wants it so badly, she can keep it. I don't want it anymore.

I call Manny at home. He seems happy to hear from me.

"How you been, Doc? You okay? You work things out with your ex?"

"I don't know." I tell him about April and Ben.

"That's cold. No wonder he did himself."

I tell him about the encrypted report, the passwords and my suspicion that someone changed the recommendation. "If I could prove someone changed the report, it might help me. I talked to Eddie. He doesn't know anything about computers. He told me to call you. That you were a computer whiz and might be able to tell me how to find out who changed the report. I don't know much about computers myself. I don't want to get you in any trouble. Think it over and call me back."

"I don't have to think it over. Three people have gone down behind this, Ben, you and Eddie. This is not just your problem. I don't want to work next to somebody I can't trust because they're loco. Whoever changed this report put us all in danger and for what, I don't know. But I'd like to find out."

"How?"

"Unless we're talking CIA level encryption, which I doubt, all you need is a file recovery utility. Piece of cake. You want me to do it?"

"No. I just want you to tell me how to do it."

"I could do it easily. I'm working mids. There's no one on mahogany row. I could get up there on a break. No problem."

"Absolutely not. No way. You've helped a lot just giving me this information. Please, don't do anything else. I want to talk to the chief first. I'll keep you posted."

"One other thing, Doc. There's a rumor going around that Ben sent a suicide note to the chief on email. How do you know that it was Ben who wrote it?"

"I just assumed."

"Eddie taught me never to assume anything. He used to say 'Don't assume nothing, just makes an ass out of you and me.' Get the joke?"

I laugh to be polite. The first time I heard it was in my freshman year of college. It wasn't very funny then, either.

Chapter Thirty Seven

It's 9:00 p.m., and I'm parked next to the chief's car. Police headquarters may be off limits, but no one has forbidden me from being in the parking lot.

I've been here for an hour eating Chinese take-out from a carton. My car smells like soy sauce and grease. Baxter's inside at a city council meeting, where he'll stay only until he can sneak out unnoticed. I'm dying of thirst, thinking about dashing to the local convenience store for a diet soda, when the interior lights in his car go on and I hear the locks click open. In a second, he materializes out of the dark. I scramble to get out of my car, cursing as half a carton of uneaten egg foo yung spills down the front of my suit.

"Who's there?" He wheels around, sucking air, filling the darkness between us with the blowhole sound of a surfacing whale. The street lamp behind me gives off a weak yellow light. It's enough to see that his hand is inside his jacket, gripping his gun.

"Stop! It's me, Dot Meyerhoff."

He reaches sideways into his car, grabs a flashlight, and shines it in my eyes. His hands look enormous.

"Jesus H. Christ. Do you know how close I came to shooting you?"

The pupils of his eyes are swimming in a circle of white. He drops the flashlight to his side and leans against his car. I bend over and put my hands between my knees to stop shaking.

"What in hell are you doing here?"

"Waiting for you."

"Ever heard of the telephone?"

"Would you take my call?"

"Probably not."

He straightens up and moves towards his car door."Wait. I have to tell you something. Somebody altered Ben Gomez' pre-employment psych report."

"What are you talking about?"

"It's complicated."

"Give me the short version."

"Mark's psych assistant disqualified Ben. I saw her original report."

"I don't hire people who've been disqualified. It's against the law."

"I know that. So someone in the PD changed the recommendation before you saw it."

He raises an eyebrow.

"And who would that be?"

"I don't know. I'd hoped you would. Mark's reports are encrypted. Who else besides you has the password?" He scowls, looks up as though the answer is written on the underside of the street lamp. "We can trace whoever did this with something called a file recovery utility. I don't understand how it works, but it can identify the computer where the changes were made as well as the date and time. Apparently it's not that difficult to do."

"This is total fantasy. I don't know which one of you is crazier, you or your ex." He is sweating in the cooling air, rolling the heavy flashlight against his thigh. "I've had it with you. I want you to back off and stay there." His lips are drawn up against his teeth like a dog.

"I can't. I mean I won't. Twenty-four hours. I'll give you twenty-four hours to look into this and get back to me before I go to the press."

He's in my face with two strides, leaning in so close I can smell coffee and onions on his breath."I told you once before, don't threaten me." He lowers his voice to a whisper, although there's no one within earshot. "Here's what I'm willing to do and when I've done it, we're finished. Do you understand?" He punctuates these last three words with a finger pointed at my heart. "I'm going to ask the city IT guy to look into this. If someone has altered confidential records, which I doubt, he'll take care of it. Not you. Not me." He slaps the flashlight against his leg. "You piss people off, you know that? I bet that's why somebody broke into your house."

Twenty four hours turns into seventy two. So much for my threat to call the newspapers. I have picked up the phone three times today and each time I tell myself there has to be a better way. It's not that I worry about ruining Mark's reputation or Melinda's future. Or Baxter's. They're on their own.

But I keep picturing Mr. and Mrs. Gomez, the looks on their faces when they open the newspaper and see Ben's photo, happy and smiling in his academy uniform, under a headline that says, "Unfit for duty." Their private tragedy exposed, once again, for the entertainment of Kenilworth's residents as they drink their morning lattes. On the other hand, why am I worrying about them? They lied to me, just like Ben did.

I pick up the phone and call them. Mrs. Gomez answers on the first ring. "This is Dr. Meyerhoff." I can hear her saying something to her husband in Spanish.

"Wait a minute. I'm putting on the speaker phone." I hear a click. "You have news?"

"Yes I do. The news is that you neglected to tell me some important facts about Ben and his parents. I heard all about Mr. Gomez' homeless brother in L.A., but nothing about your daughter and her husband. They didn't die in a car wreck, like Ben told me, they died of an overdose."

"Why did you need to know this? What difference would it make?"

"Because I've been thinking that Ben's death was my fault. Because—" She cuts me off before I can finish my sentence.

"So now you know why we didn't say. We're ashamed. It must be our fault. First our daughter kills herself with drugs and then Ben shoots himself."

"Why did you tell the district attorney's investigator and not me?"

"He was so nasty, that man. He threatened to arrest us."

"We didn't lie to you, doctor" Mr. Gomez says. "We just didn't say."

"Ben lied. He lied on his police application. He lied to his wife. He lied to his in-laws."

"That's my fault," he says. "There was so much publicity. The name Sturgis was everywhere. It would have followed him forever. He would never have had a chance, everyone thinking he was like his dope fiend father. I was glad Sturgis was dead. He took our daughter from us. Turned her into someone we didn't know. We adopted Ben to protect him, give him a new start. I told him, never tell anybody who your parents were. Just say they died in a car accident. Nobody will ask. And nobody did. Not until he killed himself."

A walk would help to work off the cortisol that has accumulated in my system, but it's after ten, too late, too dark and I'm too tired. My other option is the comforting ritual of popcorn and wine, although it's not wise to drink during a crisis. Alcohol will only increase the stress-related hormones in my blood stream.

Not one to practice what I preach, I pour myself a generous glass of red wine and turn on the TV. And just for the hell of it, I take out a pad of paper and begin writing down the talking points for my future non-existent press debut. Oedipus is meowing, complaining that he's been dumped outside for the night. I open the slider to my yard. He's sitting in a splotch of moonlight, his grey fur turned to silver. I bend over to pet him and my phone rings. It's Baxter, sounding surprisingly upbeat. As promised, he talked to the city's IT expert who figured out what happened to the encrypted report.

Our problem is solved, and Baxter can't wait to show me. He asks me to please come to his office right now. Evidently, I'm no longer *persona non grata*. He'll even send a car for me, if I want one, which I don't, having barely drunk half a glass of wine. "Our" problem, he had said. I feel immense relief to hear him finally take responsibility, show some ownership for this mess that I'm in.

A new desk officer buzzes me in. I wonder where Eddie is. I take the elevator up. Mahogany row is deserted, and most of the office doors are closed. From somewhere in the building, I hear soft laughter.

Manny is sitting in a chair next to the coffee table in the chief's office. He is leaning on his knees with his head in his hands. He doesn't look at me. The chief is in his shirt sleeves, his shoulder holster on display.

"An amazing thing happened, Dot. I came into the office to do some work. I get more done at night when it's quiet. And who do I find in my office, at my desk, on my computer, but Officer Ochoa? What, I wonder, could he be doing? You, of course, know the answer."

Manny looks up. "I was just looking for a quiet place to write a report."

"Shut up." Baxter picks up a plastic disc holder from his desk and waves it at me. "File recovery utility," he reads off the box. "Where have I heard that before?"

"It's mine. She has nothing to do with it. I came on my own."

Baxter whirls towards him. "Speak when spoken to. That's an order."

Manny lowers his head to his hands again. I can't look at him.

"Chivalrous, isn't he? Impressionable. Open to influence. What did you promise him? You're really something, you know that. Eddie's on his way out, thanks to you, and now you've done it again."

He leans against his desk and drums his fingers on the disc case. He looks like a child about to gleefully incinerate some insects under a magnifying glass.

"What do you want?"

"Same as before. Quit hounding me."

"If I don't?"

"This promising young officer will lose his job. Remember, he's still on probation. I don't need a reason to fire him. Plus, it would be unethical of me not to tell any prospective employers that he hacked into my computer seeking access to confidential personnel records. That's against the law. The city attorney may ask me to press charges."

"Fine. You have a deal."

"That's it? No questions?"

"No questions."

Baxter takes his gun out of his shoulder holster and smashes the computer disc with the handle, splitting it in half. He puts the two halves back into the carrying case and hands it to Manny.

"You're dismissed. For the time being."

"What about me?"

"Do whatever you want after you leave the building. Remember? You don't work here anymore."

I follow Manny down the hall to the elevator. He won't look at me.

"I am so sorry. I wish you hadn't done this."

He is red-faced, staring at his shoes.

"The file was on three computers, the chief's, his secretary's and the computer in personnel and training. Whoever made the changes did it in the chief's office at 1:00 a.m."

"Manny, please. Stay out of this. It's my problem. You'll ruin your career."

"I already have," he says as he takes the stairs, leaving me to wait alone for the elevator.

Chapter Thirty Eight

I talk to myself in the car on the way home. Giving up is a small price to pay if it saves Manny's career. I've had doubts about working for the Kenilworth police from the beginning. If I hadn't been in such a hurry to get away from Mark, I might have thought twice about taking the contract. Things were easier when I sat in an office writing books or doing assessments of virtual strangers, no involvement, no on-going relationships, no responsibility for anyone's future. Just interesting conversations. I don't belong in this cop world, not with my family background. I don't trust cops and they don't trust me, especially not now after what's happened to Ben, Eddie and Manny.

I uncork the bottle of Pinot Noir. It's 2:00 a.m., too early or too late for a drink. I don't care. I toast myself. This is an opportunity to do something different, find work where people are happy to see me coming. Work that doesn't give me nightmares. I could sell flowers or work as a greeter in Home Depot. I take a sip of wine. It's lovely. A damn sight better than the Two Buck Chuck of my future.

I take my yellow pad into the living room and start to make a list of all the possible jobs I might want. I can't concentrate. All I can think of is Manny, desolate, slumped against the wall in Baxter's office. How can he work with the threat of dismissal hanging over his head? How safe will he be if he's worried and distracted? The smart thing for me to do is to look the other way, cut my losses, and move on, like Gary's been telling me to do.

But I can't. I'm having trouble living with myself after Ben's death. How could I live with myself if I abandon Manny too? He hasn't done anything wrong. He's only a pawn in the power struggle between me and the chief. And what about Eddie, drunk, depressed, maybe suicidal?

I start another list, a catalogue of recent events. I've spent years doing research and assessments, organizing and capturing complex information about people on paper. Why can't I do the same about my own life? By 3:30, I've covered four pages with notes, and I'm having trouble keeping my eyes open.

I make a pot of coffee. It takes three cups for me to feel half awake. I should go to bed, but every time I think of Manny, my stomach skids sideways. Something's missing. Like a lost name, it hovers at the edge of my consciousness. I look at my notes. Melinda did Ben's assessment. I accept that now. And, although I hate to admit it, she did a decent job. I'm still not sure that Mark didn't take Belle Patcher's money to change the recommendation. But if he didn't take it, who did?

"Want to find the corrupt bastards?" my father used to say, "Follow the money."

I nap for three hours and call a psychologist friend who works in the mental health clinic at Kenilworth Community Hospital. I tell her a client of mine has been admitted to the hospital after a suicide attempt and her case has been taken over by a psychiatrist. We commiserate about how psychiatrists never return phone calls, especially to psychologists who want to follow their own clients in the hospital. She checks on Belle Patcher's current status and tells me she's been moved to the Prescott Residential Center for the treatment of depression.

Prescott Residential Center is a hybrid facility, part psychiatric hospital, part spa. I pull into the parking lot, the lone Honda amongst a herd of Mercedes and BMWs. Lush landscaping surrounds fountains, miniature waterfalls, teak benches and koi filled ponds. All artfully arranged into picture-perfect niches of tranquility and contemplation. At the moment, no one is partaking of such beauty, save the gardeners.

The lobby rivals a four-star hotel. Marble floors and columns, a plant filled atrium and vases of silk flowers as tall as I am. The young woman behind the front desk is reading a magazine. I drill my fingers on the marble counter top to get her attention. She tells me that all the residents — apparently she has been instructed not to call them patients—are in OT, occupational therapy. She asks the name of the resident I want to visit, checks her computer and informs me that there's only one name on the list of permitted visitors.

"I'm Belle's sister. I've just flown in from out of town. She doesn't know that I know she's in here," I whisper. "I just want to give her a hug. I won't be but a minute."

The young woman smiles unenthusiastically. "You still have to be on the list."

"Ten minutes, that's all I want. I've been up all night on the red eye. I just want her to know I'm here. Her husband begged me to come. Said it would cheer her up enormously."

Cheering up a depressed person is ill-advised, makes them feel as though no one understands the stranglehold depression has on their lives.

"Ten minutes. Please?" My eyeballs bulge with tears. I am not feigning this. I'm exhausted and maybe a little hung over.

"What's your name?"

"April."

She glances at the computer screen and tells me to wait in the seating area to my right. I sink into a glove leather sofa. There is a pile of brochures on the bamboo coffee table in front of me. The Prescott Residential Center describes itself as a renowned treatment facility with exceptional accommodations. There are photos of contented people in deep conversation. Not a depressive or a psychotic in the crowd. No mention of locked facilities, restraints, suicide watches or even medication.

I can't tell the patients from the staff. No one wears a uniform. There is a list of activities available to residents: tennis, swimming, massage, gardening, meditation and yoga. I'm tempted to have a meltdown and check myself in. I wonder how much it would cost.

There is something about the place that reeks of exploitation. Vinnie Patcher trying to buy off his guilt, Belle making him pay for his abuse. A door bangs open behind me and Belle bursts around the corner with her wobbly gait. She's wearing her silk jogging suit and her hair has been freshly permed. A leather handbag dangles from her arm. Her face is lit up like a child until she sees me. Then she collapses into a tantrum, swinging at me with her purse, kicking me in the legs. The receptionist looks at us in alarm.

"Belle, Belle," I say, "It's all right, I'm here now. I came as soon as I heard."

I get behind her, wrap my arms around her body and hold her in a bear hug. She tries to bite me.

The receptionist asks if I need an orderly. I don't recall seeing orderlies mentioned in the brochure.

"She's just excited to see me. It's very emotional for us both. She'll calm down in a minute. I'll take her outside so we won't disturb you."

"She can't leave the grounds." The young woman admonishes me. Then she shrugs and sits down behind the desk, her head barely visible over the marble counter. Whatever the residents are getting for their money, it isn't an alert receptionist.

"Get hold of yourself," I hiss in Belle's ear.

She makes some sort of grunting noise. I squeeze more tightly and propel her out the door and across the lawn to where a stand of dwarf mogu pines acts as a privacy hedge. I push her down on a bench and sit next to her, my arm around her, my fingers digging into her shoulder.

"Where is the money?"

"I want April, I want my grandbaby," she wails.

I press harder, bending the tips of my fingernails. She's snuffling, wiping her dripping nose and eyes on her sleeve like a child, kicking her stubbly little legs in the air.

"Who did you give it to?"

"No one. I'm going to use it. For me and April and the baby. For a down payment on a condo."

"April's gone. The baby is gone."

"I need it for a lawyer. To get the baby back."

"You're in a nut house. No one is going to give you a baby."

She wrenches against me, growling and gritting her teeth. A moment later she is on her feet, storming across the lawn. I grab her by the shoulders and wheel her around, back toward the bench. The receptionist opens the front door and calls out, asking if everything is okay.

I smile and wave. "She's a lot better. Back to her old spunky self."

I have only moments before a slew of burly men in white uniforms will burst through the camouflage of normalcy and haul Belle off in four point restraints. I squeeze her, pinching the soft flesh around her collarbone.

"Sit." I push her behind the hedge. "Tell me about the money. I'll tell you where April is."

"You don't know where she is."

"Yes I do. She's not hiding from me. You're the one she doesn't want to see."

"Does my husband know where she is?"

"He wants to keep you away from April, doesn't he? Tell me about the money or I'll tell him where to find her."

"You can't do that." Her hands ball into chubby fists.

"Cut the crap. You can act crazy for these people. They get paid to listen to it. I don't. I want an answer."

"You won't tell Vinnie where April is? You'll tell me first?"

"Yes."

"I gave the money to Chief Baxter. He told me that if Ben flunked the psychological, he couldn't hire him. He would have to find another psychologist who would give him a favorable opinion. And there wasn't money in the budget for that. Plus, he'd have to give Ben extra training and that would require overtime, and he didn't have money in his budget for that either. So I told him I would pay the extra."

She slumps against me, her body soft and flaccid. "I have a receipt."

"I don't believe you."

She fumbles in her purse and hands me a battered envelope. Inside is a handwritten receipt for $60,000 signed by Robert B. Baxter on police department stationery. Only a card-carrying narcissist would be arrogant enough to think he could give someone a signed receipt for a bribe and get away with it.

"Why didn't you tell me about this before?"

"Would you have believed me? You said so yourself. I'm in the nut house, and he's the chief of police. Anyhow, I'm waiting for him to give me my money back. Then April and the baby and I will move to San Francisco. April likes San Francisco."

I pocket the receipt.

"I need that," she says.

"It's safer with me. Prescott is notorious for having crooks on staff who like to steal from rich patients. Someone might take your purse. I'll send you a copy."

Two men in white uniforms are walking towards us. The gurney they are pulling leaves deep tracks in the soft, moist lawn. I stand up and start walking toward my car. Belle calls after me.

"You don't have children, do you? That's why you don't understand."

Baxter wasn't even on my radar. So much for my psychological skills. I'll have to tell Eddie that he's not the only one who can't find a bowling ball in a bathtub. Why would Baxter take such a risk? He's full of himself and not terribly bright, but he's also not stupid enough to risk his job just to curry favor with the wife of a politically powerful man.

Patcher once had important connections all over the state and the clout to help Baxter with his future, but after that scene at the Good Shepherd home, his career is over. A recommendation from him might do more harm than good. Maybe Baxter has a secret vice – gambling, women – although all he seems to do is work and lift weights. It wouldn't be drugs, his body is a temple, unless he's taking steroids, and then he would be far more jumpy and irritable.

I start my car. It's not my job to figure out Baxter's motives. He's my enemy now, not my client. My job is to hang him out to dry and get myself off the hook.

I make copies of the receipt and mail one each to Gary and Frank. I stifle an impulse to deliver Frank's by hand. A short movie plays in my head, me, Frank, and the solace of flesh. I try writing something warm on a post-it note and come up with nothing more than "Hope you're well. I'm still covered in dust."

I call Manny to see how he's doing. And because I need to ask him something. He sounds really down and tells me that FedEx is hiring drivers. He's thinking about applying. I tell him to keep that as Plan B, but to hang in there. I'm going to bring this to a close.

"When we talked on the phone a few days ago, you asked me how I knew that Ben wrote his suicide note. You made a joke about assuming things. Remember?"

"Yeah, so?"

"Supposing someone else did write it. How could I find that out?"

"Depends. You could look at the time it was written, what computer it was written on, where it was located. The medical examiner who examined Ben's body would have an approximate time of death. You could check that against the time on the email. Or you could let me do that."

"No," I say. "You are already in a ton of trouble."

"I can't make it any worse."

"Yes you can."

"Give me the name of the motel where Ben died. I'll call you back."

He calls me back in an hour. The motel owner's wife called the sheriff's department to report the body at 8:05 a.m. A deputy took the license number of Ben's car off the motel registration and put out an all-points bulletin for April. A Highway Patrol unit spotted her car in a shopping center about an hour later and found her in an internet cafe, drinking coffee and working on her laptop. The CHP officer noted in his report that April quickly closed the lid to her computer when she saw him and seemed remarkably unmoved at the news that her husband had just committed suicide. She refused an escort home and said she was fine to drive. The CHP officer had no reason to detain her, so he let her go.

"So what does this mean?"

"I asked the motel owner if there was a computer in Ben's room. She said no. I asked if Ben ever used a computer in the office. She said they didn't have one. My guess is that Ben didn't write the suicide note. April did."

"Can we prove it?"

"If she used the wi-fi network in the café, we can check the café's log, the computer logs, or the ISP logs. We'll know what time she wrote it and who she sent it to."

"Once again, Manny, you have saved my bacon. I just hope I can pull yours out of the fire."

I call him back in ten minutes. "What does LMAO mean?"

"Doc," he says. "What are you looking at?"

"April's Facebook page."

"Bitchin. You're getting to be a real computer nerd."

"So what does it mean?"

"Laughing my ass off."

"And IMHO, BTW, LOL, OMG, and WTF?" April and her friends seem to have a language all their own.

"Hang on," Manny says, "I'm getting on Facebook now. Did you check out her timeline?"

"What's a timeline?"

"Like a history. Everything she ever posted."

"You mean we can roll back to before Ben killed himself and see what she was writing?"

"Sure."

We start with the month before Ben's death. Thirty straight days of variations on a theme. April's profile photo is ANIFOC – almost naked in front of the camera. She wants to MIRL – meet in real life – with a hot guy who wants to hook-up with a preggo slut with big boobies. Her husband, soon-to-be wasband, is such an emo loser. Never wants to do anything or go anywhere. She's going to buy him a suicide bag for his birthday and hopes he'll off himself so she can go party. It's hard being married and worse being preggers because she can't drink or smoke weed.

It's a tirade of trash talk. I've never read anything like it, yet something about it sounds familiar.

"You know what, Doc? I think this meets 401 P.C."

"Manny, talk to me in English, please."

"Sorry. I'm talking about the penal code. 401 P.C. says, 'Every person who deliberately aids, or advises, or encourages another to commit suicide, is guilty of a felony.' It can be difficult to prove, but April could get some jail time for this."

If I could hug Manny over the phone, I would.

The idea of April sitting in jail in an ill-fitting jumpsuit with no make-up and no computer privileges is extremely satisfying. So is the idea of justice for poor, tortured Ben. Manny said it was possible to compare the time on Ben's suicide note with the time of his death. There was at least an hour between the time the motel owner found Ben's body and the Highway Patrol officer found April. If the time on the note coincided with April's stop at the internet café, that would mean she wrote the note. If she wrote the note before the CHP guy talked to her, then she already knew Ben was dead. There is no way she could have known Ben was dead unless she was in the room with him when he shot himself.

I get my briefcase. The copy of Ben's suicide note is sitting on top of some other papers, neatly folded. I haven't looked at it, couldn't bear to, since he died. Familiar words jump off the page. 'Eddie Rimbauer is an emo loser.' I go back to April's Facebook postings. There are four separate instances when she refers to Ben as an 'emo loser'. I telephone Manny again.

"What do you call it when someone impersonates another person?"

"Misdemeanor fraud. That's section 528.5 of the penal code, punishable by a fine of $1000 and maybe a year in the county jail."

"What about libel and defamation of character? April wrote the suicide note, and I think I can prove it. She was setting Eddie and me up for a lawsuit. She wants money. Fat chance she'd have collecting any after she ruined my reputation."

"That's civil code. I can look it up if you want."

"I want, but not right now. I've something else to do. I'll see you later tonight."

Chapter Thirty Nine

Tonight is the monthly meeting of the human relations commission. I figure it's the perfect venue for a confrontation with Baxter. No way am I going to risk being alone with him again.

The commission attracts anti-police protesters and hecklers. There are always two on-duty officers present in case of trouble plus a slew of others commanded to attend if they have any hopes of being promoted. I slip in about an hour after the meeting has started, dressed for success in my tailored gray suit.

The seats in the council chambers are arranged in rows, like pews in a church. Baxter is sitting in the back where the commission members can't see him reading the newspaper. I recognize four off-duty officers to his immediate right, including Manny. He's jumping through hoops to get out of the chief's penalty box. The higher he jumps, the more hoops I put in front of him. I owe him, big time.

I scoot in from the left, blocking Baxter's access to the aisle. He turns to see who's sitting next to him and when he sees it's me, the artificial smile on his face turns to a scowl. Before he can speak, I hand him an envelope containing a copy of the receipt he gave Belle Patcher. He opens it, unfolds the sheet of paper and reads. Except for the tiniest twitch at the outside of his left eye, he doesn't react. I wait. He puts his hand over his mouth. I think he's going to be sick to his stomach. When he turns to me, I see he's stifling a laugh.

"What do you think this is, Sherlock? A bribe? It's a donation. Belle Patcher gave it to me in honor of her son-in-law. For the police associations' widows and children's fund."

"Check the date. Odd that she gave it to you before he died."

"I'll repeat myself. It was in honor of him, not in memory."

"So when I ask the association, they'll have a record of it?" His neck muscles tighten just slightly.

"I haven't gotten around to giving it to them yet. Too busy chasing ghosts and defending myself from wacko psychologists."

"This is a bribe. Belle Patcher will swear to it."

"Belle Patcher is a bona fide mentally disordered person."

"That may be so, but do you really want to start a war with her husband? You took money from his wife without his knowledge. Imagine how that will go over with him."

A woman in the row in front of us turns and gives us a dirty look, her finger pressed against her lips.

"Sorry" Baxter says and stands up. I prop my feet against the back of the seat in front of me, blocking his exit. He motions me out of his way.

"We're disturbing people," he says. "Let's go to my office."

I shake my head. He turns to his right and pushes past the officers sitting next to him. They all move aside except for Manny who is leaning forward, his elbows on his knees. Baxter bumps Manny's leg with his knee, then pushes on his shoulder. Manny doesn't budge. Baxter bends over and whispers something in his ear. Manny holds his position. People in the surrounding rows are turning around, looking at the disturbance. Whoever is speaking at the microphone stops. Baxter returns to his seat. The edges of his ears are flaming scarlet. He's cornered.

I lean in, close enough to feel the heat of his body."There are four reporters in the front row. I have enough copies of the receipt and the letter disqualifying Ben Gomez for each of them, all the members of the HRC, the mayor and the city manager. Plus, I sent copies to two of my friends."

The woman in front of us turns again, glaring.

"Sorry lady," I say. "This is police business. Find yourself another seat."

She makes a show of disgust and bangs her way down to the front of the room. Baxter eyes the vacant place she has created. He looks hinky, as cops like to say, ready to jump into the next row and run. I put my hand on his arm.

"We're going to work this out, here and now."

Small rivulets of perspiration trickle down in front of his ears and across his cheeks. I can see blood pumping at his temples. He turns to me, his broad shoulders obscuring my view of Manny and the other officers.

"I never took a dime in my life. Not even a free cup of coffee. She gave it to me. She knows we have a limited budget. Told me to do something good with it. Add it to the fund for the new public safety building."

"Hoping they'll name the building after you?"

That would be the kind of thing a narcissist would risk everything for.

"What's wrong with that? I gave my whole life to this goddamn department. As soon as I walk out the door, I'm just a P.O.W., a picture on the wall."

"Are you planning to walk out the door anytime soon?"

This is an option I hadn't considered.

"Don't get any ideas. I'm not leaving until I max out my pension."

Who knows how intuition works? How patterns emerge out of some chaotic nowhere of crashing ideas. I came here today to expose him, with no hope of anything beyond the immediate satisfaction of seeing him pilloried in the press. And now, I see a way to use his vulnerabilities to form an exit strategy that will be, in the cheery vernacular of pop psychology, a win-win solution for the two of us. I can hardly keep from smiling.

"I'm going to give you a choice, just like the one you gave Ben Gomez. Resign now or be terminated, because that's what will happen when this gets out. There will be an investigation and not just into Ben's case. Remember those officers who are out on leave? What are the investigators going to find when they look into their cases? Negligent hiring? More donations?" I pat my purse with one hand and hold the shoulder strap against my chest with the other. "Think about it. How will your pension be affected if you're fired? Your medical benefits?"

Drops of perspiration drip off his chin, leaving shiny streaks on his jacket.

"I have no reason to resign."

"Just say you want to spend more time with your family."

"I have no family. The department is my family."

"Personal reasons, then."

"Such as?"

"You don't have to say. That's why they call them personal. I'm giving you a one-time only opportunity to craft your exit. Cooperate with me and you'll get to leave the legacy you want."

The Commission chair hits the gavel and asks if there are any more public comments.

"Time is up." I stand, my purse under my arm. "So, who takes the microphone next, you or me?"

Chapter Forty

I am awake at dawn. Long fingers of pink announce the sun as it comes over the horizon. I bunch my bathrobe closed against the morning chill and open the front door. I walk down the front path in my bare feet. The concrete is cold and scratchy. A lone jogger wearing headphones and black running shorts races past, his lips moving in sync with music only he can hear. I pull the newspaper out of its plastic sleeve. Shopping inserts and circulars flutter to the sidewalk. The front page headline reads: "Police Chief Stuns Commission with Resignation."

"In a surprise announcement at the end of last night's human relations commission meeting, Police Chief Robert Baxter gave notice of his intention to resign immediately. Despite appearing to be in robust health, he cited medical problems as the reason he is leaving. He indicated that his present state of health assures a full recovery from his undisclosed medical problems. He apologized for the abruptness of his departure and assured everyone that the transition to a new chief would be swift and have no adverse impact on public safety. He left the auditorium without further comment. Chief Baxter was seen earlier in the evening engaged in intense discussion with Dr. Dot Meyerhoff, former department psychologist, leading some to speculate that Chief Baxter's health problems may be psychological. The city manager has declined to comment."

On the morning of Baxter's hastily concocted retirement ceremony I marshal my courage and call Ms. Hudson to inquire about the status of April's complaint against me. She informs me that the complainant has failed to respond to letters or phone calls. Relief slides down my body from my chest to my knees. I start to thank her and she interrupts. "However, your case will remain on file for three years from the date Mrs. Gomez made her complaint. For future reference."

I hang up with no clear sense of what it means to be on file for future reference. Is there a little icon of me on her computer desktop? Will she be following me or flying over my head, her painted red talons illuminated in the sun, a vulture in search of fresh carrion?

The phone rings. I jump and slosh hot coffee on the counter. It's Mark calling to tell me that Melinda has delivered a healthy baby boy. With an alliterative flourish, they have named him Milo. Mark has read this morning's newspaper and wonders if I had anything to do with Baxter's decision to retire. As always, he hopes that we can remain friends and colleagues. I tell him I'd sooner be friends with Adolph Hitler.

His voice grows sulky until he remembers that he's really calling to ask if I'm still planning to report him and Melinda to the Board of Psychology. It would be a pleasure to deliver the lovebirds into Ms. Hudson's bony hands if I could do so without drawing her attention in my direction at the same time. It's not a decision I need to make right away. The statute of limitations for filing complaints with the board gives me seven years to make up my mind.

Mark gives a hoarse sigh. Seven years, he says, is a long time to have the threat of an investigation hanging over their heads. I tell him, with absolute sincerity, that I couldn't agree more. Still, Mark has far worse troubles to face than Ms. Hudson. Unless I'm way off base, and I doubt it, his future with Melinda will resemble Vinnie Patcher's present.

I'm tempted to wear something black to Baxter's retirement ceremony as an ironic fashion statement, but I don't want to further add to the travesty or give the appearance that I am mocking his downfall. I choose, instead, my default gray pants suit.

People are straggling into the auditorium and taking their seats. It's 2:00 in the afternoon. There are a lot of retirees in the audience, a few workers from city hall, some reporters and a homeless man who rushes to the back row with his backpack and junk filled paper bags and promptly falls asleep.

I sit with Mr. and Mrs. Gomez and their grandchildren. She is wearing the same clothes she wore to Ben's funeral. I doubt this is by accident. She hadn't wanted to come to the ceremony after I told her about Baxter and the bribe. She had wanted to call a lawyer and start a lawsuit. But Mr. Gomez put her off. He wasn't sure, given Ben's early family history, that they could win a lawsuit claiming Ben's employer was responsible for his suicide. Furthermore, he thought they should direct all their energies to raising their remaining grandchildren. But, out of respect for Ben and to keep his memory alive, the entire family would attend the ceremony and sit in the front row, where the chief could see the traces of Ben's face in their own. They have lost a lot, these people – a daughter, a grandson, and, in all probability, a great grandchild.

Barely ten minutes have gone by when the city manager decides that the small crowd is all that's coming and asks us to take our seats. There are half a dozen cops in the audience, including Manny. Baxter comes in from a side door and mounts the podium.

He is wearing his Class-A dress uniform. He's playing this like a politician, waving and smiling at phantom friends in the audience. No one waves back. There is the usual squeal of protest from the microphone as the city manager announces that an interim chief will be appointed within the week after which he will authorize a nationwide search for a new chief. The mayor, a tall, elegant man with silky snow white hair, presents Baxter with a framed resolution in appreciation of his years of service. He apologizes for the absence of the other elected officials, all of whom, it appears, had previously scheduled appointments they were unable to change. He bends to shake the chief's hand and they pose for pictures, holding the resolution between them. The photographer has to turn his lens sideways to get them both in the frame.

It is Baxter's turn at the microphone. He adjusts it downward, producing another shattering electronic squeal. He taps the head of it with his fingers and says, "I hate these things. I'd rather be chasing crooks than making speeches, any day."

He hasn't chased a crook in years. His forehead is glistening with sweat as though he had oiled himself for a weight lifting contest. He pulls a folded piece of paper from his pocket and spreads it open on the podium. "Thank you everyone for coming today on such short notice. It has been my honor and privilege to serve and protect the people of Kenilworth for so many years. No matter where I go or how far I travel, Kenilworth will always be my home and the good people of the Kenilworth police department will always be my family."

"Bull shit." Eddie stumbles down the center aisle and flops into a seat. He's wearing his dress uniform. The jacket hangs open and his shirt gapes at the buttons. His chin is pocked with gray stubble and he's not wearing socks. "You don't deserve to wear the uniform, you ignoranus."

The sheen on Baxter's forehead tinges with pink. His nostrils flare, in and out, like miniature bellows. He smiles broadly, splitting his face in two.

"Allow me to introduce Eddie Rimbauer, one of my most senior officers."

"Know why you're an ignoranus, Baxter? Not only are you stupid, you're an asshole too."

Eddie doubles over with laughter, tipping sideways out of his seat. A slender thread of drool falls from his lower lip onto the floor. Manny appears at the back of the room, vaults down the aisle and pulls Eddie to his feet.

"Manny, you young turk. My best ever recruit. Helluva cop."

Eddie raises Manny's hand like a winning boxer and tries to turn him around for the audience. Manny retracts his hand, presses it firmly against Eddie's broad back, and pushes him toward the door.

Baxter watches their exit, staring after them, his flinty eyes sparking in the overhead lights. His face is a mask, except for the rhythmic twitching of his nostrils. Silence fills the room like glue, viscous and sticky.

Baxter snaps to attention and parries the moment to his advantage. "Know what I'll miss about this place? The laughs. Nothing like cop humor. That Eddie Rimbauer is a master comic. Kept me in stitches for years."

He looks down at his notes, dragging his thick fingers over the page, until he finds his place. People are shifting in their seats. The mayor steals a look at his watch.

"If my health problems weren't the way they are, I'd probably stay on the job forever. But that's not to be. So let me cut to the chase. I've been to a lot of retirements. Nothing but long speeches, bad food and even worse jokes. People have been asking me what I want for a parting gift and I told them nothing. This community has already given me so much. What I want is to give something back. Therefore it is my privilege to announce the formation of the Robert Baxter Foundation for the prevention of police suicide." He pulls an envelope from his pocket. "To kick things off, I'm going to contribute $60,000 of my own money." There is a smattering of applause. "The foundation will fund programs to provide education and counseling to officers and their families. To design and administer this program, I've asked Dr. Dot Meyerhoff to end her sabbatical and continue in her position as department psychologist."

He turns to where I am sitting in the audience with the Gomez family and motions for me to join him on the stage. It takes me a minute to catch on because I'm still stunned at his chutzpah, firing me and calling it a sabbatical. I climb to the stage and offer my hand, hoping to avoid having to hug him. He rejects my hand with feigned hurt and pulls me forward, embracing me with his bulbous arms, digging his stubby fingers into my back. The cold metal microphone presses against my neck like a gun. His breath hisses in my ear. I squirm and he tightens his grip, pressing his body against mine, stretching the moment into something lurid.

I know what he's doing, he's teasing the press, encouraging them to speculate that there is something prurient about the way I got my job back. He releases me and shoves the microphone into my hand. My cheeks are inflamed and my heart is pounding. I can't hide my breathlessness. I turn to the audience and exaggerate my panting.

"That's a hug I won't forget." They twitter politely, looking at me with a collective expectant eye, wondering what the two of us have been up to. I turn my back to Baxter and walk to the front of the stage.

"I'm honored to continue serving the needs of the officers and civilians who work at the Kenilworth Police Department and to serve as coordinator of this new program for the prevention of police suicide. I've discovered something for myself in the time I've been here. I like working with cops more than I like writing about them."

There's a burst of applause from the cops in the audience.

"As administrator of this program, my first official act is to rename the foundation in honor of Benjamin Gomez, the young officer who took his life several months ago. Ben's suicide was the first in this department's history. It is my mission to see that it is the last."

There is an eddy of movement in the front row as Mrs. Gomez stifles a sob with her handkerchief.

"I want to acknowledge Officer Gomez' grandparents, Lupe and Ramon Gomez. Their presence today is a reminder that this occupation affects families. Police officers, like other emergency responders, could not work the long hours or take the physical and emotional risks they do without the understanding and support of those at home. It will be my job to see that police officers take as good care of their families and themselves as they do of the rest of us. I thank you for this opportunity."

I hand the microphone to the mayor who invites the crowd for cake and coffee. I leave via a side door to avoid Baxter and the press. Over my shoulder I see people swarming the Gomez family, offering their condolences. They are nodding, smiling, shaking hands. Baxter is standing by himself, waiting for someone to cut the cake.

Sgt. Lyndley follows me. "Hey, Doc, got a minute? Any chance you can come to the FTO meeting day after tomorrow? We don't have any new recruits to discuss, probably won't get any until we get a new chief, but I have a couple of announcements to make, and I'd appreciate it if you were there."

"That's mysterious. What's up?"

He pats my shoulder before going back into the auditorium. "Curiosity killed the cat. See you when I see you."

We file into the briefing room, coffee cups in hand, and take our places at the table. Lyndley is the last to enter. Manny is behind him. My heart sinks. Manny is still on probation. Probies don't attend FTO meetings, not unless they're in big trouble. I can't look at him.

"Morning everyone," Lyndley says. "Anybody catch the Chief's retirement ceremony?" No one responds. "Don't know what this means for the future except that we get a break, no new trainees for a while. Takes a while to find a new chief, especially if they're going outside to look."

There's mumbling. Someone mutters "Doesn't make any difference who's chief. We do the work."

"Which brings me to the reason I called this meeting." He turns to Manny. "Stand up here with me, please."

Manny grimaces and gets up.

"Officer Ochoa, on his own initiative, and with the assistance of Dr. Meyerhoff," – everyone turns to look at me – "started an investigation into the circumstances surrounding Ben Gomez' death. He did an excellent job despite some major challenges. Last night, he and I arrested April Patcher Gomez on charges of fraud and abetting a suicide." Everyone applauds. Manny is looking at his shoes. "After our D.A. finishes her investigation, there may be additional criminal and civil charges brought to bear. Any questions?"

"How did it go down?" someone asks.

Lyndley raises an eyebrow and asks Manny to answer the question.

"She wasn't exactly happy to see us. She said she tried to stop Ben from killing himself. That she was scared he would kill her too so she left him alone in the motel. She admits she wrote the suicide note. Didn't think it would do any harm because he was already dead. She needed money to get an apartment and her father wouldn't give her any."

"And then all hell broke loose," Lyndley says. "She and her father went at each other like wildcats. We had to call the locals for back up. It took four of us to get the situation under control. Patcher got hauled off to his own jail, and April was so crazy we 5150'd her and took her to Prescott because there weren't any beds for psychos available at the county hospital."

"Oh my God," I say. "Did you know her mother's in Prescott?"

"We do now. Mrs. Patcher was folk-dancing in the lobby with the other inmates when we dragged April in. Like daughter, like mother. They both went berserk, started throwing things, beating on us, beating on each other, beating on the staff. They amassed so many felonies for d.v. and assault and battery against a police officer, it will take two judges to try them all."

Lyndley bends to the group. "Here's the corker. Prescott has one locked ward. Guess who gets to be roommates? I hope the orderlies have hazardous duty pay."

"Cat fight, cat fight." A small chant goes up from the group.

"One more thing," Lyndley says. He clamps Manny on the shoulder. "This young man has done such a good job, I'm cutting him loose from probation early. You're on your own buddy, congratulations."

They shake hands. We all clap.

"Thanks, Sarge. Thanks, everyone." Manny raises his hand to quiet us. "Like the Sarge said, I didn't do this alone." He points at me. "If it wasn't for the Doc, I wouldn't be standing here, and Ben would be forgotten. We talk trash about shrinks behind her back, but she's one determined lady. She may be small, but she has a big brain and a big heart."

Lyndley asks me if I want to say anything. I do, but I can't, not without crying.

Chapter Forty One

We are on our way to Pinky's, a 28 day residential treatment center for cops with drinking problems. Fran is driving her van, I'm in the passenger seat and Manny is sitting behind me, keeping his eye on Eddie who has passed out in the back seat.

"So, Doc. We picked up the kid who's been vandalizing houses in your development. Probably the same idiot who trashed your place."

And stole my tennis bracelet? I think to myself. I don't ask because Patcher remains my prime suspect. It doesn't matter now. He's facing bigger problems than a simple B & E. So is Melinda, my other suspect, although she seems an uncommon vandal, given her aesthetic sensibilities. More than likely she demanded that Mark buy her one like mine and he did, the poor love sick fool. He never was much of an original thinker.

Eddie snorts, startles himself awake, and passes out again. He hasn't had a drink since we ambushed him early this morning at his apartment and begged, pleaded and threatened until he agreed to accept help. The smell of booze rises off his body like the stink off an old kitchen sponge.

Fran lowers her window. The air outside is cool and smells of grass. We are heading north through the wine country. Grapevines inch along the wires that run between wooden posts. Straw-hatted farm workers move along rows of plants, inspecting the new crop. I can see tiny rainbows bobbing in the wake of the powerful spinning sprinklers.

Pinky's isn't the total answer, but it's a start. A safe place where Eddie can face his demons without having to worry that the person sitting next to him is someone he once arrested. There will be 24 hour support from a cadre of cops who have been there before him and know every trick in the book when it comes to alcoholism.

"You can't bullshit a bullshitter," is what the man on intake told me. "Haul the sonofabitch up here. We'll fix him."

We are quiet on the way home. None of us wants to stop to eat. We have a victory that we don't want to celebrate.

"I can't get the picture out of my head, Eddie sobbing like a baby when we drove away, running after us, so scared and confused." Fran wipes her eyes with the back of her hand. Manny leans over the seat and puts his hand on her shoulder.

"He's better off. Safer. The way he's been drinking, he'll be dead unless he stops."

Fran looks at me. "What do you think, Doc?"

"We did the right thing. Now it's up to Eddie."

I'm exhausted by the time Fran drops me off. My stomach is rumbling with hunger, but I'm too tired to eat. My house is dark. I need a glass of wine and a good night's sleep. More than that, I need some human warmth. I pick up the phone and call Frank. It's been weeks since we've talked. Plenty of time for him to forget about me and find someone else. The phone rings four times before his voice fills the quiet room like a spicy fragrance.

Author's Postscript

There are many myths about police suicide. Here is what I know. More officers kill themselves than are killed in the line of duty by a multiple of two. On the other hand, when you control for age, gender, race, marital status, and state of residency, officers may be less likely to kill themselves than the general population. Whatever the statistics or the reasons that push cops to kill themselves, every suicide is a tragic loss affecting many people, often for generations to come. The following resources may help:

Books

Emotional Survival for Law Enforcement by Kevin Gilmartin, Ph.D., (E-S Press, 2002).

Cop Shock, Surviving Posttraumatic Stress Disorder (PTSD), 2nd ed. by Allen R. Kates, MFAW, BCECR (Holbrook Street Press, 2008).

I Love a Cop: What Police Families Need to Know by Ellen Kirschman, Ph.D., (Guilford Press, 2007).

Websites

badgeoflife.com – dedicated to psychological survival and suicide prevention for police officers. Resources include a nationwide listing of alcoholics anonymous-type groups for first responders only.

tearsofacop.com – information about police suicide and home to Survivors of Law Enforcement Suicide (S.O.L.E.S.) .

Additional resources

The West Coast Post Trauma Retreat (www.wcpr2001.org) – a peer driven, clinically guided retreat for first responders suffering with post traumatic stress.

Preventing Law Enforcement Officer Suicide – An interactive CD containing sample suicide prevention print materials, presentations, videos and reference publications compiled by the Police Psychological Services Section of the International Association of Chiefs of Police. Free from the IACP at http://psychtheiacp.org.